PRAISE FOR THE FIGURE SKATING MYSTERIES

Death Drop

"This series is light reading, with a lot of self-deprecating humor tossed in by the protagonist, Bex Levy. I like the returning characters with all of their quirks, and the light sense of romance that is included, as well as the eye-opening information and the behind-the-scenes look at a popular sport." —*Gumshoe Review*

"A well-written whodunit murder mystery with plenty of suspects and twists and turns." —*MyShelf.com*

Axel of Evil

"Bex is a great character . . . As always, the author puts her insider knowledge of the skating world to good use, filling in the background and participants with very realistic details. A new Bex Levy mystery is a real treat; so settle in for an evening of skating, murder, and entertainment." —*The Romance Readers Connection*

"Fans will score Alina Adams with 9s and 10s for her superb figure skating murder mystery." —*Midwest Book Review*

continued . . .

On Thin Ice

"Fans of figure skating will laugh out loud at the descriptions of the skaters, attitudes, costumes, and stunts. Nonfans will revel in the finely crafted mystery. Bex Levy is a great protagonist who is prone to talking to herself, putting her foot in her mouth, and slashing at people with blades of sarcasm. Alone, the humor in *On Thin Ice* makes it a good book; combined with the interesting characters and suspense, it is a great book."   —*The Best Reviews*

Murder on Ice

"If you are even a casual fan of figure skating, you will love this book. The author . . . really knows the behind-the-scenes dish . . . The character of Bex is one of the best amateur sleuths to come along in some time . . . The mystery is interesting, and the investigation is so entertaining that you'll be glad you're along for the ride. I'm already impatiently awaiting the next book in this series."
          —*The Romance Readers Connection*

"Alina Adams gives a glimpse into the rivalries, the animosities, and the bickering that goes on in the world of amateur figure skating. The protagonist scores a 10 as one of the better leads to come along in years. She is perky, has a delightful sense of humor, and leaves no stone unturned in her quest to find a murderer . . . *Murder on Ice* is a winning amateur-sleuth tale starring a delightful self-deprecating heroine."
          —*The Best Reviews*

Skate Crime

ALINA ADAMS

BERKLEY PRIME CRIME, NEW YORK

THE BERKLEY PUBLISHING GROUP
Published by the Penguin Group
Penguin Group (USA) Inc.
375 Hudson Street, New York, New York 10014, USA
Penguin Group (Canada), 90 Eglinton Avenue East, Suite 700, Toronto, Ontario M4P 2Y3, Canada
(a division of Pearson Penguin Canada Inc.)
Penguin Books Ltd., 80 Strand, London WC2R 0RL, England
Penguin Group Ireland, 25 St. Stephen's Green, Dublin 2, Ireland (a division of Penguin Books Ltd.)
Penguin Group (Australia), 250 Camberwell Road, Camberwell, Victoria 3124, Australia
(a division of Pearson Australia Group Pty. Ltd.)
Penguin Books India Pvt. Ltd., 11 Community Centre, Panchsheel Park, New Delhi—110 017, India
Penguin Group (NZ), 67 Apollo Drive, Rosedale, North Shore 0632, New Zealand
(a division of Pearson New Zealand Ltd.)
Penguin Books (South Africa) (Pty.) Ltd., 24 Sturdee Avenue, Rosebank, Johannesburg 2196,
South Africa

Penguin Books Ltd., Registered Offices: 80 Strand, London WC2R 0RL, England

This is a work of fiction. Names, characters, places, and incidents either are the product of the author's
imagination or are used fictitiously, and any resemblance to actual persons, living or dead, business
establishments, events, or locales is entirely coincidental. The publisher does not have any control over
and does not assume any responsibility for author or third-party websites or their content.

SKATE CRIME

A Berkley Prime Crime Book / published by arrangement with the author

PRINTING HISTORY
Berkley Prime Crime mass-market edition / December 2007

Copyright © 2007 by Alina Sivorinovsky.
Cover art by Jeff Fitz-Maurice.
Cover design by Lesley Worrell.
Hand lettering by Iskra Johnson.
Interior text design by Kristin del Rosario.

ISBN: 978-0-425-21803-7

BERKLEY® PRIME CRIME
Berkley Prime Crime Books are published by The Berkley Publishing Group,
a division of Penguin Group (USA) Inc.,
375 Hudson Street, New York, New York 10014.
The name BERKLEY PRIME CRIME and the BERKLEY PRIME CRIME design are trademarks of
Penguin Group (USA) Inc.

PRINTED IN THE UNITED STATES OF AMERICA

10 9 8 7 6 5 4 3 2 1

Prologue

The second week in July, Bex Levy received two proposals.

One took her by surprise. Still, she said "yes" immediately.

The other left her dumbfounded. To it, she had no idea what to say.

"I think we should get married," suggested Craig, the man who Bex guessed might technically be called her boyfriend.

The reason Bex still stumbled, even mentally, over Craig's exact designation was because, while they had been dating for almost six months—doing all of the expected boyfriend/girlfriend things like going out, staying in, having phone conversations so long that the receiver was actually hot after being set down, and racking up way too many miles on their respective cars driving from Bex's apartment in Manhattan to Craig's house in the Pocono Mountains of Pennsylvania to see each other—there was still, on a semantic level, no way that Craig Hunt could be reasonably described by anyone as a boy.

For one thing, he was thirty-four years old, which made him a decade Bex's senior (though, having recently turned twenty-five, she could pretend that the age gap was actually growing smaller, with Craig not due to turn thirty-five for another seven weeks). For another, he was one of those people that, Bex suspected, had never really been young. A foster child who'd become an adoptive father himself (under some very bizarre circumstances) at the age of twenty, Craig was currently the widowed, single parent of a fourteen-year-old son.

Everyone Bex had dated prior to Craig, regardless of age, had been a boy, and thus a "boyfriend" candidate. Craig Hunt was a man. Which meant Bex had absolutely no idea how to refer to him.

Not that apt monikers were, at the moment, her greatest concern.

She and Craig were sitting inside her studio apartment. An apartment so small that once Bex unfolded the sofa bed and angled it so that the frame's edge didn't scrape the side of her desk, the room was effectively filled. Only a foot on the left side near the window and a foot on the right beside the door to the bathroom remained as actual, available floor space. Bex and Craig were sitting on the bed. Not due to any romantic intentions, but merely because there was no place else to do so. And they had to sit somewhere to eat the roasted chicken Craig had miraculously managed to coax out of her Easy-Bake kitchen, where oven, fridge, and sink appeared to have been built for the exclusive use of Hobbits and/or Oompa-Loompas.

It wasn't exactly where and how Bex had expected a proposal of marriage. And it most certainly wasn't when. So she blurted out the first thing that came to her mind. She had a tendency to do that.

"Why?" Bex asked.

There—where, how, when, and why, all nicely covered. Wasn't she the good journalist?

"Because," Craig said, apparently so used to her blurts that he didn't even bother to politely fake being phased, "I like being married."

"To me?"

"I don't know." Again, not phased. "I've never been married to you. I would, however, very much like to be."

"I mean . . ." Slowly, the power of sentence construction was returning to Bex's tongue. Not coherent sentence construction, mind you, but enough to drive her foot even deeper into her mouth. "I know you liked being married. Before. But that wasn't to me. You're talking about Rachel. But Rachel's only been dead—"

"I know how long Rachel has been dead."

"It hasn't even been a year."

"That's the number I've got, too, yes."

"How can you—what about Jeremy?"

"A part of this is because of Jeremy. Look, Bex, it's not that I mind driving up to see you, per se. But I can't very well bring Jeremy with me here, and neither one of us wants you staying over at the house when he's there—"

"God, no."

"So, it's awkward. If we were married, I wouldn't feel like we were sneaking around."

"We're not sneaking around."

"What are we doing, then?"

"We're . . . dating."

"To what end?"

She shrugged. It was either shrug or admit, "I dunno." And, under the circumstances, a shrug seemed more mature.

"I love you, Bex," Craig said softly. "But this 'dating' thing, this tiny-apartment-take-out-food-just-out-of-college lifestyle . . . I'm too old for it. I've done *Barefoot in the Park* already."

"With Rachel," Bex reminded.

"Yes. With Rachel."

"And now you want the house, the nine-to-five job, the kids. Good-bye *Barefoot in the Park*, hello *Brady Bunch*. Craig Hunt *is* Robert Reed. Cue theme song and moppets."

"You seem to know a lot more about what's going on in my head than I do, Bex. Theme song and all." She couldn't tell if Craig was joking or not. "How do you figure that works exactly?"

"It's what I do for a living."

"Read minds?"

"No." Technically, Bex was merely a figure skating researcher for the 24/7 television network. "But the biggest part of what I do is extrapolate a big picture from small details. I collect a bunch of facts about a given person or situation, and then I turn it into a comprehensive story."

"A three-minute up-close-and-personal segment wedged in between televised short programs can hardly be considered comprehensive. Not everything is necessarily as simple as it seems on the surface"

"But it is, it is," she insisted. "A well-put-together three-minute segment features just enough pertinent, telling details so that our viewers can draw their own big picture. People aren't that complicated. They're mostly predictable. Telling their stories is what I do, even when the people themselves don't know that there is a story."

"Well, it's certainly what you're doing to me, right now. Though you'll forgive me if I don't exactly agree with the conclusions you've drawn about how I feel or what I want."

"Are you saying you're not at a point in your life where you're looking for this idyllic family existence?"

"Would that really be so bad?"

"I don't know. All I know is, you're not looking for a new life. You're looking to recreate a life you already had. With Rachel."

"Yes," Craig said, again unashamed. "Though may I remind you that what Rachel and I had was hardly normal or traditional. And, for the record, I may be trying to recreate the broad strokes of a life, but I am not trying to recreate *her* with *you*. Rachel was Rachel, and you're Bex. I don't suffer from any confusion on that part."

"What about my job?"

"What about it?"

"I work in Manhattan. And . . . other places." Bex's job not only required that she report to 24/7's midtown offices, but, during the October through March skating season, it also demanded she jet off every four weeks to glamorous locations ranging from Moscow, Russia, to Beijing, China, to Fort

Worth, Texas. It wasn't the kind of gig she could do part-time from a Martha Stewart–decorated home in the suburbs.

"And you'll continue working in Manhattan. And other places—if that's what you want. We can find someplace to live that works for everybody. What, do you think I'm a total idiot?"

"I don't want to have kids. I mean, not right away. Not in the near future. Not soon. I don't know when."

"Fine. I asked you to marry me. I didn't say anything about kids."

"Why are you being so reasonable?"

"Because I want you to say yes."

"And if I don't?"

It was the first thing she'd blurted out all evening that appeared to genuinely throw him. "What do you mean?"

"I mean, what if I don't say yes? Is that it? Are we over? Are you giving me an ultimatum? Or do we just go on pretending you never asked and I never refused and everything is okay and the same as before?"

He thought about it. Bex guessed the possibility of her saying no had never crossed his mind. Bex didn't know whether to be flattered or offended.

"I—I don't know," he finally said.

"So you might dump me?"

"I don't know."

"Well, then, I . . . then I . . . I don't know, either."

They sat just looking at each other for a long moment. Finally, Craig said, "This went well."

"Am I on a time limit? Do I have to give you an answer in a certain amount of time?"

"You mean, like *Jeopardy*?"

"Yes, Craig, exactly like *Jeopardy*. Want to hum that theme song while you're at it?"

He smiled, "Now you see why I love you."

"I love you, too."

"Then it seems like this should be easy."

"And yet it's not."

Craig said, "Look. How about this? When I dropped

Jeremy off at the rink this morning, Toni told me about this thing, this tribute thing, they're having for Lucian Pryce out in Colorado next week. The Figure Skating Hall of Fame is honoring his fifty years of contributions to skating. It's a major shindig. Dignitaries, Olympic champions, former students are flying out to lay wreaths at his feet, or on his ice or whatever. Toni is going there to talk about when she and Lucian skated Pairs together. She suggested taking Jeremy with her. She thinks Lucian could really work with him on his presentation, knock it up a level. Now that Jeremy's competed at his first Worlds, Toni says the judges are expecting him to stop skating like a Junior, blah, blah, blah—you know the drill. I was against it. After everything that happened with Rachel and Robby and Felicia, and well . . . everything, the last thing I wanted was my son in Lucian Pryce's clutches. Not that Toni wouldn't look out for him the best she could, but Toni and Lucian have their own history. I had no intention of getting Jeremy in the middle of that." He sighed. "On the other hand, what if I go out there with him? I can keep an eye on Jeremy, and you can take—what is it, a week? Ten days?—to . . . think. I won't bother you. I won't put on any pressure. Take all the time you need to figure out what you really want."

"As long as it's a week to ten days," Bex clarified.

"Hey," Craig said, shrugging, "none of us are getting any younger."

No. Thanks to the adult decision he was expecting her to make in a week to ten days, Bex felt older already.

𝔅𝔢𝔵'𝔰 second proposal came about an hour after Craig decamped for home. When the phone rang, she thought maybe it was him, saying he'd reconsidered the whole thing and yeah, let's give Bex's pretend-it-never-happened idea a shot. But it wasn't Craig. It was Bex's 24/7 boss, Gil Cahill. If Gil was calling Bex on a Sunday night at home, the news couldn't be good. Actually, if Gil was calling, period, angst was destined to follow.

Bex knew it was Gil on the other line because she picked

up the receiver, and he was already in the middle of a conversation. No small talk, no salutation even.

"Mollie let me down," he raged. "Some nonsense about bed rest or whatnot, one of those women things. So this is your big chance. You want it or not, Bex?"

Bex said, "Hi, Gil." It seemed safest under the circumstances.

"Summer is always such a dead time for skating, which is why we agreed to pick up this Lucian Pryce special thing. Something to plug the hole and get those teenage girl demos the chief keeps saying we need to balance out the male ones."

"You're covering Lucian Pryce's tribute?"

"No, Bex, pay attention. You are."

"I am?"

"I had it all set up. Got a director flying out next week to shoot the actual show, but Mollie was going to go up early, do the features, local color, background, that sort of thing. Of course now, because her uterus can't behave itself, I've got no feature producer, and everyone else is booked covering real sports. That's why I thought of you. Well, actually, Ruth here in my office did. She figured you've already done the research on most of these guys, and you're always itching to be a producer, so this is your big chance, right? You want it or not?"

"I want it," Bex said without thinking. Like Pavlov's dog, she'd started mentally salivating at the words "producer" and "big chance." She'd do it.

It was only after she'd gotten off the phone with the travel department to set up her plane ticket to Colorado for the next day and hurriedly began tossing articles of clothing that screamed "distinguished producer" rather than "lowly researcher" into her well-worn suitcase that Bex allowed herself to realize that a trip to Colorado to further her heretofore rather undistinguished career meant the designated week "off" with Craig was officially . . . off.

She considered calling to tell him. But she didn't know what to say exactly. And she didn't know what he would say in return.

As always under such indefinite circumstances, Bex chickened out.

She figured her arrival would be a surprise. As would whatever happened next. A big surprise for both of them.

One

𝕭𝖊𝖝'𝖘 plane touched down in Colorado Springs at 8:15 PM.
By the time she'd taken the cab to her hotel a few blocks from

the Olympic Training Center, the one usually used to host athletes, coaches, officials, and fans at times of major competitions, it was 9:10 PM. When she finished unpacking her suitcase, it was 9:13.

Bex figured it was too late to call Craig and let him know she was in town. In his hotel, as a matter of fact. Not that Bex knew for sure that Craig and Jeremy were staying at the official hotel. They might be bunking in the skaters' dorms on the grounds of the OTC. Or in some other hotel miles away. Bex didn't know that hotel's number. And she didn't know if Craig had his cell phone on him. Although, as a rule, he usually did.

Besides, Bex had stuff of her own to do. Her first assignment was to meet Lucian Pryce at his home, bright and early at 5 AM the next morning. Bex would follow him to the rink, where, before the morning session commenced, she and a locally hired film crew would tape him on the ice. Footage they could later use as b-roll and interstitial material for the special.

If Bex expected to be at Lucian's at five, that meant she would need to rise at least by 4:15 and get herself ready. Which meant she had no time for superfluous phone calls.

Bex went to bed, turned off the lights, and ordered herself to get a good night's sleep. By the time she rose, in advance of her wake-up call, at 4:10 the next morning, she'd slept, by her calculations, easily a refreshing eight to nine minutes.

With that kind of rest deficit, Bex did the best she could with what she saw in the mirror. She pulled her chestnut hair back into a ponytail, scrubbed her face first with cold water, then with an astringent cleanser to close her pores. Followed by a moisturizer to open them up again. The one-two punch seemed rather self-defeating to Bex, but the perky girl who did makeovers at the mall on the outskirts of a small town Bex could no longer remember the name of had insisted that it would all somehow add up to great beauty. Some day.

Bex pulled on a pair of blue jeans, rejecting the long johns she usually donned underneath on the argument that it was summertime and she didn't need to suit up quite as intensively as she usually did for wintertime work in Moscow or even

New Hampshire. She decided to go with layers for the top half: a light green T-shirt, followed by a dark green linen blazer. A bit *Miami Vice*, but it was the most businesslike attire she owned. The rest of her wardrobe consisted mostly of sweatshirts with the names of competitions she'd covered sprayed across the front and a host of "24/7"-labeled merchandise she periodically borrowed from the supply closet at work.

At 5 AM on the nose, she was on the doorstep of Lucian Pryce's two-story suburban home. Bex wondered whether to ring the bell or knock. On the one hand, she had been invited. On the other, it was 5 AM. Then again, this was a skating household. Five AM was practically midday for them. Then again-again, she had no evidence that only skaters were in residence. Perhaps the Pryce household also consisted of some—what were they called? Oh, yes, normal people.

She settled for knocking. But firmly. When no one answered, Bex bit the bullet and rang the bell. The door was instantly answered, but not by Lucian.

It was his wife, Olympic champion Gina Gregory, five feet tall, freckle covered, frizzy red hair sticking out in every direction, and, if Bex remembered correctly from her research manual, over thirty years younger than her coach-turned-husband. Bex's first reaction was that it was a bit disconcerting to catch Gina like this. From the time she won her first World Championship medal on the way to Olympic Gold, Gina Gregory always appeared on television perfectly coiffed, her hair shellacked into place, her freckles evened out and obscured by a nonobtrusive tint, her skirt and blouse neatly pressed, hose aligned, lipstick and nail polish color coordinated, preferably with her purse. In fact, the only reason Bex even guessed that the early-morning disheveled figure currently standing in front of her was, in fact, Gina Gregory, was through the process of elimination. What other thirtysomething woman would be opening Lucian Pryce's door at 5 AM wearing a bathrobe?

A second later, however, Bex had just cause to reevaluate her assumption. Over Gina's (not Gina's?) shoulder, she spied

another woman of approximately the same age, also wearing
a robe and the grumpy appearance of someone rudely awak-
ened from a sound sleep.

Bex wondered just what sort of situation she'd stumbled
into here. Lucian Pryce and his all-singing, all-dancing, all-
skating harem?

However, when the second woman turned briefly in profile
to stumble through the swinging, ridged wooden door into
what Bex glimpsed as the kitchen (complete with life-saving,
percolating coffeemaker), the mystery of her identity became
somewhat clearer. The jut of her nose and chin, combined
with the near-translucent blue eyes and cascade of mink black
hair pegged her as the daughter of Lucian Pryce and his
first wife (not to mention first Olympic champion), Eleanor
Quinn. Her sharp features and mirror eyes came from Daddy.
The hair was all Eleanor.

The age, however, appeared closer to her stepmother's.
Bex vaguely recalled that there was only a year's difference.
Though she couldn't remember in which direction.

"Bex Levy!" Gina exclaimed, as if they were old friends
rather than people who'd briefly glimpsed each other across
foggy ice rinks in various parts of the world. "Come in, come
in. Lucian will be right down. Can I get you something? We
have coffee, but I can also make tea if you like. Plenty of hot
water for both. Would you like a Danish?"

"Hi," Bex said cautiously.

As she was dragged through the living room into the
kitchen, Bex caught a glimpse of various medals and silver-
plated platters mounted on all four walls, as well as, above the
fireplace, an enlarged copy of the cover *LIFE* magazine ran
after Eleanor Quinn's death: "Farewell to America's Ice
Princess." It showed Eleanor the year she won the Olympics,
standing on the top step of the podium, waving to the crowd,
gold medal around her neck, dressed in a pale pink skating
dress, a matching ribbon shaped into a rose and woven
through all that incredible hair piled on top of her head.

"So did you say coffee or tea?" Gina plopped Bex down on
a chair at the edge of the table. "This is Lucian's little girl,

Sabrina." She indicated her stepdaughter, who right then was cautiously blowing on a cup of steaming coffee prior to figuring, what the heck, and just downing half in a single gulp. Bex wondered if Gina thought that referring to the grown woman as "Lucian's little girl" might hide the lack of age difference between them.

"Hi." Bex went with the line that had obviously won her such instant acceptance back in the living room. Sabrina may have nodded in Bex's direction. Or she may have simply momentarily nodded off. Her body language didn't suggest that the shot of sizzling caffeine had done much good.

"Sabrina flew in especially for Lucian's tribute, didn't you, Sabrina? She lives in San Francisco. She's very successful. In the Internet and all that. That's what they do out in San Francisco mostly these days, the Internet. Sabrina is very busy. But she made the time to come and see her father honored, didn't you, Sabrina?"

This time, Lucian's daughter definitely nodded. But she didn't seem particularly enthused by either the gesture or what she was agreeing to. Meanwhile, Bex wondered how many cups of coffee Gina had already ingested.

"We, Lucian and I, that is—well, Sabrina, too, I'm sure— we're very excited that 24/7 decided to broadcast our show. It's such an honor. I'm sure you must have so many other important sporting events just clamoring for your attention."

"We like to cover all the bases," Bex said.

"It's going to be wonderful. So many of Lucian's champions are coming to perform. And Toni Wright. Do you know Toni Wright? She and Lucian were National Pairs champions together. You can imagine what a scandal it was forty-five years ago, an interracial Pairs team. The Ku Klux Klan actually protested them when they competed in Atlanta. They said it was a horrible example to set. And when Lucian and Toni went to the Olympics, some of the Southern television stations didn't show their performance. Just didn't show it. Don't know what they showed instead. And it must have looked so strange, not to show the Americans. Of course, that kind of thing is hardly a problem today. Why, no one blinks an eye at it today. It didn't even come up when we were planning the tribute show. Not that Lucian and Toni will be performing. But Toni is already here in Colorado. And other people are coming today and tomorrow. It's going to be a great show."

"Gina!" The voice from their doorway made both Gina and Bex jump.

Sabrina didn't even deign to turn her head.

Lucian Pryce took a single step into the kitchen. He was wearing a white waterproof warm-up suit, with "Colorado OTC" stitched in red over the right breast pocket and up the right pants leg. His turtleneck sweater under the warm-up jacket was red, with "Colorado OTC" stitched in white along the corner of the neckline. His grey hair was combed neatly to the side, and his face boasted the ruddy complexion that on any other man would have bespoken a drinking problem but, in Bex's experience, in this particular world, simply meant too much prolonged exposure to the cold.

He said, "Gina, calm down. You're giving the girl whiplash."

Bex wouldn't have put it quite so bluntly, but yeah, she kind of was.

"Let's go, Bex." Lucian turned without checking to see whether his command had been obeyed. "We can talk in the car."

They didn't talk in the car. Or, rather, Bex didn't. Lucian monologued the entire ten-minute drive over to the rink. He listed his Olympic champions for Bex. He listed his World champions for Bex. Then his World medalists. Then his National champions. Bex listened, dutifully impressed, but mostly by the fact that, when he got to the names Robby Sharpton and Rachel Rose, Lucian at least had the grace to look slightly sheepish. Courtesy of a piece Bex had produced on the pair the previous fall, she knew exactly what role Lucian Pryce had played in their eventual downfalls.

Which, of course, didn't mean he hadn't made champions of them.

Which, of course, was what really mattered.

Bex's camera crew—a cameraman and a soundman—were waiting for them in the parking lot. The rink wasn't open yet. Lucian unlocked the door, flicked on the lights, and told them to wait a second, he'd just go fetch his skates from the coaches' lounge and be right back. The plan was to get some footage of him stroking in circles, showing how, even at age sixty-five, he still had it.

While Lucian was putting on his skates, Bex slowly walked around the ice surface, pretending that she could tell which angle would make a better shot. Producing features for a primetime 24/7 special was the biggest career break she'd gotten since coming to the network, and she was determined to take full advantage of it. This was her career they were talking about. This was important. Especially since she was about to have no personal life to speak of.

Bex sternly told herself that this was no time to think about Craig. She was working. She walked around the ice surface again, looking extra thoughtful.

On her third go-round, the cameraman suggested maybe they should all get on the ice with Lucian, since the six-foot-high Plexiglass surrounding the rink (to keep stray pucks from knocking teeth out in the stands during hockey games) meant they couldn't shoot from the floor without getting a horrible glare, anyway.

Bex nodded to indicate not only that she thought it an excellent suggestion, but also that she had been just about to make the same one herself.

When Lucian exited from the coaches' lounge, he was wearing his black skates, the blades covered with dark purple plastic guards to keep them from getting dulled by the padded floor. He paused at the gated entrance to the ice to take off the guards and lay them neatly on the barrier.

Lucian pushed off, hesitating for a second and glancing briefly down at his feet before shaking off whatever it was that had bothered him and asking Bex, "So, what do you need me to do?"

She suggested he just stroke around for a bit and let them

get some full body shots. Lucian acquiesced, leaning slightly towards the inside of the rink and taking off backwards. It didn't matter how long Bex covered skating, she was certain she would never get used to the fact that, in order to go backwards, skaters had to put one foot in front of the other. It didn't make any kind of sense, though it sure was pretty to watch.

She had to admit that on the ice, Lucian moved like a much younger man. She wouldn't have thought a sixty-five-year-old with two artificial hips could appear to float above the surface, but Lucian was doing just that, his shoulders still and steady, his head slightly turned to look over his shoulder, despite the fact that he was the only person on the ice.

On his second lap, Lucian saw Toni walk in through the door. She paused at the main barrier, a few feet above the northernmost tip of the oval. Toni was wearing her traditional rink uniform of dark wool pants, a padded blue parka over a cashmere sweater, and a woolen hat pulled down over her ears. Lucian raised a hand to wave and Toni waved back. The smiles on both their faces seemed surprisingly genuine.

Not that Bex had any reason to think they shouldn't be. It was just that, at least at competition time, there wasn't an authentic grin to be found. And during practice—well, if you were smiling, you probably weren't sweating, and if you weren't sweating, why the heck were you there? Which meant that a true expression of pleasure while skating was a rare bird indeed.

Lucian yelled to Toni, "When did you get in?"

"Yesterday afternoon."

"You bring the Hunt boy?"

Toni nodded. Bex fought the urge to ask how the Hunt boy's father was.

"Good. Kid's got a lot of potential. We'll mine a lot of gold out of that boy, you mark my words."

"That's what we came for. The tribute was just a clever way to get the Hall of Fame to cover my plane fare," Toni said. But at that point, Lucian was at the southernmost end of the rink and had to struggle to hear her over the rhythmic swish of his blades on the ice.

He turned his head abruptly in her direction, asking, "What did you say, now?" when his feet suddenly slipped out from under him.

It all happened in less than a second. One moment, Lucian was upright, talking, and the next, his body was crashing to the ice. He didn't even have time to bend at the waist or throw out his hands to try to cushion the fall. First his left knee, then his hip, then his elbow, then the side of his head crashed into the ice, all in one equally fluid motion. He hit the ground and then slid until he hit the barrier. And then he didn't move at all.

Bex gasped. But it was all she did. Toni was the one who instantaneously ran down the embankment to the entrance, stepping out onto the ice in her street shoes and cautiously half running, half skidding her way over to Lucian. She knelt on her knees, touching her palm to the side of his head. It came away covered with blood.

"Call an ambulance," Toni ordered Bex over her shoulder.

Bex nodded mutely and proceeded to do her own half run/half skid, much more awkwardly than Toni had, towards the rink's office. On her way, she did manage to notice that the camera was still running. Ethically speaking, she knew she should tell the crew to shut down. Practically speaking, Bex knew that if she did, Gil would have her head.

She tugged on the office door. It wouldn't give.

"It's locked," Bex yelled to Toni.

"Try the coaches' lounge. There's a phone in there, too."

Luckily, Lucian had left it open after he'd changed. Bex was able to step right in and find, amidst the couches that had seen better days, the stacks of student bills to be sent out, and the piles of programs going back to Regional competitions from the 1970s, an old-school rotary phone. Obviously, this was not a room that saw a lot of redecorating with the changing seasons.

She reached 911 after two rings, only to realize she didn't know the rink's exact address. Fortunately, the dispatcher was familiar with the Olympic Training Center. Bex wondered how many calls for help they fielded a week.

"Ambulance is on its way," she assured Toni, rushing back towards the rink.

But, from the look on her face—not to mention those of the cameraman and sound guy—Bex quickly realized that 24/7 was now the proud owner of exclusive video footage documenting Lucian Pryce's death.

Two
Toni

$\mathcal{A}$t the age of eight, Toni Wright stood alone at the entry gate to New York City's Wollman Outdoor Ice Rink in Central Park, waiting for her turn to pay the twenty-five cent admission and take a spin around the slick oval in her brand-new Christmas skates. She wore—at her mother's insistence—her waterproof rain pants. But Toni, frankly, had no intention of falling down. For the past year, she'd watched other boys and girls glide gracefully across the rink and she felt certain she would be able to do the same.

When it was her turn, Toni plunked down the required two dimes and a nickel, and was already pushing the door with her shoulder when the girl working the window leaned over across the cashier's sill and grabbed Toni by the arm. Toni turned her head slowly and gazed at the older teen with the same look Toni's mother unleashed on any salesgirl, waitress, or taxi driver unfortunate enough not to realize whom they were dealing with.

"Is there a problem, miss?" But unlike her mama, who had no patience for dealing with fools, Toni followed her Daddy's instructions to always be polite. Especially to the ignorant. He

said it was their job to teach them, in particular, the right way
to behave.

Either the girl wasn't accustomed to being addressed as
"miss" or she didn't realize the query was directed at her. She
yanked Toni backwards and announced, "No niggers allowed."

Toni sighed. So this was to be another case of her needing
to educate somebody. Well, Daddy did say it was their burden
to bear.

As politely as she could manage—her seven-year-old patience not being quite as sturdy as Daddy's—Toni explained,
"This is a public facility. You are not allowed to make rules
like that."

"It is a rule," the girl insisted.

"Please show me where it's written, then."

"It's a rule."

Toni yanked her arm free. It wasn't very ladylike, but she
couldn't figure out any other way to do it. The girl had hurt
her, squeezing so tightly. But Toni would never let her see
that.

She said, "I've given you my money, and now I am going
skating."

Before the cashier could make another lunge at her elbow,
Toni slipped through the door and walked over to the bench,
sat down, and without looking at any of the faces now staring
curiously in her direction, proceeded to take off her shoes and
slip on her skates. She waited until she'd taken a few wobbly
step on the ice and come crashing down on her bottom—
Mama had been right about the waterproof pants, after all—
before allowing a couple of tears to slip free from her eyes.
She figured those people watching would think she'd just hurt
herself.

That first day, Toni fell down fourteen times—she counted.
But she came back the next day. There was a different girl at
the window. Either she'd heard about Toni from the day before or she didn't subscribe to the same unwritten rule of ex-
clusivity, because she let Toni in without a word of protest.

She just sniffed rather haughtily, but even Mama didn't consider those sorts of slights worth her while.

The second day, Toni fell only nine times. By the end of the week, she felt she'd gotten the hang of going forward. Now, she thought it was time to tackle the backward strokes that most of the older kids were doing, the ones that permitted them to fly like the wind. Toni tried it by herself for almost a month. She watched the others as closely as she could—hopefully without them noticing; if they did and glared at her, Toni scurried away as fast as she could, realizing that, in this instance, she was actually the one in the wrong—and attempted to replicate exactly what they were doing. But going backwards by crossing her foot in front proved much too confusing. She would master a step or two, then lose her rhythm and find her ankles tangled in a hopeless muddle. She said to Daddy over dinner that maybe it was time to get herself a coach. He set down his fork. He didn't say anything.

The Wright family lived along Striver's Row in Harlem, in a four-story row house built by no less than David H. King, the same contractor who'd built Madison Square Garden and the base of the Statue of Liberty. They boarded one live-in girl to keep the house tidy on a daily basis and had another come in once a week to do what Mama called heavy work, beating the carpets, washing the windows, scrubbing each bathroom until it gleamed. When Mama and Daddy threw dinner parties, they'd even have another girl in to help with the cooking and the serving and the cleaning up.

Daddy said there was no shame in hiring people to help with what you couldn't do yourself. It was a blessing on them and on you.

Which was why Toni couldn't understand his hesitation about hiring her a coach for skating. Surely Daddy had seen how hard Toni was working. She wasn't being frivolous, like her friend from next door, who took up ballet dancing, then horseback riding, then oil painting, only to drop each within the course of a month. Toni was determined to stick with her chosen endeavor. She merely needed some help, that was all.

Daddy asked, "Any colored teachers at that rink there?"

"No, sir."

"Antonia . . ."

"Yes, sir?"

"I say this: You find yourself a coach willing to teach you, and I will pay her price. But you need to come to me with an agreement first. Does that sound fair?"

"Yes, sir," Toni said, still unsure why Daddy seemed to think this would be so difficult.

It proved rather difficult.

As he must have known, none of the teachers at Wollman was willing to take Toni on. They didn't give a reason. They simply said no. But, then again, to actually give the reason out loud, well, as Mama liked to say, that would have been an insult to both their intelligences—if the latter had any, that is.

Toni was ready to give up, to tell Daddy that maybe, like her friend from next door, she'd like to try dance lessons, after all. There was a lady on Hamilton Heights who gave classes, and those were for colored girls only, so there would surely be a space for Toni if she asked.

But that was before the boy that came right up to her at the rink as she was taking off her skates after another fruitless day of attempting to master backward crossovers and asked, "You got a lot of money?"

He was about twelve, maybe thirteen years old, with hair so blond he might have been a ghost and eyes so blue they looked like mirrors reflecting the summer sky. His chin had a point at the end, and with every word he spoke, it looked as though he was jabbing it right in Toni's direction.

"What's it to you?" Toni asked, knowing that she sounded common, and happy that Mama wasn't around to hear her.

"I heard you going around asking everybody for lessons. You got money to pay for them?"

"Not that it's any of your business, but, yes. Yes, I do."

"Where'd you get it?"

"From my daddy, of course."

"Ha! Never heard of a rich colored man."

"That is likely because you are ignorant." Toni heard

Mama's voice coming out of her mouth and decided that made up for sounding so cheap earlier.

"Where'd he get all his money? He a thief?"

"Of course not! For your information, my father runs the Wright Funeral Homes of New York City. Two in Harlem, one in Queens, two in the Bronx, and we're opening another in Brooklyn next month!"

"So he's a vampire!"

Toni knew she should be offended. But the image of her daddy with bat wings and sharp teeth just made her giggle.

"So you're really rich, then?"

Toni shrugged. Well-brought-up young ladies didn't discuss money in public. It was even more common than bad grammar.

"I have an idea," the boy said. "About how you can take skating lessons."

She knew she shouldn't be listening to him, but Toni couldn't help it. She said, "How?"

"Okay, well, see, here's the thing: I could teach you."

"You're just a boy!"

"I'm almost thirteen! And I've been skating, well, since I was a baby almost. See, my ma and dad, they run the Arthur Murray Dance Studio on West fifty-ninth—that's practically right down the street, in Hell's Kitchen. So I've been dancing since I was a baby, too. I'm good. Ma says I could be a ballroom champion, maybe. But dancing, that's nothing like skating. Skating is everything you do in dance, but harder and faster and . . . and . . . better. It's just better, you know?"

"I know," Toni said softly.

"Now, my folks, they can afford a lesson for me here and there, but if you want to be a champion, you need lessons every day. My folks don't have the money for that. So I thought, it's like this . . . I thought I could give you lessons on what I know and you don't, but since I can't take money or I wouldn't be an amateur skater anymore, your daddy can pay the money for my lessons to my coach for her to teach me. Then I take what I learn and teach it to you, you understand?"

Toni thought she did. But . . . "Your coach doesn't want to teach me."

"No, she doesn't. But I bet she wouldn't mind taking money from you for me, especially if she knows it's the only way I could afford it."

When Toni later told her daddy what the boy had proposed, he chuckled, but he didn't look particularly happy when he agreed, "No, I suspect she wouldn't mind, at that."

"So can we do it, Daddy? Can we do it this way?"

"Well, I would like to speak to this boy first. What did you say his name was?"

Toni had to sheepishly admit she had no idea.

The next day, Daddy came to the rink in person. Toni pointed out the boy with the pale hair and mirror eyes. He was on the ice, running backwards at top speed, then leaping into the air and splitting his legs so high, his toes were nearly up to his shoulders when he touched them with his fingers.

Daddy beckoned him over and the boy came instantly. He said his name was Lucian Pryce.

"Lucian, huh?" Daddy noted. "That's quite the mouthful."

"My ma is French, sir. Well, first Russian, then French. She's from a long line of ballerinas that ran away from Russia between the wars and ended up first in France, then America. Dad's just a regular mick, though. Nothing fancy there."

Toni wasn't sure if Daddy actually heard the gist of Lucian's explanation. He still seemed a bit dumbstruck that a white boy had called him "sir."

Daddy told Lucian he would speak to his coach, but if she agreed with Lucian's idea to pay for his lessons, then Daddy was for it. Lucian grinned and winked at Toni. She knew that winking was very common. But she couldn't help winking back.

Lucian's coach did Daddy the great favor of taking his money. She hesitated a bit before actually, physically accepting it, but, in the end, like Daddy always said, "The color green wins out over any other."

And Toni began taking lessons from Lucian.

Their first day, he taught her the backwards crossovers.

Their first year, she had mastered every single revolution jump, up through the Axel (which was actually one and a half turns in the air). By the second year, she could spin so ferociously, Daddy said it was like seeing a spool of movie film slip out of its projector. By the third, Lucian told Toni he thought she was ready for real U.S. Figure Skating Association competition. There was only one problem. In order to compete, she had to join the USFSA. And the USFSA did not—Lucian had actually called their headquarters and asked; he would apply for her father to cover the long-distance bill later—have any colored members.

Toni asked Lucian for a copy of the form to join the USFSA. She read it closely. She said, "It doesn't ask anywhere if you're colored or not. It just says what the dues are to join."

Lucian read the form, too. "You're right," he said.

At eleven years old, Toni was a dues-paying, official member of the U.S. Figure Skating Association. Now she could take the necessary figure and freestyle tests to qualify for competition at the Regional, Sectional, maybe even the National Championships. When she filled out her paperwork to take the test, it didn't ask whether or not she was colored, either. But when the three judges assigned to mark her test arrived at Wollman Rink, they could see for themselves. One refused to look at her figures at all. The other two simply marked her "Failed" before she was even through demonstrating.

"This is a problem," Lucian said.

"Is it a problem that can be solved with money?" Daddy asked him.

"Maybe . . ."

"Then I expect you to let me know how to solve it."

Lucian called the USFSA headquarters—this time, he simply used the Wrights' phone, to make the reimbursement easier—and asked for a list of every qualified judge in the country, plus their contact information. He then proceeded to call over two hundred of them, until he found three willing to judge a little colored girl's tests. On a warm April morning a few weeks before Toni turned twelve, as the outdoor rink's ice was beginning to melt in the spring thaw, three USFSA judges—one from Maine, one from Vermont, one all the way from the aptly named Great Falls, Montana—arrived in New York City—plane fare courtesy of Wright Funeral Homes— to judge one Antonia Wright's figure and freestyle tests.

Daddy told her, "I don't plan to do this regularly, so you better make sure you get this right the first time, you hear me, Antonia?"

"Yes, sir," she said.

"That goes for you, too, Lucian."

"Yes, sir," he said. And Lucian made sure that when Toni took her tests, they were loop and bracket and Choctaw perfect, so that, in the space of that one morning, she passed all of her tests up to the Junior level.

"That means you're qualified to compete at Nationals!" he told her excitedly.

"Don't I have to place at Regionals and Sectionals first?"

"Technicality," Lucian said. "I'm going to go to Nationals in Senior Men, and you're going to go in Junior Ladies. It's all over but the medal ceremony, really."

Toni was the fifth girl in her group of twelve at the Regionals. She skated in a purple velvet dress and white tights to music from Broadway's *Showboat*. Lucian had picked and edited the tunes himself on a special record. The first, fast part was to "Can't Help Lovin' Dat Man," the slow middle section was to "Ol' Man River," and then for the big, dramatic finish she skated to a Charleston. Toni landed all of her double jumps and wrapped up with a change-leg camel/sit/scratch spin. She placed twelfth out of twelve in the free skating, just as she had in the figures.

"This is a problem," Lucian said, looking at her scores.

"Is it a problem that can be solved with money?" Daddy asked.

"I don't know, sir," Lucian admitted.

"Then you'd best figure it out and tell me. Soon."

"Yes, sir."

To Toni, Daddy said, "Now, the only solution I personally

can see to this problem is for you to get yourself twice as good, three times as good, whatever it takes, so that those judges can't keep on ignoring you like this. You think you can do that, Antonia?"

"I don't know, sir."

"Then you'd best figure it out and tell me. Soon."

After a few days of thinking about it, Lucian said, "I think I may have a solution."

"What is it?"

"You're going to skate Pairs." It wasn't a question. It was a pronouncement.

"With who?"

"With me." Another pronouncement.

"You know, Lucian, even in a Pair, I'll still be colored."

"Yes. But it will matter less. Trust me. Plus, the judges have already shown they like me. I won my group on all seven cards, and by a wide margin, too. If they like me by myself, they'll like me with you."

"Why would you want to give up skating Singles to skate Pairs with me?"

"Because I'm good by myself, but I can be great with you." Lucian smiled. "What do you say? Have I ever steered you wrong before?"

Toni hesitated. "I . . . Let me talk to my father."

"Of course." He appeared utterly unconcerned about what her answer would be. Toni wished she knew her own mind as well as he seemed to believe he did.

When she told Daddy about Lucian's plan, he thought about it for a moment, then observed, "You've told me all the reasons why young Master Pryce thinks you should skate Pairs. But I have yet to hear whether this is what you want, Antonia."

"I . . . I . . . ," Toni stammered. So many contradictory fireworks were going off in her head simultaneously, she felt as though she couldn't quite articulate anything that she wanted—or didn't want—at the moment. "Lucian thinks—"

"Lucian thinks. Lucian thinks. Lucian says . . . Tell me, Toni, do you do everything Lucian tells you to?" Her father's voice was gentle. But also, for the first time ever, Toni heard an edge in his tone that had never been there before. He seemed to be asking her more than what he was simply asking her. But, under the circumstances, it just became another bottle rocket in her head, and she let it go without following up.

"No, of course not, Daddy," Toni said, knowing it was exactly what he needed to hear. "But he's smart. He knows a lot about skating. And that he's willing to give up his Singles career for me, well, it must mean he really believes we can be good as a Pair."

"Lucian Pryce is smart. Smart enough to understand that if you were to grow frustrated as a result of your poor placing and quit skating, then there go his own prospects as well. I highly doubt he can convince another parent to assume the financial responsibility I have these past few years. By suggesting that you switch to Pairs, he is acting in his own interests, no one else's. You'd do well to remember that, Antonia, for the present and future. Ultimately, everyone acts only in their own interests. Especially those who spend a great deal of time explaining how they are acting in yours."

"I want to skate Pairs with Lucian, Daddy." Toni made up her mind on the spot. She hoped her tone didn't reveal just how fresh the decision was.

"You're certain?"

"Yes, sir."

"All right then. I wish you all the luck in the world."

His words proved prophetic. A year later, thirteen-year-old Toni and eighteen-year-old Lucian were competing at the World—well, the Junior World—Championship as the number-three Pair out of the United States. They were not expected to win a medal, and they didn't. But that wasn't the point. The point was—even Daddy had to admit it and he was happy to do so—that Lucian had proven himself right. Again. Pairs was the way to go. For both of them.

It took them two seasons to win a Junior medal internationally, and then another before they made the World Team as Seniors.

At the Nationals where they finally won their first Senior U.S. title, a vocal group of spectators in the stands made monkey sounds when Toni stepped on the ice for warm-up. In the front row, directly across from the judges, another handful of people made a point of turning their backs to the rink as soon as Wright and Pryce were announced as taking the ice. In her hotel room at that Nationals and at several subsequent ones, Toni got scribbled notes slipped under the door, threatening both her and Lucian with all sorts of anatomical tortures she hadn't even known were possible. Toni dutifully turned each of the missives over to the police in whatever city they happened to be visiting. And then proceeded to never hear from the authorities again.

She didn't care.

And this time, she wasn't just pretending not to care, like she had that day over ten years ago at Wollman Rink, when she waited until an opportune fall gave her the chance to cry with honor. This time, she really, truly, utterly didn't care. Because at this point, the only thing that genuinely mattered was the skating, the progressing, the winning. And Lucian.

Lucian mattered. Of course, he always had before. But it was different now. Toni wasn't sure when she had fallen in love with him. She only knew that when she asked him if it was a problem, he grinned and said, "Now *this* isn't a problem at all."

They never talked about keeping their relationship a secret. They simply did. Because neither one of them was an idiot. Lucian's parents liked Toni well enough, and Toni's parents, she suspected, actually even respected Lucian quite a bit. But both knew that like and respect were a long way away from tolerate or condone.

Toni suspected her father knew something was going on. Because, all of a sudden, he would out of the blue tell her, "Those folks down in Virginia, those folks called Loving— isn't that the name? Dragging their miscegenation marriage nonsense all the way up to the Supreme Court. What did it get them but heartache? All well and good that they can get married now. But I ask you, where do they think they're going to live? In Narnia? In Nod? In Oz, maybe?"

Sarcasm was rarely her father's weapon of choice. Toni had to presume that he was trying to tell her something, without flat out asking her something. Because if he asked, he knew his daughter well enough to understand that she would tell him the truth. And then he would have to hear it.

But Toni didn't need her father's lectures on the wisdom of the Loving v. Virginia decision of 1967. She was perfectly well aware of the court case. Mainly because she had recently made Lucian perfectly well aware that fun was fun and laughs were laughs and love may have been a many splendored thing, but if they intended to progress beyond the fun and the laughs and the basic splendor, they would need to get married first.

"Is that a problem?" she asked him.

"Not at all," he replied.

They decided to wait one more season. It was an Olympic one after all, and both agreed they needed to focus all their energy on defending their U.S. title—and pretty spectacularly at that—if they intended to make any kind of challenge for a Gold medal on the international stage. So far, they'd finished sixth in the world, then fourth. A Gold medal wasn't a given, but neither was it an impossibility.

That year at Nationals, a petition no one would admit to starting or signing, yet one everyone claimed to have seen, circulated in the arena, asserting that assigning a team like Wright and Pryce to the Olympics would send the wrong message to the world about what America stood for. For a petition everyone swore not to have signed, it reached three single-spaced pages by the start of their Free Skate.

Lucian and Toni still won it. But the judges split five to four in their favor, with four of the votes going to a brother-and-sister team that had previously finished no higher than eighth. Only one season earlier, Toni and Lucian had won every judge. This was not a good sign, and they both knew it. At the Olympics, when even the Soviet judge put them in third place, their own U.S. judge had them fifth. Toni and

Lucian understood it was over. They'd been humored long enough, but now that America had an adequate replacement team—she was blonde and he was blonder—ready in the wings, it was time for Toni Wright and Lucian Pryce to move on.

So they did. No complaints, no press conferences, no finger pointing. It wouldn't have occurred to either of them to act in such a manner. Toni because it was hardly a classy way to behave, and Lucian because he knew that aggravating skating's powers that be was an excellent way to insure never having a professional career. And both he and Toni had agreed they wanted one. For a few years at least.

As reigning U.S. Pairs champions, they expected they could have, if not their pick of the touring, high-profile skating shows, at least a decent offer or two to consider.

None came.

Ice Capades simply passed without explanation. Holiday on Ice conceded that there were "issues" but declined to articulate what they might be. The Tour of World Figure Skating Champions offered them a dozen dates over the course of the year—but all of them outside of the United States.

It wasn't that Toni and Lucian objected to touring Europe. But they'd had their hearts set on America as well. Finally, they turned to a smaller outfit, Sullivan's Skating Stars, a company not known for its headliners. Sullivan's tended to play smaller arenas and decamped in towns the big tours never bothered visiting. But they'd expressed some initial interest.

Negotiations got as far as the contract stage where, as part of outlining exactly what accomodations they'd be needing while on tour, Toni casually mentioned that she and Lucian planned on getting married prior to departing.

That brought Mr. Sullivan himself up short.

"Hmm," he said.

Toni and Lucian exchanged looks. Both realized that Mr. Sullivan's "hmm" was the equivalent of Lucian's "This is a problem."

"What, exactly, is the problem?" Toni asked, sparing him the trouble of actually introducing the topic.

"Hmm," Mr. Sullivan said again. "I'm afraid . . . the problem is . . . it wouldn't be possible. . . . I can take one of you," he said. "One, not both. I'm sorry. It's one thing, just the skating. People can overlook just the skating. Maybe. But a married couple such as yourselves . . . We play a lot of small towns, you see."

They saw. They said they would think about it. They both did.

The next morning, Lucian called Mr. Sullivan to tell him his circumstances had changed. It seemed that he would be available to take the offered headlining spot on his own. Miss Wright would be pursuing opportunities elsewhere.

A few months later, the *New York Times*, in its regular "Weddings" section, carried an item announcing that Lucian Pryce, former U.S. Pairs champion with Antonia Wright, while on a hiatus from his role as principle headliner for Sullivan's Skating Stars, had wed a young woman he had also recently started coaching in Ladies' Singles, by the name of Eleanor Quinn.

Toni Wright didn't attend the wedding.

Three

**SKATINGANDSTUFF.COM
MESSAGE BOARD**

FROM: SkateGr8
Posted at 9:44 AM

Anyone know if Antonia Wright is going to be at the Pryce tribute?

FROM: IceIsNice
Posted at 9:57 AM

I would totally not blame her if she didn't show. Everybody knows Pryce completely dumped her for Eleanor Quinn because Miss Wright wasn't the right enough shade for Pryce's country-club set. What a jerk! He doesn't deserve a tribute, IMHO.

FROM: LuvsLian
Posted at 10:11 AM

I heard it wasn't because Toni was black, but because she couldn't do anything more for Lucian's career that he dumped her. They'd already been US Champions, this was before there was a Pro circuit for them to compete on. So Toni was out and Eleanor in. She could bring Lucian Gold.

FROM: SkatingFreak
Posted at 10:33 AM

So you're saying Pryce wasn't a racist, just a dirty old man. Great defense. Sure makes me love him now!

FROM: LuvsLian
Posted at 10:47 AM

I didn't say he was a dirty old man.

FROM: SkatingFreak
Posted at 10:52 AM

What do you call a guy who dumps his partner, who is practically—well for Lucian anyway—his own age, and takes up with a teenager? Then, soon as she gets too old for him, Lucian starts macking on Gina Gregory, who is younger even than his daughter.

Toni was on her knees, on the ice, next to Lucian. She'd yanked off her gloves and tossed them over her shoulder, desperately digging into his neck for a pulse with her bare fingers. Bex felt like she should be doing something but, from the look on Toni's face, didn't think there was much to be done. Instead, she went outside to look for the ambulance, flagging them down as they rounded the corner and leading them towards the ice surface. She needn't have bothered. They were clearly old pros at this.

Toni stepped aside when the experts swept in, but didn't leave the ice. She merely stood by the barrier, watching, oblivious to anyone else's presence, even Bex's when Bex helplessly handed Toni her cast-aside gloves. Toni took them without so much as a thank-you. When Toni Wright forgot her manners, Bex knew the situation was dire.

The paramedics didn't look back at either of them. But neither did they attempt CPR. When they loaded Lucian onto the stretcher, there was no neck brace. He was obviously dead weight.

Finally, one of the medics slowly turned around and asked the assembled, "Who's in charge here?"

"He was," Toni said, without a trace of irony. Without a trace of anything, really.

Her use of the past tense clued the guy in that there was no need to make the final pronouncement. So instead, he merely said, "Police are on their way. They'll have to file a report, paperwork, that sort of thing."

"Of course."

"They'll need to ask some questions."

"We'll be here to answer them," Toni reassured. "I feel certain no one is planning to flee the jurisdiction in the next few minutes."

It was apparently exactly what the paramedic needed to hear, because he smiled gratefully and took off, with only a final, "Yeah, you know, sorry about your loss, folks," to freeze and crack under the chilly air in his wake.

Toni watched him go. They all did. The four of them stood staring at the rink door as it clanked shut, no one budging an inch or making a sound until Toni, realizing it was up to her, softly told the camera crew, "You might as well get your equipment off the ice, gentlemen. I don't believe you'll be needing it anymore today."

They humbly did as bidden, whispering to Bex they'd be out in the parking lot packing up the truck, and to holler if she needed anything.

Bex said that she would, but her focus was on Toni. The older woman eased her way off the ice, moving as gracefully across the surface in shoes as she did atop skates on those occasions when she still slipped them on to teach a lesson. The moment her feet hit the carpeting, though, Toni seemed to lose all energy, practically collapsing on the nearest bench and holding on to the back of it as if lacking the strength to so much as remain upright. Bex hurried over, terrified that Toni might be having stroke of some kind.

"I'm all right," Toni assured, waving away Bex's concern even as she struggled to take a full breath. "I'm all right. Just . . . stunned. Yes, stunned, that's the correct word."

"I don't know what happened," Bex stammered. "He was fine. I mean, he looked fine. He was just skating around. . . ."

"He fell."

"Well, yes, but . . . skaters, don't they fall, like, a million times a day?"

"The body bounces back a lot easier at fifteen then at sixty-five, my dear."

"Still . . ."

"I'm sure the coroner will figure it out. Not that it matters, does it? What does it matter how he died? Lucian is dead. That's what matters."

"What about the tribute?" Bex said the most inappropriate thing possible under the circumstances. She was like that. Or, more to the point, Gil Cahill had helped to make her like that. She would have to call Gil and tell him his woman-ratings-driving prime-time TV special had just hit a little . . . snag.

Toni took no offense. She simply repeated, "The tribute . . ."

"Excuse me." A policeman's voice echoed inside the cavernous rink. "I'm here to talk about Lucian Pryce's death."

"Of course." Toni rose and regally went to greet him, all her frailty of a moment earlier magically gone in the service of politeness. "How may we help you?"

Bex tagged along like a well-trained puppy. She did her best to answer the cop's questions about who she was, why they were there at such an ungodly hour, and what, to the best of her knowledge, had just happened. Toni backed up Bex's story, explaining that she'd only been there for a minute, but as far as she could tell, Lucian had slipped and hit his head and . . .

"Did he have a history of head injuries?" the policeman asked.

"Of course," Toni answered.

The certainty of her confirmation took both the policeman and Bex by surprise.

Toni explained, "Hairline fractures, concussions are second nature to a skater. And it's even worse in Pairs. I've lost track of how many times I must have hit Lucian on the side of the head with my skate. He was only hospitalized twice. With most injuries, unless there's heavy bleeding or bones protruding, we didn't even bother seeing a doctor. When I had my first son thirty years ago, they asked me at the doctor's office, 'Did you know you had three hairline fractures on your pelvis and one on your tailbone that never healed right?' I had no idea. We just skated through the pain. What else could you do?"

"But isn't there a danger of reinjuring—"

"Skating is a dangerous sport," Toni said firmly, indicating that she would be accepting no judgments from a civilian on the matter.

"The paramedics told me it looked like the skull cracked on impact with the ice. Probably sent bone fractions into his brain like a couple dozen toothpicks."

Bex winced at the description, but Toni only nodded sagely, as if she'd been expecting something like that.

"A dangerous sport," she reminded.

"Now, we'll need to notify the next of kin. . . ."

"Gina," Toni said. "Gina Gregory, that's his wife. And Sabrina Pryce, she's his daughter. Sabrina was supposed to be in town for this. I wonder if she's—"

"She's here," Bex interrupted. "I saw her at the house this morning."

"Gina and Sabrina, then. They're the next of kin."

"If you give us the address, we can send a squad car—"

"No!" Toni piped up. Then, getting control of herself, softly repeated, "No. Can I—would you mind if I did it? I've known them both for a very long time and—"

"That will be fine, ma'am. We'll let you both know if we need anything further."

Toni nodded, realizing the interview was over, and stood up when the policeman did. As he headed towards the door, she headed towards the coaches' lounge, not looking over her should to even check whether he was out of the building.

Bex's head swiveled from one to the other, not sure which to follow. She finally decided to go with the policeman, waiting until they were both in the parking lot and out of Toni's hearing range before asking, "When do you think the coroner's report will be ready?"

"What now?" He hadn't realized he was being tailed and appeared a bit startled to find her on his heels. "Oh, that. A few days, I suppose."

"So you'll interview Gina and Sabrina, then?"

"Gina and Sabrina?"

"The wife and the daughter," Bex reminded.

"The wife and . . . I thought Miss Wright there said she would take care of—"

"Well, yes, but your detectives will want to get their statements."

"About what?"

Bex felt like they were speaking two different languages. "The murder, of course."

"Murder, ma'am?"

"You'll need motive, means, opportunity. As I mentioned, I'm from the 24/7 network and I would really appreciate being kept in the loop."

"What murder?"

Definitely two different languages. "Lucian's!"

"Lucian Pryce's death was an accident, ma'am."

"Of course it wasn't." That fact was blatantly obvious to Bex. She wondered why an officer of the law was having trouble . . . Oh, of course! "Right. You want to keep this quiet for now. I understand. With a murder in such a public place, the last thing you want is curiosity seekers coming by and tainting your chain of evidence. Believe me, I can be very discreet. Especially if you promise to let me know as soon as you're ready to make a statement about the investigation. I'd like to be first to report it. Maybe we can make a trade. Our exclusive footage of the death in exchange for, say, a six-hour news window for 24/7 to run with the story?"

"Miss Levy?"

"Yes?"

"What are you talking about? There was no murder here. Lucian Pryce died in an accident. There's your exclusive. Take all the time with it you need."

"Can you believe it?" Bex ranted to Toni, catching the older woman as she was exiting the rink just after the black and white police car pulled out of the parking lot. Bex's 24/7 crew had left as well. "These hick cops actually think Lucian's death was an accident!"

Toni paused at the door of her car, key halfway in the lock to ask, "And what do you think it was, Bex?"

"Why, murder, of course. Isn't it obvious?"

"Murder . . ."

"You don't think it's terribly convenient that Lucian should turn up dead on the eve of a tribute to him? Doing something he's done how many millions of times in his life?"

"Convenient? No, Bex, I wouldn't say it was exactly convenient."

"I didn't mean it like that."

"I'm afraid I'm not sure what exactly you meant, then."

"Do you remember at Worlds? Not this Worlds, the one before it. When that judge, Silvana Potenza, died."

"Of course."

"Well, everyone was saying that was an accident, too. But I wanted to know, what would a judge at a World Championship be doing in a dark, dirty room, standing in a puddle of water and getting electrocuted? Especially when it was her vote that gave Gold to a Russian girl half the arena thought should have come in second. I kept digging and digging and digging, and sure enough, it was murder."

"I hardly think this is the same kind of thing."

"Igor Marchenko, six months ago at that Pro-Am in Russian. It looked like a heart attack. Turned out to be poison."

"Again, Bex . . ."

"How do we know Lucian wasn't poisoned? I mean, what made him fall like that? It's not like he was trying some fancy trick. He was skating backwards. How hard can that be?"

"It's actually rather difficult."

"For someone who'd been doing it for over sixty years?"

"Bex, I'm afraid . . . I think . . . Maybe you should consider the possibility that some of the things you've been through over the past year or two may possibly have colored your judgment when it comes to—"

"Don't you want to know who did this to him, Toni?"

"Frankly, dear, I can't imagine anyone who'd want to."

"He must have had enemies. Everybody does, especially someone as successful as Lucian. There have to be people who wanted to do him harm."

"Like whom, for instance?"

"Other coaches, former students, you . . ."

That last part slipped out. As so many things Bex said were wont to do. Though, if she were truly honest with herself, Bex would have to admit that a part of her was dying to check out Toni's reaction to the pseudo-accusation.

"Me," Toni repeated.

"Um, yes."

"I poisoned Lucian to make him fall?"

"Well, I'm not certain about the poison angle. That's up to the coroner. I just mentioned that Igor Marchenko—"

"And why did I do this, exactly? We'll get to the how, when, and where later."

"Well, I—there's your past."

"I killed him because we were National Pairs champions?"

"I meant, your more personal past."

Toni bristled. "You don't know what you're talking about, Bex."

"I do. I mean, everybody does. It's hardly a secret that you two were engaged, and then he dumped you so he could skate in an ice show and marry Eleanor Quinn. It's practically a matter of public record."

"You don't know what you're talking about," Toni repeated, this time much more firmly, and slid into the front seat of her car.

Bex would have left it at that. Except that, with Lucian dead, Bex also had no way of leaving the rink. She had to ask Toni for a ride back to her hotel.

It was rather humiliating.

They were in the process of driving, in frosty silence, towards the direction Bex had requested, when she suddenly piped up, "Oh, wait a minute. Toni, I'm so sorry. I just remembered I forgot some things back at Lucian's house. Since you're going there anyway, do you think I could tag along?"

Toni surveyed Bex out of the corner of her eye. She said coolly, "How about this, Bex? You try not to insult my intelligence, and I'll let you come along when I tell Gina and Sabrina about Lucian. How about that?"

Bex didn't stand that many inches over five feet as it was. Courtesy of Toni's tongue lashing, she now felt exactly one centimeter tall. Bex wondered if it was actually possible to shrivel up and die on the spot from embarrassment, or whether she would simply spontaneously combust from the heat inflaming her cheeks, instead.

"I'm sorry," she said.

"It's all right. I could use the moral support." Toni pulled into the Pryce driveway. "This isn't going to be easy."

Especially since, when Bex and Toni got to the house, Gina and Sabrina weren't alone. In the few hours Bex and Lucian had been gone, both women had gotten dressed, Sabrina in a pair of tailored gray slacks and a pink cashmere sweater, her hair swept back with a plastic headband, and Gina into tight-fitting blue jeans with a purple T-shirt that showed off her unnaturally toned midriff. She may have tried to do something with her hair, but it appeared to Bex as unruly as ever.

Still apparently tripping on the excess coffee of the morning, Gina swept Bex and Toni into the house with a frenetic beckon of the hand and a shrieked, "What a terrific surprise! Toni, how nice to see you! Look who's here!"

The frenetic hand shifted from beckoning to pointing as Gina giddily indicated a couple sitting on the couch.

Bex recognized Christian Kelly right away. The thirty-eight-year-old Englishman was Lucian Pryce's most decorated skater, a multitime British, European, and World, but, most importantly, two-time Olympic Men's champion. He was almost six feet tall standing up, slender and long limbed, with dark brown hair and green eyes, dressed as nattily as if for a precompetition banquet in neatly pressed khaki pants, a white shirt with no tie and the top button undone, and a sports jacket. It was a look, Bex noted, very similar to the one Lucian himself employed twenty years earlier, when Chris was under his tutelage.

Bex introduced herself to the champion, shaking his hand, then waited for him to identify the woman sitting beside him. She had the typical former skater look, small and slight, with shoulder-length blonde hair pulled back into a French braid. She appeared about a decade younger than Chris, somewhere between Bex's age and Gina/Sabrina's.

"Gabrielle Cassidy," Chris explained, without looking at her.

"Oh!" Bex exclaimed. "Dr. Cassidy! Hi, I'm Bex Levy. We spoke on the phone last year when I was researching my piece about skaters who dropped out of the sport at seemingly the top of their game, remember? You told me about how you'd opened your new training center based on your PhD thesis proving that elite, champion athletes could be produced without pressure or stress."

At that bit of blasphemy, Sabrina looked uninterested, Gina incredulous, and Toni amused. Chris was the only one who actually snorted out loud.

Gabrielle said, "Even after a year of working for me, Mr. Kelly still has a bit of a theological problem with the concept."

"You work there? For her?" Bex clarified.

"Oh, yes," Gina said. "Chris and Gabrielle just flew up together this morning from California so they could both be with us for Lucian's big evening. . . ." The mention of her husband's name triggered a quizzical, "Where is Lucian? Did he stay back at the rink?"

Bex glanced nervously at Toni. The older woman had been content to lurk in the background up to that point, obviously happy to put off the inevitable for a few more moments. Now, Toni stepped forward, reaching one arm for Sabrina, the other for Gina. Neither took the proffered hand. Both sensed something was wrong. Sabrina inched a nervous step back and—was it subconsciously?—snuck a peek at the picture of her late mother above the fireplace. Gina, for her part, actually stopped talking.

"Toni?" Chris was ultimately the one who spoke first. "What is it, darling?"

"There was," Toni said slowly, "an accident. Lucian was skating—"

"That's ridiculous," Gina interjected. "Lucian hardly ever gets out on the ice, anymore. He teaches mostly from rinkside."

"I asked him to," Bex said. "It was for the tribute show. We wanted footage of his skating. Then and now."

Toni said, "He fell. He hit his head."

"Is he all right?" Gina demanded.

"Is he in hospital?" Chris asked, already standing up in anticipation of heading straight there.

Only Sabrina calmly guessed, "He's dead."

"Oh, shut up, would you?" Gina snapped, turning on her stepdaughter in a fury. "We all know your issues with your father, but this old song is getting very boring, and now isn't the time for a new verse, all right?"

Sabrina didn't respond to Gina's outburst. She simply kept looking at Toni and calmly asked, "I'm right, aren't I? He's dead."

"Yes," Toni said.

Of all the people in the room, Chris seemed to take it the

hardest. The skin around his eyes instantly turned red and blotchy. He raised one hand to cover his mouth, inhaling harshly and holding his breath. Sabrina remained frozen to the spot, eyes locked with Toni's, while Gina spun around abruptly, so that no one could see her reaction. Gabrielle merely seemed uncomfortable, not too shocked, not too saddened, not too anything except concerned that a reaction was expected of her, and she didn't have an appropriate one to offer. Toni stepped forward and wrapped one arm around Sabrina, but the younger woman didn't yield to the embrace. After a moment, Toni awkwardly let her go. Chris stepped over Gabrielle's legs to rest his hand on Gina's shoulder. She shrugged him off and he didn't try again. Bex and Gabrielle exchanged uneasy looks. Both realized they were out of place, but neither knew exactly how to either join in or extricate themselves from the situation. At least in Bex's case, she had a professional reason for observing the scene. Gabrielle looked as though she'd bought a ticket for one movie and accidentally stumbled into a screening of another.

Trying to get them all off the hook and dissipate the unbearable tension building in the room, Bex offered, "The coroner's office, they have Lucian's body right now. You should be able to claim it as soon as they finish the autopsy and determine cause of death."

"What are you talking about?" Gina spun back around to face them all. Bex noted that her eyes were dry, her hands steady, and her voice as shrill as ever. "What determine cause of death? Toni said he fell and hit his head. What's there to determine?"

"It was an accident," Toni agreed, glaring daggers at Bex.

But sticks and stones weren't too good at stopping Bex when she was on a tear. Mere words had no chance. She said, "It might not have been."

"Then what was it?" Chris demanded.

"It could have been . . . I mean, it's possible . . . The circumstances . . . There's a possibility it might have been . . . well . . . murder."

Chris snorted again. He was very good at that. Bex wondered if all English people were. "What rubbish."

"Why?" Sabrina piped up. "Do you think Lucian was so universally loved that no one could have even entertained the possibility?"

"Darling," Chris began.

"Oh, don't 'darling' me. I'm not still that big-eyed nine-year-old you can pat on the head and tell to go play nicely in her room." She addressed Bex. "So you think my father was murdered?"

"I'm just saying it could have happened."

"He wasn't murdered," Toni said.

"How?" Sabrina challenged. "How did it happen?"

"Well, there are several possibilities," Bex admitted. "Until the coroner comes back with some kind of verdict, there's really no use in guessing—"

"Okay, then, by whom? You don't need a coroner's report to take a stab at that, do you, Miss Levy?"

"I—I don't know. I'd like to ask some questions, maybe—"

"Well, I know," Sabrina announced.

"You do?" That certainly got everyone's attention.

"I do," Sabrina crowed. "Or, rather, I know who didn't do it. Other coaches may have hated my father. Other skaters, big-time officials, judges, heck, even a good number of disgruntled parents. But the one thing my father always had was the love and devotion of his precious students." She waved an arm to encompass Gina, Chris, Gabrielle, and any others who may have been lurking on the periphery, or were at least represented in abstentia by the multiple trophies, plaques, and ribbons on the walls. "My father's students were nuts about him. They were like the children he never had. Present company included, of course."

Four

Sabrina

Until she was six years old or so, Sabrina Pryce never knew that she was, technically, an only child. That's because everywhere she looked, there were pseudo-sibling rivals about. If they weren't clinging to Lucian's arm at the rink (he let the littlest ones practice their Axel jump by holding onto his finger and rotating), then they were badgering him off the ice with their incessant questions as he sat in the lounge taking off his skates or in the office finessing the master coaching schedule.

"Mr. Pryce, will you cut my music this weekend?"

"Mr. Pryce, can you just take a quick look at my camel spin? I think I got it now."

If they weren't at the house for a costume fitting, then they were on the phone, and if they weren't in the back seat of the family car being given a lift to the rink, then their photos were strewn about the living room, waiting for Lucian's approval before they sent them in for inclusion in the latest competition program.

And then, of course, there were the ones who just moved in.

Every season for as far back as Sabrina could remember,

there had been some skater or two ensconced in their guest room. They might just be spending the night to make getting to the rink for an early morning practice session the next day easier, or they might be there for the school term or the summer to have Lucian work on a particular troublesome element before sending them back to their regular coaches. Or they might be there for the long haul.

Christian Kelly moved in when Sabrina was nine. At first, he was merely a videotaped presence, but even then, he consumed a good chunk of Lucian's time. Sabrina's father had received a videotape in the mail from a fellow coach in England extolling the virtues of her prodigious pupil and asking if Lucian would consider taking the fourteen-year-old boy on as a student—and as a charity case. It was that last one that prompted Lucian to watch the tape over and over again, trying to make up his mind.

Pointing at the television screen where, for what seemed like the umpteenth time, Chris was performing his interpretation of "The Flight of the Bumblebee," Lucian told Eleanor, "Boy's got talent, there is absolutely no question about that. Look how he moves, he's a natural. Nice spring, nice sense of music. And his technique isn't bad, not too many lousy habits for me to break. If they could afford it, I'd snap him up in a second. But, Nancy says there's not a penny to be spared. Parents are split up and working class, and in any case, they've practically disowned the kid for wanting to skate. Not that Nancy thinks the pair's any great bargain, says the boy would be better off away from them for the long haul. That's why she came to me. If that's the case, though, she's not just asking me to train him and fund him, she's practically asking us to raise him. He's fourteen! Boys at fourteen, Ellie . . ."

"Is there money in the scholarship fund?"

"A bit. Enough for one more this season, probably, yes. Question is, should this be the boy?"

After another week of back-and-forth and near constant tape viewing, Lucian decided that yes, it should be.

Chris arrived on a Saturday night, while Sabrina and her mother were at the movies. When they returned, Lucian introduced them all. Chris shook hands with Eleanor and said it was nice to meet her. He said hi to Sabrina and then went upstairs to finish his unpacking. Sabrina hated him on sight.

She thought he looked funny. Like his arms and his legs were longer than the rest of him. She thought he talked funny, pronouncing "garage" like "gahr-age" and "can't" as "cah-n't." She thought he smelled funny, like the pungent mint gel that he was always smearing on his knees to keep them from swelling. She even thought his name was stupid. If his name was Christian, then his nickname shouldn't have been Chris, it should have been "Chrish." Any dummy could see that.

Plus, there was the fact that Sabrina's father liked him best.

She wouldn't have blamed Lucian if it were just about the skating. Well, she would have blamed him, but she'd have understood it, nonetheless. Despite her nearly legendary lineage, Sabrina had never taken much to skating. Her parents put her on the ice when she was eighteen months old. And promptly took her off when she commenced screaming at the top of her lungs for close to a half hour.

"No like it!" was all they ever got in the way of an explanation.

They tried again when she was three and when she was four, too. "No like it," remained the sentiment, even if she did become more articulate in expressing it.

By the time she was old enough to remember, Sabrina could no longer recall what exactly had prompted her reaction. All she knew was that the thought of putting on ice skates filled her with a stubborn conviction not to. No reason why.

So if mere skating were all Lucian and Chris had in common, Sabrina could have accepted it. But it was more than that. Lucian and Chris were . . . for lack of a better term, buddies. They hung out. They talked about things. They talked about . . . life. And they left Sabrina out of it completely.

"Christian is older than you, honey," her mother tried to soothe. "Of course he and Daddy have things to talk about that aren't for you. But when you're bigger . . ."

"No," Sabrina said. Even at ten years old she knew when she was being spun.

Chris ended up living with them for four years. When he finally moved out, Sabrina thought maybe now she'd have a chance at a normal family, without a perennial outsider hanging around, drawing focus. But, within a week of Chris leaving, there was another skater. And then another and another and another until, ultimately, it was Sabrina who moved out to go to college and a relatively normal living experience for the first time in her life.

Though, as she would tell her therapist years later, Sabrina supposed she could have, one day, forgiven her father for always putting his students ahead of her. What she couldn't forgive Lucian for was killing her mother.

At the time of their marriage, Lucian and Eleanor Quinn Pryce were not quite yet skating royalty. Lucian, after all, was only half of a Nationals-winning Pairs team—and a pretty controversial one, at that—while Eleanor was a former Novice and Junior Ladies' champion looking to make a name for herself in the Senior ranks.

She'd only been coached by Lucian for a few months when she earned her first U.S. medal, a Bronze. Then, a year later, she came back to win the whole thing—as an entirely new person.

It wasn't only that her name was now Eleanor Quinn Pryce. It was that, in twelve short months, Lucian had seemingly created a different skater. At eighteen, even nineteen years old, she'd been what the pundits loved to describe as "coltlike," all raw energy and sinewy limbs and a style that consisted of unbridled enthusiasm over everything else. At twenty, under Lucian's guidance, she was suddenly calm, controlled, graceful, balletic, and poised. Her music, instead of a frantic Khachaturian "Sabre Dance," was now Beethoven's meditative *Moonlight* Sonata. Her costumes went from almost practice-quality blacks and whites to an assortment of soft, flowing, chiffon pastels.

Her hair, which she once wore plaited into two braids and looped over the top of her head not unlike Heidi or one of the *Sound of Music* moppets just to functionally keep it from flopping in her face, was now piled in a glorious concoction atop her head, prompting spectators to sit in equal awe at her skating and at her ability to keep the carefully constructed edifice from tumbling down. She had become, quite simply, a work of art. Lucian Pryce's own, personal Galatea.

When Eleanor won the Olympics—and the hearts of the television audience in the process; she received so many congratulatory telegrams after the event that the Olympic Village was required to create a special storage area just for her—she and Lucian ascended to the ranks of Golden Couple. Reporters wanted to interview them. Magazines wrote cover stories on them. There was even a children's book on Eleanor that featured Lucian quite prominently in the middle photo section, and when Eleanor wrote her own autobiography, Lucian was credited as the coauthor. Everyone wanted to know, what was next for Eleanor Quinn Pryce?

Lucian let them in on the game plan: Eleanor would turn professional immediately after the post-Olympic World Championships (which she would, of course, win), she would accept a contract from the most prestigious ice show in America, tour for exactly four years, retire from performing a few weeks before the new Olympic champion was crowned, and then focus her attentions on starting a family.

Which was exactly how it happened—to the letter. Even Sabrina did her part, being born nine months following the Olympics that dethroned her mother. Though, as Lucian liked to point out, that was hardly her achievement, now, was it?

By the time Sabrina was old enough to recognize what was what, Eleanor had long ago stepped out of the limelight. She only skated on special occasions, mostly for charity events, primarily if they were televised, or for herself, just for fun. She might help Lucian out periodically by consulting on a skater he was working with, but she never coached full-time. Her chief identity, as far as Sabrina could tell, was being

Lucian's support staff. She kept his house, she kept his schedule, she kept his child, and she kept him happy.

When Sabrina was little, she didn't question it. After all, her mother serving her father's every whim at home also meant that she was usually there at Sabrina's beck and call, too. Which was nice. Sabrina would never deny that it was quite nice. But by the time Sabrina's know-it-all teen years hit in conjunction with the women's movement, she felt enlightened enough to be properly outraged and insulted on her mother's behalf.

"How can you let Daddy treat you like that?" she demanded.

"Like what?" Eleanor usually spoke softly. But, as her daughter grew shriller and more strident, Eleanor would lower her voice even more, in a subtle attempt to encourage Sabrina to do the same.

Unfortunately, when Sabrina was a teenager, the technique only served to inflame her, and she cranked up the volume. "Like you're his personal slave or something. All you care about is Lucian this, Lucian that, Lucian, Lucian, Lucian. What about you? Don't you matter? You're a person! Heck, you're a celebrity!" To Sabrina, that last one seemed to be the biggest insult. How dare her mother yield to her father like she did, when Eleanor was the true star in the family!

"And Daddy is the head of this household," Eleanor responded with what, to Sabrina, was a nonanswer. It nevertheless meant "Discussion over."

There was a lot of that going around the Pryce domicile. Whenever Sabrina wondered out loud why her mother seemed so tired, or where she kept disappearing in the afternoons, she got a nonanswer/"Discussion over" brush off. It probably would have gone on that way indefinitely if Sabrina hadn't come home unexpectedly early from school one day because of a teachers' development meeting and caught her mother sitting in the car, in the driveway, not getting out, not moving, not doing anything.

She might have been the Eleanor Pryce wax museum figure commissioned after her Olympic win and still on exhibit in London. Only that figure was more animated, caught frozen in Eleanor's trademark layback spin and giving off an illusion of life and motion. This version's hands were on the steering wheel. She was staring straight ahead at the garage door, not even blinking, barely breathing it seemed.

When a terrified Sabrina knocked on the driver's side window—well, more like pounded the glass, really, so confused was she by the sight—Eleanor turned her head ever so slowly to respond, as if having a hard, almost drugged, time waking up. She looked at Sabrina questioningly. And then she started to cry.

Sabrina had never seen her mother cry before. Lucian believed it was a wasted activity that served no purpose and so strongly urged his students never to succumb. "You put your pain in your pocket, and go" was the phrase his acolytes liked to repeat to each other, even as blood gushed from a perennially opening blister or bone ground against bone in a joint where the cartilage had long gone missing. Before she was Sabrina's mother, before she was Lucian's wife, Eleanor had been his student. And she subscribed to his philosophy as much as anyone.

Yet here she was. Crying. And out in public, in the driveway, where anyone could come by and see. Sabrina may have been at what she then believed was the pinnacle of her dislike for Lucian and his little aphorisms. But that didn't mean they hadn't been internalized with every breath she'd drawn since infancy. She yanked open the car door, grabbed her mother by the arm, and practically dragged her inside the house. Eleanor followed along meekly.

But by the time they'd crossed their front stoop, Sabrina was already wondering if she'd imagined the whole incident. Because, once inside their living room, Eleanor had pulled herself together like the champion she was. The tears were gone. So was the inertia as well as the daze. She was herself again. Crisp, chipper, efficient, and determined to act as if nothing had happened.

"My goodness," she bubbled, removing her coat and moving to hang it up in the closet, making certain Sabrina couldn't see her face as she did it. "I must have fallen asleep at the wheel. Fortunately, I had the good sense to do so in my own driveway instead of on the highway somewhere. That would have been a mess, wouldn't it? Ah, well, all's well that ends well. What are you doing home so early, sweetheart?"

"Teacher development. Half day," Sabrina answered automatically, determined not to buy a word of this, yet already questioning her own judgment.

"Ah. I guess I'd forgotten."

"Mother . . ."

"Yes?" Now Eleanor was rotating the coats in the closet, brushing imaginary lint off the sleeves, still not looking Sabrina's way.

"What just happened?"

"You mean outside?"

"Yeah . . ."

"I told you. I fell asleep. It was a late night last night. Mrs. Gregory called and Lucian wasn't home, so I got to listen to the day's laments in his stead, and you know how she can be. And then, after your father left for the rink this morning, I just couldn't get back to sleep for the life of me, so . . . that's what happened."

"I thought I saw you . . . Were you crying?"

"I fell asleep," Eleanor reiterated firmly. "My eyes may have watered. I'm fine, Sabrina. Everything is fine. Come on. You can help me get lunch ready. Your father should be home soon. We don't want to keep him waiting."

For the rest of the day, Eleanor acted as if nothing in the world were the matter. But Sabrina, for the first time in her life, refused to take it on faith. Something was clearly going on. Something neither Sabrina nor Lucian were supposed to know about. And the notion of knowing something her father didn't proved even more enticing to Sabrina than simply wanting to discover what her mother was hiding.

The following day, Sabrina turned detective. She went off to school pretending everything was normal—after all, what

was good for the goose (her in-denial mother), etc., etc.—but
as soon as she was out of sight, Sabrina doubled back and
took a seat in the row of bushes across the street from her
house, choosing a spot from where she could see the front
door and garage clearly. When Eleanor left for the morning,
Sabrina snuck back inside. It was a situation she kept expecting to feel 007ish, but it didn't really. What with Sabrina having her own key and all. She was hardly picking locks and
sidestepping complicated security systems here. Once in,
Sabrina proceeded to look for . . . well, she didn't know what
she was looking for. But she figured there had to be something. As she couldn't very well tail her mother on roller
skates while Eleanor drove along in the car, this was the best
plan of action Sabrina had managed to conceive.

Sabrina figured that if whatever it was that Eleanor was
hiding was a secret from Lucian as well as Sabrina, it probably wouldn't be in her parents' bedroom. And it wouldn't be
in Sabrina's room or the guest room. (Even after half a
decade, Sabrina still preferred to think of it as the guest room
rather than Chris's room. That would be tantamount to toler-
ating his presence. Or admitting it was there.) The living room
and dining room were communal spaces; the basement and
attic were more or less open to all, though hardly anybody
ever went in either. That left the kitchen as her mother's primary domain. They may all have eaten there, but Eleanor was
the only one who cooked. It was also the room where she kept
a rolltop desk in the corner by the window to sort and pay
household bills out of the allowance Lucian gave her.

Sabrina started the snooping there. She learned very
quickly that, in addition to being an impeccable figure skater,
her mother was an even more methodical bookkeeper. Each
category of bill—electric, gas, insurance, grocery, water,
medical—that she'd recently paid had its own stack, filed in
reverse chronological order. As for the bills waiting to be paid,
prior to the first of every month Eleanor wrote out the appropriate check and slipped it in its reply envelope. The date the
bill was due was then written in the upper right hand corner
of the envelope and the envelopes lined up in order. That way,

all Eleanor needed to do was cover the date with a stamp when the time came, drop it in the mailbox, and the next one would be there, waiting for its own departure. Eleanor did Lucian's billing of his students, too. She said her father had enough to worry about without needing to keep a ledger of who was paid up and who was in arrears.

Sabrina leafed through the bills, finding nothing unusual, or at least nothing that looked unusual. She was so engrossed in the task at hand, she didn't even hear Eleanor come back home. Because, in the instant that she heard her mother demand, "What are you doing, Sabrina?" in a voice harsher than she'd ever used with her daughter before, Sabrina also found the invoice that explained pretty much everything.

She meant only to show the piece of paper to Eleanor, to prove that she knew and that there was no more point in lying. But the anger at having been kept in the dark proved overwhelming, and Sabrina ended up all but hurling it at her, accusing, "You're sick. You're sick and you didn't tell me. You didn't tell anybody."

Eleanor calmly bent down to retrieve the fluttering invoice, along with its litany of lab fees and other diagnostic minutia inadequately covered by health insurance. She said, "That's right. I didn't. I would have thought you'd have respected me enough to—"

"This says its been weeks!"

"Months, actually."

"They can fix it, can't they? It's not like that stupid movie with Ali McGraw. They can fix leukemia. You just need to get the right treatment."

"Sometimes. It depends."

"On what?"

"A lot of factors."

"Like what?" Sabrina could hear how petulant she sounded, how . . . adolescent. But right now, she didn't care.

"How often you get the treatment, what kind of treatment it is, how you respond to it. There are a great many variables."

"Well, you're getting the best treatment, aren't you? Aren't you?"

"I am getting what I need under the circumstances."

Something about the way she said it made Sabrina certain she was being put off. This was yet another "Discussion over" moment. But Sabrina wasn't having it. "What do you mean? You mean you're not doing everything you can? Why, Mom? That's stupid! Is it that we don't have enough money? Is that it?"

"We have money, Sabrina."

"Then what is it?"

Eleanor hesitated, and in the hesitation, Sabrina understood. "This is something to do with Daddy, isn't it?" She didn't know how that could be possible, but she also knew it was true. Eleanor wore that particular look of devoted concern only when the issue at hand might somehow negatively impact on her precious husband. "What does Daddy have to do with—"

"This is a very important year for your father. Chris won the Europeans last year. It's imperative that he win again this year if he's going to have a chance at a World medal, maybe even the actual title. And with the Olympics being next year, Chris absolutely has to position himself—"

"This is about Chris?" Sabrina all but roared. "Chris Kelly winning the Olympics?"

"I can't let anything distract your father right now."

"Your dying would distract him!"

"I'm not going to die. I'm doing well, my doctor agrees. Putting off the most aggressive treatment for just a few months is a viable option."

"So you could be getting more treatment right now, but you're not going to because it might somehow keep Chris from winning the Olympics? God, Mom, can you hear how stupid this is?"

"Your father hasn't ever had a male Olympic champion. He hasn't had a World champion since I retired. He needs this. He's in danger of becoming irrelevant."

"Chris Kelly is irrelevant! The Olympics are irrelevant! You have to get treatment."

"I'm getting it."

"Sure, just not enough."

"This is my decision, Sabrina."

"Not if I tell Daddy." She'd never spoken to her mother in such a tone of voice, much less flat out threatened her. And yet that certainly felt like what she was doing now. "He'll make you get treatment. He loves you."

"Yes," Eleanor agreed. "He does love me. He will make me get treatment. And he'll stay home from the rink to make sure I get it, and he'll skip Europeans and Worlds to make sure I'm well taken care of, and Chris will either give up completely or he will lose ground or he will find a new coach, and either way, Daddy will lose."

"You think he'd rather lose you than some stupid Olympic title?"

"I'm doing what I think is best, Sabrina. For everybody."

"I'll tell him." It was her only weapon, and Sabrina intended to keep firing it until her mother saw how ridiculous this all was.

"If you do," Eleanor said, showing the steel that propelled her to podium after podium as she "put her pain in her pocket and went," "I will never forgive you."

Sabrina didn't want to believe that it was true. But she was also too much of a coward to find out. And so she kept her mouth shut.

And so, while her father was at the World Championships in Italy with two-time European champion Christian Kelly, Eleanor died.

Sabrina wasn't the one who called to tell him in Rome. It was actually Toni who did the deed; Sabrina was too shell-shocked. And too angry.

Sabrina didn't know what they talked about, or what Lucian said or did or thought in the next twenty-four hours. All she knew was that Lucian didn't call home to find out how Sabrina was doing. And when he was interviewed live on television the next day prior to Chris's Long Program, he flung one arm around their perennial houseguest's shoulder and told everyone watching, "This wonderful boy is the only reason I had for getting up this morning."

Five

**SKATINGANDSTUFF.COM
MESSAGE BOARD**

FROM: GoGoGregory1
Posted at 9:44 AM

I think Gina is a couple years older than Sabrina—Lucian's daughter is still in college or just out.

FROM: SuperCooperFan
Posted at 9:56 AM

GUYS, GO LOOK AT GOOGLE NEWS RIGHT NOW!!!!

FROM: LuvsLian
Posted at 9:57 AM

OMG!!

FROM: SkatingFreak
Posted at 9:57 AM

Do you think it's true?

FROM: LuvsLian
Posted at 9:58 AM

Of course it's true, it's on the news! Do you think they'll still do the show?

FROM: GoGoGregory1
Posted at 9:59 AM

Oh, I hope so I've already got my flight booked they've just got to go on with the show it would be very inconsiderate to the fans IMHO who've already made plans and taken time off from work and spent a ton of money to be there if they don't.

The police arrived a few minutes after Toni finished breaking the news of Lucian's death. They said they needed to speak to Gina and Sabrina in private, and pretty much shuffled everybody else out of the house. Before she was unceremoniously tossed onto the driveway, Bex managed to ask her old friend, the officer in charge, "Does this mean you're finally ready to officially declare this a murder investigation?"

He sighed. He shook his head. He said, "This is not a murder investigation, Miss Levy. We simply need some paperwork signed." He completed the unceremonial tossing onto the driveway.

Toni, Chris, and Gabrielle were already there. They waited politely for Bex before preparing to disperse to their respective cars. Chris appeared to still be in a bit of shock, because it fell to Gabrielle to ask an obvious question no one had yet to voice (well, except Bex, tactlessly, earlier in the day). "So, is the tribute show off, then?"

It really was an excellent question. And not as trivial as it seemed. Sure, Lucian, the honoree, was dead. But ice time had been booked, tickets sold, publicity done, and most important, television crews dispatched and prime-time space allotted. This event had taken on a life of its own. It wasn't something that could easily be canceled at the drop of a hat. Nor was it necessarily something that should be.

Toni, Chris, and Gabrielle looked to Bex for the answer. She said, "I'll call Gil Cahill and ask."

Bex hitched a ride back to the rink with Toni. By the time they got there, the news of Lucian's death had already been leaked, and the usual early morning quiet of a practice session with only the sounds of blades slicing ice and sleepy coaches urging equally sleepy students to "Pull in harder" or "Push out stronger," had been replaced with a cacophony of rumor, speculation, and innuendo. The warmly bundled mob descended on Toni as soon as she stepped through the rink's doors, demanding answers and details. While Toni tried to make out who was asking what and who deserved to be answered versus who definitely begged to be ignored, Bex slipped away into the coaches' lounge, requisitioning the rotary phone for her own usage.

She called Gil in New York and appraised him of the situation. Her boss said, "Of course the show's going on! You think I'm going to take a bath on this?"

Well, no, she most certainly hadn't thought that, but . . . "We're going to put on a show to honor someone who isn't around to be honored?"

"Absolutely! This makes it even better! With a live honoree there's always a danger of them doing or saying something stupid to taint the whole thing. A dead guy . . . A dead guy is gold, Bex!"

She sighed and said, "And I suppose you expect me to figure out who murdered him before we go live with the show at the end of the week?"

Gil had a habit of demanding such tight turnarounds. At the World Championship in San Francisco, he'd wanted Bex to discern who'd killed the judge who gave first place to the Russian diva over America's sweetheart in time for them to reveal it live during the Exhibition Show. At the U.S.A. vs. Russia made-for-television competition he'd wanted the same information about the coach who'd been poisoned, and at the last Nationals, it had been find out who fathered the baby of a former Ice Dance champion now swinging from a belt in the costume room—oh, and who strung her up that way as well. Bex had delivered all three results (plus solved an earlier mystery featuring a kidnapped Jeremy and his dead mother) as requested. For the first time since Gil started sticking her with these macabre assignments, she finally felt confident enough to believe she could do it.

"Are you nuts, Bex?" Gil asked.

"I—what?"

"There's no murder here. Old guy takes a tumble and cracks his skull. Kind of hard to ferret out a conspiracy."

"But—"

"Look, Bex, I gave you a chance to produce some pieces for this special because I thought you were ready for a shot at the big leagues. But if you're just going to use it as an opportunity for self-aggrandizement . . ."

"Wait a minute, I'm not—"

"No one likes a show-off, Bex. This isn't about you. Stop trying to be the center of attention all the time. It's really unattractive."

"I thought you'd want—"

"What I want is a tear-jerking tribute show with a line around the block of world-famous skaters sobbing about their sainted, dead coach and how much he meant to their lives and careers. You got that? I don't want any nasty insinuations from you to mar the genuine beauty of the moment. Understand, Bex? Beauty? Moment? Tear-jerking?"

"But, Gil—"

"If you can't deliver the damn tears, Bex, I'll send someone up there who will. You following me?"

"Yes, Gil . . ."

"Excellent."

"Well, hello, stranger."

Bex had to confess. In all the fracas over Lucian's mur—

Lucian's death; she needed to remember that it was Lucian's *death*—she'd forgotten a key detail of her trip to Colorado. Craig was there, too. Not just in the vicinity but, at that moment, actually physically at the rink with Jeremy. Not just at the rink, but standing in the doorway of the coaches' lounge, arms crossed against his chest, peeking in, smiling and observing. "As soon as I heard there was a death in the skating community, I had a feeling I'd be seeing you. How in the world did you get here so fast? I thought Lucian only fell this morning?"

Oops. This was going to be a little awkward. Bex admitted, "I flew in last night. I'm producing features for the tribute show."

Craig cocked his head to one side. "You were coming to work the tribute show? And you didn't let me know?"

"I was going to. . . ."

"Oh," he said. Bex had no idea how to interpret the interjection.

"I really was. It's just it all happened so fast. Gil called me right after you left my apartment on Sunday, and then I had to get ready to fly out at a moment's notice and—"

"It's okay. The whole point of this week was supposed to give you space. I'm sorry if I sounded like—"

"You didn't."

"Well, I'm sorry anyway. Hey," Craig said, smiling that sincere smile that always made her melt, "feature producer. That's awesome. You've been working so hard to get that promotion. Congratulations."

"It's not exactly a promotion," she admitted. "More a dry run. If I don't screw up too horribly, Gil might start thinking about thinking about promoting me. Sometime."

"In any case, I'm happy for you."

He turned to leave, and suddenly, more than anything, Bex wanted him to stay.

"Craig!"

"What?"

"I—I really was going to tell you."

"It's okay. You've got work to do."

"Not really." Bex wasn't sure why she said that. At first, she assumed it was just another desperate attempt on her part to keep him from walking out. But, as she started with her babbling, she realized that what she was really craving was for somebody to hear her out. "I mean—Gil doesn't think Lucian was murdered."

Craig, who'd had one foot out the door, stopped and turned all the way back in. "Does anybody think he was?"

"Yeah," Bex sheepishly admitted.

"Who?"

"Me?"

Unlike Toni and Gil and Sabrina and Gina and let's not forget the police detective, Craig gave the matter due consideration. He said, "Well, your instincts have never been wrong before."

"Except that time I thought you killed Rachel."

"Except then, yes."

"You really think I could be right?"

"I don't know. But I believe you'll get to the bottom of this, one way or another."

"You know, you're really way too nice to me."

"Yeah. That's one of the side effects to being in love with you."

She blushed so furiously, Bex was surprised the rink's cooling system didn't kick into overdrive just to keep the ice from melting. Craig was always saying stuff like that. Unexpectedly and un-self-consciously, too. And Bex never knew how to react. She wondered if it was simply a matter of maturity—and her lack thereof. Or whether it was something more sinister. And a much deeper, fundamental lack.

"Sorry," Craig apologized again. "That wasn't exactly space giving."

"It's my fault. I'm acting stupid."

"I'll leave you alone."

"Please don't."

Craig apparently found her bipolar disorder amusing. He smiled. "Okay."

"I just feel so . . . blah."

"That's an interesting state of mind."

"I feel like there's something going on here. Something more than what it seems. But everyone is acting like I'm nuts. And not just Gil. That I'm used to. Toni says there is absolutely no reason why anyone would want to kill Lucian. And his daughter, Sabrina, she did this whole dramatic thing about how all of his students adored him so it's not like they'd lift a finger to hurt him. Now I'm sure this was more about her own issues than about any particular thing I brought up. But it's hard not to feel like you're the crazy one when everybody around you is insisting the guy you think was murdered was categorically loved by one and all and—"

"Lucian Pryce was hardly loved by one and all, Bex. Yes, he had his obsessive acolytes, like well, Eleanor Quinn and Gina Gregory. I'd say marrying the guy was pretty obsessive. And Chris Kelly and Robby Sharpton—though you know how well that last one turned out in the end. But for every Chris and Robby you had a Felicia Tufts or a Rachel Rose— remember them? Obviously, neither is here to do the deed. But do you doubt that they'd at least considered it over the years?"

Bex recalled the hell Lucian had reportedly put both his former skaters through, and she grasped the wisdom of Craig's point. However . . . "Like you said, neither one of them is here. Neither, for all I know, is any other student with an axe to grind. I mean, if they hated him, they wouldn't exactly show up to skate in his honor, would they?"

"What about Gabrielle Cassidy?"

"What about her?"

"Gabrielle is a couple of years younger than Rachel, but their training time with Lucian overlapped by a few years. They didn't know each other that well; Pairs and Dance don't share sessions. But I could have sworn there was some incident between Lucian and Gabrielle that he tried to hush up. I remember Rachel mentioning the name for sure, and some scandal."

•   •   •

Gabrielle Cassidy was staying at the same official hotel as Bex and everyone else who'd come to town for the tribute. Bex cabbed it back to home base and, without bothering to call first, went knocking on the good PhD's door. She'd learned a long time ago that forewarned was forearmed with a better lie. Truth tended to come out smoother when served as a side dish to ambush.

Of course, Bex didn't leap right into the cross-examination. She opened with, "I spoke to Gil Cahill. He said the show will go on as scheduled. It will still be a tribute to Lucian's life and career. Just posthumous now."

"Great!" Gabrielle enthused. She obviously bounced back from the shock of death rather quickly. "Chris and I have actually prepared a number to do together. It was like pulling teeth, believe me. You know how those Singles skaters are. They think sure, ice dancing belongs in the Olympics—the Special Olympics. But since my partner, Todd Zamir, died a couple of years ago, Chris agreed to step in and do a few moves with me. To honor Lucian. He'll still skate a solo, too, of course. But we did work pretty hard on our routine. I'd hate for it to go to waste."

"I'm surprised," Bex said.

"About Chris? He could have made a pretty good ice dancer, you know. But there's more glory in the Singles."

"No. About you."

"What about me?"

"That you're here."

"Without Todd?"

Bex had never been to a psychologist (though many had suggested it might be an excellent idea), but she couldn't help feeling she was getting a bit of that treatment now. Was Gabrielle messing with her?

"No," Bex replied patiently. "That you agreed to skate at a tribute for Lucian. I hear you two didn't get along too well."

Gabrielle shrugged. "That was all a long time ago. I was a kid."

"Still . . ."

"Still what?"

"It must be hard for you, being around everyone who thought so highly of him."

"The same people who thought highly of Lucian a decade ago still think highly of him now. And, amazingly enough, even people who didn't think highly of him then, once he made them a champion were able to miraculously reassess their opinions."

Ah, there's that bitterness Bex was eagerly awaiting.

"So you weren't one of his bigger fans?"

"Look, let's stop beating around the bush, okay? You're here to dig up dirt for the TV special, I get that. I also get that no matter how hard Lucian tried to pretend nothing happened, everyone in skating knew then and knows now what I did. I'm not trying to hide it. If anything, that's why I opened my own training center."

See Bex. See Bex lose the conversation's narrative thread. Backpedal, Bex; backpedal to figure out what you just missed.

"Excuse me?"

"I want to prove to the world that you don't have to drive a child to mental and physical collapse before you get a result out of him or her. Champions don't only have to be made the Lucian Pryce way. You can train an athlete under calm, nurturing conditions and still get the best out of them."

"Right," Bex said. She'd read the brochure for Gabrielle's facility when it first opened. She remembered the pitch.

"I thought parents would be happy to send their children someplace where we cared about them as people, not just little skating drones."

"They're not?"

"Well, not enough of them . . . I mean, we get regular inquiries, especially from parents of kids who have burned out elsewhere. But, the problem is, our competitive record . . ."

"Isn't very competitive?"

"You could say that. In three years, none of my students has made it out of Sectionals. That's not the kind of result destined to drive customers to your doorstep. That's why I wanted to skate this tribute so badly. I wanted to get the word out about my training center. I thought the more people who knew about it, the more likely it was we'd attract like-minded people to enroll."

"So paying homage to Lucian was a marketing opportunity for you?"

"And it wasn't for 24/7?" Gabrielle challenged.

Bex shrugged. "Hey, I'm not judging, just trying to figure stuff out."

"It's pretty simple. Lucian Pryce ruined my life. I figured the least I could do was take his to help put mine back together."

Six
Gabrielle

Gabrielle Cassidy's parents were not wannabe athletes who lived their frustrated ambitions out through the accomplishments of their four children. Gabrielle's father had been High School All-City in tennis, swimming, and track. He'd qualified for the Olympic Trials in the pentathlon in college and, as an adult, earned a seeded spot in both the New York City and Boston marathons. Gabrielle's mother had been a nationally ranked Junior golfer at the age of twelve, a collegiate champion at eighteen, and she continued to play semi-professionally while raising her family and serving as a circuit court judge. The Cassidys didn't force their children into sports. They simply could not imagine a happy, fulfilling life without them.

To that end, they allowed each child to experiment with a variety of activities until they found the one destined to be a lifelong passion. Naturally, the possibility that such an epiphany might fail to occur never crossed their minds. Their older son gravitated towards baseball, the younger to gymnastics. Their older daughter picked up a bow and arrow and proceeded never to put it down again. And then there was the case of the baby, Gabrielle. Gabrielle ended up in figure skating because it was clearly the activity she had the most aptitude for. Which, to her parents, was the same as enthusiasm.

Not to Gabrielle.

Sure, gliding and turning and brackets and Choctaws and Mohawks and twizzles came easy for her. Sure, she could do them without thinking while other girls spent hours upon hours with tongues clenched between their teeth just trying to get one of the tricks to flow smoothly. So what if, after only three months of lessons, she passed the tests for twelve compulsory dances and qualified for the Intermediate level of competition on her first try? It didn't mean she liked it. Neither did the fact that, by the time she was ten, Gabrielle had made it up to the Senior and International level by passing her Austrian Waltz, Cha Cha Congelado, Golden Waltz, Midnight Blues, Ravensburger Waltz, Rhumba, Silver Samba, Tango Romantica, and Yankee Polka.

To her parents, though, it meant that Gabrielle was clearly ready for the same sort of intense, specialized instruction they'd been so happy to give their other children in their respective sports. Those three had eventually needed to move away from home to elite training centers to continue with their concentrated lessons. Her parents understood that Gabrielle would have to do the same.

Whether or not Gabrielle wanted to do this never came up. Years later, when her dance partner, Todd, asked, "Why didn't you tell your parents you didn't like any of this?" she'd answered truthfully and somewhat confusedly, "They never asked."

In the same way in which her parents believed they'd never pressured Gabrielle in which sport to take up, the Cassidys also believed it was Gabrielle's choice as to which coach she wanted to take lessons from. The summer between seventh and eighth grade, they piled into the family camper and took a road trip across the country, visiting various training centers, meeting coaches, and allowing Gabrielle to decide which one she thought would be best for her.

The first coach she auditioned was a world-famous

Russian defector who looked at the five-foot-two, eighty-three-pound Gabrielle and told her parents, "Girl needs a bit more of the skinny, yes?"

The second asked her how long she practiced every day. When Gabrielle told him two hours before school and two hours after, he snorted and judged her not disciplined enough yet to join his group.

The third said Gabrielle had been coached all wrong, she would need to relearn every dance again from the beginning, while the fourth said her technique was too European and the fifth insisted it was much too American.

All of them stressed that the hours would be long, the training excruciating, and the atmosphere less than collegiate—"Competition between students, that's the only way to bring out the killer instinct. Physical and mental. Once a skater gets complacent, it's all over." However, if Gabrielle's parents were ready to pay, the coaches were ready to train her.

Gabrielle's sixth tryout was with Lucian Pryce, then based in Connecticut.

He gave her a twenty-minute lesson during which he never left the barrier, never put down the lit cigar he was holding (or bothered to blow smoke in the opposite direction of her face whenever Gabrielle came up for feedback on what she'd just done), and never offered a remark beyond, "Do it again. That wasn't it."

By the time Gabrielle got off the ice, she felt as though she'd been pummeled. Although, to be fair, Lucian hadn't laid a hand on her.

"So you didn't like Mr. Pryce, either, Gabby?" Any other parent might have been frustrated or even discouraged. But the only time either of her parents acknowledged the existence of such words was at spelling bees (which they didn't consider a real sport, but good, competitive fun, nonetheless).

"Not really," she admitted.

"Well, we've got you booked to spend the night at the training center's dorms, anyway. Why don't you check out how you like it, and we'll regroup in the morning to reassess where we stand. Okey-dokey, Smokey?"

"Okay," Gabrielle said.

The dorm rooms at the Connecticut Olympic Training Center were more or less in line with what she'd already visited all across the country. Four girls to a room, two bunk beds, one closet, two tall dressers with a minimum of one drawer standing open. A pile of discarded socks, hair ribbons, and unmatched shoes in the corner, a bathroom down the hall. The girls, also, were more or less standard issue. In this case, two were white, one Asian. No one was over five feet tall or one hundred pounds—including skates. They slept in size-large T-shirts with either the word "Regional," "Sectional," or "National" emblazoned across the silk screen of an abstract skater doing a layback or a stag jump. All three were adequately polite, saying hi to Gabrielle, asking how she liked the center, then ignoring her completely. Gabrielle didn't particularly mind. She had as little to say to them as they did to her. Besides, she didn't intend to stay.

When it was time to get ready for bed she pulled out her own size-large T-shirt, this one from her sister's last archery competition. It got Gabrielle a few curious looks, followed by an ultimate shrug of indifference. She crawled under the scratchy blanket, not surprised to discover it smelled of a combination of bleach and vague dampness, and waited to find out which abstract sound would be keeping her awake this night. Because there was always something. If not a renegade car alarm, then a heating system going on and off arbitrarily with a hammering clang. If not a snoring roommate, then a coughing one.

Here in Connecticut, it proved to be a combination of the Asian girl mumbling in her sleep, "Cross behind, then turn. Cross behind, *then* turn," and, around midnight, an unexpected crash that seemed to emanate from somewhere down the hall. Then a pair of raised voices, not quite arguing, but not exactly keeping it down, either.

Gabrielle stayed still for a moment, wondering if this was par for the course. No one else seemed disturbed by the racket. Then again, Gabrielle was willing to bet no one else was nicknamed "The Princess and the Pea of Sound" by her family thanks to an uncanny ability to wake up at the slightest pin drop somewhere in the same area code.

The shouting continued, piquing Gabrielle's curiosity. What was so important that it necessitated an argument in the middle of the night? Especially since it was very likely that the participants needed to be up in a mere few hours for the first ice session of the day. Figuring she wouldn't be getting to sleep until it was over anyway, Gabrielle slipped out of bed, shrugged on her terry-cloth robe, and, barefoot, padded down the hall.

The last room before the stairs leading to the next floor proved to be an office. At least that's what Gabrielle assumed it was used for during a normal day. At the moment, it looked more like the aftermath of a tornado. Papers were scattered over and around the desk as if somebody had snatched them up in wild handfuls, then flung them in the air. A chair lay on its side, not tucked in the nook of the desk, but by the door. Shards of glass sparkled on the floor next to broken picture frames that had clearly been ripped off the walls and smashed. Amongst the carnage stood Mr. Pryce, dressed in a jogging suit of baby blue bottom and dark green top, indicating that Lucian had thrown on the first things he got his hands on without worry for color coordination. His hair was uncombed and one of his sneakers flapped off and on as he tramped about the room, apparently trying to calm down a student in the middle of a hysterical rampage.

The student, it took Gabrielle a moment to recognize, was the Olympic champion Christian Kelly. Despite being in the skating world, Gabrielle wasn't particularly a fan of the sport. Not like her siblings, who worshiped the respective winners in their fields and plastered their rooms back home with posters of assorted champs mid-spectacular-action. Gabrielle would under normal circumstances be hard-pressed to identify the winners of last year's World or National Championships. But Chris Kelly was different. He'd won the Olympics the season before. And in the Cassidy household, watching the Olympics—Summer and Winter—was a nonnegotiable event, like tooth brushing or looking both ways before crossing the street. So she'd had her fill of Chris Kelly. On the ice, off the ice, skating, interviewing, strolling about the Olympic Village deep in cinematic thought.

Right now, however, he appeared to be deep in borderline psychotic meltdown.

It was obvious from the way Lucian was fruitlessly struggling to pin Chris's arms to his sides and grabbing him from behind as if in a wrestling hold, that Chris was responsible for all the damage to the office. And he wasn't using only his hands for the rampage. He kicked a solid wood chair to knock it over. He was wearing sneakers. Gabrielle couldn't imagine how a blow of such magnitude didn't send excruciating pain shooting all along his foot and straight up to Chris's spine. He twisted his upper body, trying to wrench out of Lucian's grip, but the older man had gotten a better grasp this time around and managed to keep him pinned. He shook Chris from side to side, trying to calm him down, and then yelled, "Christian! Christian, listen to me!"

Chris continued struggling. But he did inch his head ever so slightly in Lucian's direction. Clearly, after years of automatic compliance to Lucian's instructions, it was a tough habit to break, even amidst hysteria.

"Listen to me, son." Lucian's voice, commanding only a split second before, grew softer, almost hypnotic. "There is nothing you can do about it, do you hear me? You can rage all you like. You can curse and you can flail and you can promise revenge, but in the end, there is absolutely nothing you can do to keep some idiotic, moronic, irresponsible drunk driver from taking to the streets and recklessly plowing into your wife's car." Chris whimpered at that, but Lucian kept talking. "Just like there is nothing you can do to stop an insidious, cruel disease from taking her away from you before you even know it's set to happen. There is nothing that men like you and me can do about those things. They are out of our control. They are arbitrary and capricious and merciless. But you know what we can control? We can control you. We can control your training, your physicality, your performance. The rest of the world, they're out of our influence. But what you do on the ice is not. That's why the only way to respond to what goes on out there, is for you to return back here. This is where you belong. This is the only place on Earth where your life and your fate are your own. Do you understand me, son? This is the only place where you can be in charge of your destiny. Do you understand what I am telling you?"

Chris stopped struggling. After a moment, he went limp, letting Lucian catch him before he hit the ground in a heap. Chris nodded meekly.

And, unseen in her hiding place outside in the hall, Gabrielle did as well.

She didn't know what they were talking about exactly. But Lucian's words made a sense to her that Gabrielle had never thought of before. She could not control whether or not she would skate. All she could control was where and how and with whom. It would have to be enough, if she ever expected to stop feeling like a badly addressed letter, sent from place to place with no say in the matter.

The next morning, Gabrielle told her thrilled parents that she'd changed her mind. She'd decided to stay in Connecticut and train with Mr. Pryce after all.

It wasn't until weeks later that Gabrielle was able to piece together the full story of what she'd witnessed that first night at the center. Thanks to her mandatory viewing of the Olympics, Gabrielle was aware that Chris Kelly, immediately after winning the Gold medal, had taken off and eloped with his girlfriend, a woman named Lauren. The media had all but ripped each other to shreds to be the first to present this romantic fairy tale to the TV-watching public prior to the conclusion of the Games. Even though both the win and the elopement happened within the first ten days of the event, the network continued cutting away from their less popular sports—biathlon and luge seemed to be particularly unloved stepchildren—to "take another up-close-and-personal look" at the story of Christian and Lauren Kelly, breathlessly asking the question "What Are They Doing Now?" Chris's competition over, the answer proved to be "Nothing much." But that

didn't stop the cameras from following them around in anticipation nonetheless.

Now, less than a year later, Lauren was dead, a victim of,
as Lucian put it, "some idiotic, moronic, irresponsible drunk
driver." And Chris was a shell-shocked widower at the age of
barely twenty-two. The only time Gabrielle ever saw him was
either at the rink, or coming and going. She had no idea what
he did with the rest of his time, but, judging by how much
weight he'd lost and how all-around haggard he looked, she
couldn't imagine it was eating a balanced diet or taking care
of himself in any way.

She felt suitably sorry for him, especially considering the
horrible breakdown she'd witnessed him experience the night
Lauren died. But him being a Singles skater and eight years
older than she to boot pretty much assured their paths rarely
crossing.

Besides, eventually Chris snapped out of his mourning—
and with a vengeance, too, as far as Gabrielle could tell from
his suddenly very busy dating life. And, by that time, Gabrielle lacked the emotional resources to feel sorry for anyone
but herself.

Lucian found Gabrielle a dance partner within three
months of her arrival at the center. Gabrielle's roommates,
who previously hadn't paid her much mind, emerged from the
stupor of indifference to wonder what made her so damn special.

"She's passed all her dance tests on the first try; that's what
makes her so damn special," Mr. Pryce snapped. "When you
stop tripping over your own cloddish feet in the Viennese, we
can talk about you finding someone, too."

Some of the other girls at the rink had been looking for a
suitable partner for years. Boys in skating were incredibly
hard to come by. Usually, the girl's family had to commit to
picking up his training expenses, plus costume, equipment,
and travel, and if that wasn't enough, they sometimes even
agreed to move to a training facility of his choice. The fact

that Gabrielle got a partner so quickly, a partner who not only was located where she already was but who also wasn't demanding payment of an extra surcharge ("the boy tax"), didn't make for a very comfortable living arrangement.

But her living arrangement, where nobody spoke to her or acknowledged that she was in the room, was still the most pleasant part of Gabrielle's day.

Because all the other parts of her day were spent at the rink.

Todd, her partner, turned out to be a godsend. He was eighteen and thus mature enough not to get into the kind of squabbles other, more similarly aged partners tended to engage in. On any given day, Gabrielle witnessed a girl pulling her hand away at the last minute, leaving her partner clutching at thin air before going sprawling on his stomach. She saw partners who kicked each other with their blades viciously enough to draw blood, then helplessly shrugged and insisted it was an accident—*prove that it wasn't*. She saw girls deliberately dropped, head first, out of lifts, and boys kneed in the groin, all done with a barely hidden smirk, covered by a cough. Todd didn't go in for those kinds of games. He was sweet and hardworking and quiet. He never argued with Gabrielle. But then again, he never argued with Lucian, either. Whatever their coach said, went. Even when what their coach said led to bleeding blisters and hairline fractures and muscles strained so badly they could barely limp, much less walk home.

After several years of skating with Todd, Gabrielle had suffered two broken wrists, one concussion, and three wrenched vertebrae in her back that required shots of cortisone just to keep her upright. Todd had dislocated his shoulder so many times he'd learned to snap it back in himself, with a sickening, rink-resounding crunch that made everyone in the vicinity shudder upon hearing it. Both his knees had worn out their cartilage, and neither he nor Gabrielle could recall a day without a stuffy nose, sore throat, or low-grade fever. But they were also the U.S. Junior champions and then, the following year, the U.S. Senior Silver medalists. So Gabrielle and Todd were stenciled in on the plus side of the OTC's judgment column. After all, unlike other skaters with dislocated body parts, they hadn't been forced to go home without a title.

In fact, Gabrielle and Todd were favored to win the U.S. title at Nationals, which meant a trip to the World Championship, and who knew what could happen there. They were in the best shape they'd ever been. Judges, both national and international, said they loved their new Free Dance. And word from the former Soviet bloc was that the breakup of their government meant a breakdown of the all-powerful Soviet sports machine. The title was no longer automatically assumed to go to those "skating while Russian." The field was supposedly wide open now. This could really be the Americans' year to make a bold move to the top of the podium.

Every day leading up to the Free Dance at Nationals, someone else told Gabrielle that this was a huge season for her. They wanted to know, was she nervous? Excited? Psyched? They told her the whole country was counting on her and Todd to pave the way for a U.S. domination in Ice Dancing the way that they now dominated Men's and Ladies' Singles. They jokingly warned her not to let them down, then, not so jokingly added, no, really, don't let us down, Gabrielle, you hear me?

Gabrielle heard them.

She heard them all. And she heard Lucian bellowing more and more complicated instructions in one ear while the fans cheered in another and TV reporters kept asking her if she was nervous and her parents gushed how proud they were and the days flew by and it was the morning of the Free Dance and Gabrielle and Todd were in first place after the first two phases of the competition, first place from every judge on every dance, and they were ready to take it all.

Standing in the bathroom, painting the whitening treatment on her teeth to make sure they sparkled for her big day, Gabrielle wondered how she could make everything slow down. Just for a bit, just so that she could take a breath and think for a minute and not hear her heart hammering so relentlessly until she was afraid it would come vomiting out of her chest along with everything she'd eaten for the past few years.

And then she remembered something Lucian had said.

It wasn't about winning and it wasn't about training and it wasn't about never, ever dropping her elbow, especially in the Waltz because that, apparently, was a fate worse than death. It was about control.

It was Lucian, his voice mesmerizing and hypnotic and unwavering, preaching, "The rest of the world is out of our influence. . . . That's why the only way to respond to what goes on out there, is for you to return here. . . . This is the only place on Earth where your life and your fate are your own. Do you understand me? This is the only place where you can be in charge of your destiny. Do you understand what I am telling you?"

Gabrielle understood.

And that was why, in the interest of taking control of her own life and her own destiny and not leaving her fate in the hands of strangers, she picked up her razor blade and, unhesitatingly, made a definite, crimson slash down the length of both her wrists.

Seven

SKATINGANDSTUFF.COM
MESSAGE BOARD

FROM: GoGoGregory1
Posted at 11:09 AM

I called the OTC they said the show is still going on as scheduled phew I would have hated to try and cancel all my travel
plans at the last minute I asked them who was going to be
skating and they said Chris, Gina, also somebody named
Gabrielle Cassidy and that Toni Wright will be there this is
going to be so good!!!!

FROM: SuperCooperFan
Posted at 11:11 AM

Who the hell is Gabrielle Cassidy that she gets billing with
Chris and Gina?

FROM: SkatingYoda
Posted at 11:14 AM

Gabrielle Cassidy was a Pair skater of Lucian's. I think she skated with Robby Sharpton?

FROM: TwirlyGirl
Posted at 11:16 AM

No, that was Felicia Tufts. They were Nat. Pair champions. Don't remember this Gabrielle Cassidy.

FROM: JordanRocks
Posted at 11:30 AM

Robby skated with Rachel, not Felicia. She's Jeremy Hunt's mother.

FROM: SkateGr8
Posted at 11:39 AM

Robby skated with BOTH Rachel and Felicia. He won Nats with Rachel, though. Gabrielle Cassidy was an ice dancer. I think she won a medal at Worlds, don't remember the color, but it wasn't gold.

FROM: GoGoGregory1
Posted at 11:40 AM

So this stupid dance medalist is being lumped in with Chris who won two Oly golds and Gina who is still the reigning US Oly Gold medalist who the heck did she sleep with to get such a sweet deal?

FROM: SkatingFreak
Posted at 11:41 AM

<<who the heck did she sleep with to get such a sweet deal?>>

Considering who we're talking about here, my money is on Lucian. She's younger than Gina, right? Time for him to trade up!

"Do you mean your suicide?" Bex clarified, wanting to make sure she and Gabrielle were on the same page about this one detail, at least.

"More like my botched suicide," Gabrielle snorted. "Another link in the Grand Canyon–sized evidence chain whispering that I can't do anything right."

"Oh," Bex said. "Sorry."

"It's okay. I'm over it. Amazing what you can accomplish with a little fortitude, perseverance, moxie, and a decade of twice-a-week therapy." In response to Bex's still guilt-ridden face, Gabrielle insisted, "No. Really. I'm fine. That's why I can make jokes about it. I really am out of the tunnel."

"But you *were* referring to your suicide attempt when you said that Lucian ruined your life?"

"It wasn't all his fault," Gabrielle conceded. "There were lots of factors. But, yes, he did lead the charge."

"So what did you mean then about figuring the least you could do was take his in exchange?"

Gabrielle asked, "What's this about, Bex? Your questions. Are you trying to get me to say or confess to something—"

"It's nothing. I'm just doing my job. Trying to get a complete picture of the man. For the tribute show."

"I don't think anyone can ever really get a complete picture of anyone. The Lucian Pryce Gina knew and knows now is different from the Lucian Sabrina knew, or Toni. And the Lucian Chris knew is certainly different from mine. We all become different people depending on the circumstances, don't you agree?"

Philosophically speaking? Absolutely.

But Bex was more interested in the concrete world at the moment.

"What you said before about taking Lucian's life to help you put yours back together . . . What did that mean, exactly?"

Gabrielle sighed. "All right, here's the thing: After I quit skating—I know, I know, it's a pretty neutral way to describe cutting my wrists, but the fact is, that's all I was trying to do.

To quit skating. One way or another. After I quit, I really didn't know what to do with myself. I didn't have any friends. No boyfriend. My family tried to be supportive, they really did, but they had no idea what to do or say, so we all just kind of ended up avoiding each other, more out of consideration than anything else. I started college and I got a degree in psychology, but that was mostly because psychology, thanks to my own therapy sessions, was about the only thing I had even a passing interest in. Everything else, at school and at home, just felt so unreal. Like I was passing through a series of moving train cars without so much as looking around. The ground was moving under my feet and I kept moving so I wouldn't fall, even though, frankly, I didn't have a lot of reasons to remain upright, either. And then, about six years ago, Todd, my former dance partner, he got sick. AIDS. No surprise. What was surprising was how he reacted. He saw it as an opportunity. He saw dying as this reminder to make his life more meaningful. He and his parents always had a good relationship—they were actually great, none of that 'never darken my doorstep' stuff with them. But having a death sentence over his head, he really reached out to them, got to know them on this deep, profound level. Same thing with me and with everyone else in his life. Todd saw his illness as this amazing chance to turn something horrible into something wonderful. He inspired me so much. I went back to school, got my PhD, and as soon as I got out, I started working to open my training center. I was going to take all the pain that Lucian and skating put me through, and I was going to turn it into a place where other kids would be safe from all that."

"That's great," Bex said, thoroughly lost but convinced that anything that kept Gabrielle talking was ultimately a good thing.

"Yes, in theory, it's awesome. But in practice, a dozen more paying customers or so would be nice, too."

"Which is why you volunteered to do the show."

"I just thought I'd follow Todd's example. Take the most awful thing in my life, my years with Lucian, and try to turn them into something good—PR for the center."

"You were using his tribute to promote your own cause?"

"Yup." If Gabrielle felt guilty about the subterfuge, she was hiding it beautifully.

"And now?"

"Now? You said the show was still on. So, as far as I know, so are my plans. In fact, this makes it even better. I was wondering how I would react, coming face-to-face with him again after all these years. What he would say, what I would say. This way, I'm off the hook."

"You don't think it's . . . awkward? You're kind of dancing on his grave here."

"Nope."

"So Lucian's death, it's kind of a lucky break all around for you."

"Yup," Gabrielle agreed.

After the somewhat morbid conversation with Dr. Cassidy, Bex went down the hotel hall to Chris Kelly's room, ostensibly to tell him that the tribute show was still on, but actually to find out what exactly he knew about his employer's less than charitable feelings towards their former coach.

Chris wasn't in, so Bex shifted to Plan B and, after ordering a cab, took it over to the Pryce home. Sabrina let her in. In the few hours since the police had ordered the rest of them out of the house, Lucian's daughter had pulled herself together enough to greet Bex if not with a chipper mood, at least with one no more sullen than the snit she'd appeared to be in even prior to her father's death. She looked neither pleased nor displeased to see her and, in response to Bex's question as to whether Gina might be around, jerked her thumb in the direction of the stairs.

"Second door on the right."

Bex followed the instructions to what she guessed was Gina and Lucian's master bedroom. There was an unmade king-size bed, a dresser, two end tables, a vanity with oversize mirror, and, by the window, a walk-in closet the size of Bex's studio apartment. The door to the closet was open. Gina sat on the threshold, surrounded by what at first glance appeared to be a cream and otherwise earth-toned pile of Jil Sander, Max Mara, Alberta Ferretti, Ralph Lauren, Christian Dior, and Calvin Klein silk, linen, and cashmere skirts, sweaters, and blouses. Which she was rather meticulously pruning with a pair of gardening shears.

Bex was initially so bowled over by that particular anomalous sight it took her a moment to register that the figure towering above the hunched-over Gina was Chris Kelly. From the way he was leaning over her, tugging on the partially shorn clothing, it was difficult to tell if he were trying to stop her endeavor or help it along.

Bex cleared her throat. Rather loudly. Gina and Chris looked up, surprised, but neither particularly embarrassed. Almost as if both believed what they were doing was perfectly natural, and Bex was the odd one for appearing confused.

She couldn't help it. She had to ask. "What are you doing?"

"Spring cleaning," Gina said brightly.

"Cutting up your clothes is spring cleaning?"

"They're all last season," Gina explained, though her tone suggested Bex should have already known that.

"Our Gina has had a rather difficult day," Chris jumped in, meeting Bex's eyes with a look half forceful, half pleading. "She isn't—she's not herself. It—Lucian—it's been rough on everybody."

"I understand," Bex said. And she did. In the abstract. Of course a woman who'd just lost her husband was allowed an eccentric reaction or two. The only problem was, of the three people currently in the room, Gina was looking the most tranquil. Unable to think of an appropriate follow-up, Bex decided to change the subject completely and asked, "What did the police want?"

"Just, you know, they had some questions about Lucian and his overall health and his skating routine, that sort of thing. For their report. The police love their reports."

"So they're still treating this as just an accident?"

"Oh, what is your problem?" Gina snapped.

"Jeans . . ." Chris sounded like he was warning her about something, but Gina plowed right over him.

"I mean, really, Bex, I know all about you and your super-skating-sleuth skills, but come on, sometimes a cigar is just a cigar, you know what I mean?"

Chris slid his hand under Gina's elbow and attempted to help her up. "Come now, let's take a break. You need to calm down."

"I'm calm!" she screeched. "Why doesn't anybody get it? I am the calmest I have ever been in my whole damn existence!"

Chris took a step back, arms raised as if in surrender. "It's all right, luv."

"Well, thanks for telling me. Now I can get on with my life."

"I was only trying to—"

"I know what you were trying to, okay? If there's one thing I'm finally real, real clear on, Chris, it's what you're trying to."

Chris looked apologetically at Bex. "She's . . ."

"Stressed. I know. I understand."

Chris leaned over and tried to kiss Gina on the cheek. Gina jerked away. Chris nearly lost his balance but was able to use the catlike grace that had saved many a triple jump from going wonky to retain his dignity. He said softly, "I'm going to take off now, all right? I'll check in on you later."

"Whatever."

Chris asked Bex, "Did you ever get an answer, then? Is the tribute show to go on as scheduled?"

"Oh!" Bex remembered her initial excuse for coming over, feeling silly for having forgotten it in all the excitement. "Yes. Yes, it is. Still going on as scheduled. Obviously we're going to have to tweak some of the copy. But the special is still set for broadcast."

"Whoop-de-doo," Gina said and threw what once might have been a black, floor-length silk skirt up into the air.

Clearly unable to match such a dramatic sentiment, Chris

merely nodded. "Fine. We'll get to rehearsing, then. I suppose I should speak to Toni about the rink's practice time availability?"

"I guess," Bex agreed.

"I will see you both later," Chris said, though his eyes never left Gina until he was actually out the door. Bex wondered what he expected Gina to do in his absence. And then she wondered what Chris was so afraid she would do in his absence.

Bex said, "I guess you and Chris go way back. Winning the Olympics the same year and all."

Gina shrugged. "It was his second time. I was the virgin. Pretty sure it didn't mean as much to him as it did to me."

Bex didn't need a degree in comparative literature from Sarah Lawrence—which she technically did not have, but could have considering how many courses she took in the subject—to understand that Gina's phrase probably covered a bit more than mere skating.

She was about to pursue the topic further when Gina stood up, kicked the piles of clothes aside, and blurted, "You know yet what you're going to want me to say?"

"What do you mean?"

"At the tribute. On TV. You said you're going to tweak the copy. So, I figure at some point the teary-eyed widow's got to make an appearance and sob something for the cameras. Otherwise, how are people going to feel they got their money's worth?"

"I—I thought there'd be something you'd *want* to say."

"Oh, there's lots I *want* to say," Gina assured. "Starting with: Hey, Mr. and Mrs. American and All the Ships at Sea— do we still have ships at sea? Should I say 'rockets in space' or something? Hey, Mr. and Mrs. America, this is Gina Gregory. Yeah, Gina Gregory. Not Eleanor Pryce. Did you know that? I bet it was hard to tell, what with me skating like her and dressing like her and talking like her and marrying her husband. I bet you all never knew I was a different person, did you?"

Once again, Bex didn't need a degree to pick up on the veiled subtext. What with it not being so veiled and all.

She said, "Lucian tried to turn you into Eleanor?"

"What gave it away?" With her foot, Gina kicked the pile of clothes. With her free arm, she indicated the pile of cosmetics on the vanity.

"Why?" The question was out of Bex's mouth before she knew what sort of answer she was hoping to receive. All she knew was what answer she was most certainly not hoping to receive.

"Because," Gina spoke as if to a dullard. "He wished I was her."

And there that answer was. Even a dullard could see it.

"How—how can you be certain?"

"The part where he tried to turn me into the mirror image of his dead wife, Bex. Were you listening?" Gina's response was flip. But, when she saw the look of utter devastation on Bex's face, her demeanor suddenly turned serious and, as if actually, genuinely concerned, Gina asked her, "Why are you so interested?"

"What? Me? No, no reason. I'm just doing research. For the special."

"Yeah. And I'm just doing spring cleaning," Gina said.

Bex waved her hand in the air, fingers splayed, striving for a nonchalance that, even if she had managed to pull it off, wouldn't have fooled anyone. "It's just that, the guy—the guy that I'm dating now. He's—he's a widower, too. And he's older than me. Not a lot. But enough. And he has a kid. And—"

"He skates?"

"No. Not that." Bex attempted a laugh, demonstrating how not seriously she was taking all of this, then sheepishly admitted, "His kid skates, though."

"Oh, well, in that case, it's a totally different matter."

Bex looked up hopefully, only to realize Gina was being sarcastic. She'd known that. She'd just been . . . hoping . . . she wasn't.

"I know it can be hard," Bex admitted. "Trying to follow in the footsteps of somebody else. Especially somebody he was really crazy about."

"It's not hard," Gina said.

"No?"

"It's impossible."

"Oh."

"Every time he says something to you, you wonder, did he say the same thing to her? Every time you do something and he doesn't like it, you wonder, did he like it better when she did it? And even when he does like it, you just wonder, is it because I remind him of her?"

"All the time?"

"All the frigging, every minute of the day, time. It can drive you crazy. You start second-guessing yourself about every little thing."

"But you stayed married to Lucian," Bex pointed out. "You didn't need to. You could have left. You could have moved on. It's not like, once you say yes to marriage, you're trapped for life."

Gina sighed. "Eventually, it gets so hard to think for yourself—because of all the doubts—that you just give it up. You do what he says, how he says it, when he says it, and you don't fight it. And then he's happy. And you're miserable. If there is still a you left to feel anything at all."

Following her delightful conversation with Gina, Bex left the bedroom, walked down the stairs and towards the front door on the equivalent of automatic pilot.

She practically bumped into Sabrina as they both rounded the same corner at the same time from different directions, barely recognizing her, so lost was Bex in her own thoughts.

"So what did the stepmoron have to say for herself?" Sabrina asked lightly.

Bex, as if waking up still groggy from anesthesia, merely shook her head and continued walking towards the door.

"Bex. Wait." Sabrina thrust out her arm to block Bex's path. "Do you have a second? I—I need to talk to you."

Bex paused. She may have been trapped in a vision of a future even more hellish than anything Dickens dreamt up for Ebenezer Scrooge, but that didn't mean the research part of her was totally out of commission. If there was one thing she'd learned over the past few months of amateur snooping, it was when someone wanted to speak to her—especially if they seemed cryptic and hesitant about it—it would behoove Bex to listen.

She stopped. She said, "I'm listening."

Sabrina looked around, as if expecting eavesdroppers. When none materialized, she let out one breath, took a second, deep one, then let it out slowly, the air from her mouth ruffling her bangs. She said, "You're the only one . . . I mean, you said earlier. No one else . . . The police, they're acting like . . . You're the only one who seems to think my dad's death wasn't an accident."

Bex nodded. She wanted to hear what else Sabrina had to say.

After a mutual moment of silence, Sabrina demanded, "Is it true?"

"I don't know. I'm trying to get more information but—"

"Well, you won't get anything useful out of Gina."

Actually, Bex felt like she already had. But it probably wasn't what Sabrina had in mind. On the other hand, overbearing husbands *did* have a nasty tendency to end up dead. And their put-upon wives were, more often than not, at least in the vicinity.

Bex said, "Gina seemed to have a lot of . . . anger . . . towards Lucian."

"What? Did she give you the 'it gets so hard to think for yourself that you just give in and do whatever he likes' speech?"

"Um . . . well, yeah."

"Yeah. It's a classic. We've all heard it. The only problem is, Gina forgets her giving in and obeying Lucian has little to do with my father, and even less to do with my mother. It's all about Chris Kelly."

"Chris Kelly," Bex repeated.

"Everything Gina does, one way or another, comes back to Chris. Heck, I'm pretty sure she even only married Lucian because of what Chris did to her."

Eight
Gina

Unlike 99 percent of the students who came under Lucian's—or, frankly, any skating coach's—elite tutelage, Gina Gregory possessed something the rest did not. Gina genuinely and completely and unabashedly loved to skate.

She loved it when she stepped onto the ice for the first time at the age of three. She loved it through group lessons and private lessons and reconstructive surgery on her elbow after she broke it trying a Double Axel when she could barely do a single. She was always the first girl at the rink when it opened in the morning and the last one off the ice, even as the Zamboni was rumbling out of the gate to signal an end of session for the night. She was always the one eager to try a trick once more to get it perfect, never complaining about injuries or not having enough time to do other, normal-kid things.

Gina Gregory would have been the perfect student. Except that, like 99 percent of the students who came under any skating coach's elite tutelage, she also had something the rest of them did—a mother keenly interested in her child's progress.

Tina Gregory was the reason Lucian Pryce initially refused to take on Gina. Yes, he saw how talented the girl was. Yes, he saw how teachable she was and how easy to deal with. But her mother was a horror. And Lucian was no fool.

It wasn't until Gina was twelve years old and picked one morning when Lucian was teaching another skater to circle him incessantly and keep doing Double Axel after Double Axel after Double Axel until Lucian was dizzy—even if she wasn't—that he threw up his hands, laughed, and gave in.

For the next decade, he had cause to regret it every day of his life.

Not because of Gina. Gina was exactly what he'd expected. But because of Tina. Because Tina was exactly what he'd expected, too. (When a woman tells you she named her only daughter after herself—G[regory] + [T]ina = Gina—you kind of know what you're in for.)

Tina Gregory wasn't just content to, like the other mothers, sit rinkside every day and coach her daughter from the sidelines—even though she was ostensibly paying Lucian good money to do the same thing. Serious money. Top dollar, as a matter of fact. (Lucian believed customers understood they were getting the best only if they were also paying the most.) No, Tina prided herself on cornering Lucian each and every time he stepped off the ice, so they could have a little confab about Gina's progress and potential. And when Lucian came home at the end of the day, more often than not, the phone would already be ringing, and it would be Tina on the other end, with yet another question or notion. They talked about Gina's programs. They talked about Gina's music. They talked about her costumes and her diet and her ballet lessons that Lucian insisted she take to lose some of the coltish qualities that judges tended to disdain in their international-level skaters. But, most of all, they talked about the fact that Gina thought too much.

The older she got, the more it became a problem.

By the time she turned sixteen, Gina was, even in the opinion of her fiercest (and cattiest) competitors, the World Ladies' champion of the practice ice. Fortunately for her competitors, however, about half the time now, her championship moves remained right there on the practice ice. All because, when it came time for competition, Gina started thinking.

She thought about which girls might be able to outskate her, and she thought about which moves she was most likely to miss. As a result, she missed the moves and the girls she most feared did, in fact, outskate her.

Lucian realized soon enough that Gina's best performances took place when she didn't have time to overthink them. Most girls hated to draw first to skate in the Short Program. Common wisdom held that judges "saved" their marks, meaning that the skater who went first could never hope to score as high as the one who went last, even if their actual performances were identical. Lucian believed "saving" marks to be an actual phenomenon. But he also knew that it was better for Gina, and so he rejoiced when she pulled her arm out of the sorting hat with a single-digit number. Unfortunately, Gina skating so well in the Short Program meant she was usually scheduled to skate in the final group for the Long. And that left more thinking time than anybody felt comfortable with.

Since Lucian couldn't very well (no matter what his own competitors believed) fix the draw to assure Gina going early in the Short, and since he couldn't change the rules to keep her from ending up in the final group for the Long, Lucian went with the factors he thought he still might be able to affect, and banned Tina from attending competitions alongside her child. He'd believed for years that Tina and her neverending need to discuss every bit of minutia surrounding her daughter's career was what filled Gina's head with the stress and anxiety that then tripped her up. So Lucian gave Tina a choice: Either she stay away from Gina at competition (and that meant far away; not in another room, not in another hotel, but preferably in another state) or Lucian would walk away from coaching her. After several years of having paid top dollar for every lesson, Tina was adequately convinced that Lucian was the best coach available, and so knew enough to back away when faced with such an ultimatum.

Initially, Lucian's gamble worked. Without her mother

constantly whispering in her ear, Gina did grow more relaxed about such issues as her program, her music, her costumes, her competition, and her chances. She trusted that she could skate as well when it counted as when it didn't. But, without her mother to take care of the associated details like she always had, Gina replaced her previous performance anxiety with a new list of worries: What if she didn't fill out her entry paperwork correctly, what if her plane wasn't on time, what if her luggage got lost, what if she misplaced her room key, what if she missed the practice bus, what if she misread her schedule, what if, what it, what if . . . The girl was a twitching bundle of nerves and Lucian was getting sick of it. So he went with yet another Plan B. Lucian always had a Plan B in case things didn't go according to plan. He'd learned it from coaching Toni.

To execute Gina's Plan B, Lucian sent in Chris Kelly.

Chris, at this point, was the undisputed king of the Pryce skating stable. Having won Olympic Gold two years earlier, then followed it up with a World Championship that year and the next, Chris was, at age twenty-two, the best-known name in Men's skating. In addition, having obviously gotten over the death of his wife from a year before, he was the acknowledged catch in the very small pool of male skaters who were successful, good-looking, and most important, straight. And Chris knew it.

He'd gone through at least a half dozen girlfriends since Lauren, including media personalities, heiresses, and fellow skaters. He'd never given eighteen-year-old Gina a second glance. Until he showed up at her hotel room at the World Championship under strict orders from Lucian to "For God's sake, son, get that girl to relax. I don't care how you do it."

Having placed first in the Short Program and then drawn to skate last for the Long in a record field of forty-seven girls, Gina had several hours with nothing to do but think about what could go wrong before she was finally allowed to leave the hotel, catch the appropriate shuttle, arrive at the arena, change into her competition outfit, and do the one thing in the entire process that she still loved to do—skate. Equally unfortunate was the fact that these particular championships were being held in Amsterdam. Which meant they were being shown on Eurosport. Which meant that, at any time, Gina could turn on the TV and watch, live, all the lucky girls who'd already gotten their programs over with.

Gina, as it had already been established not only by Lucian but also by the U.S. figure skating press corps as well as the fans who liked to discuss such matters in grave detail each time they gathered at yet another championship, did not know how to relax.

It was up to Chris to show her.

At first, when he kissed her, Gina had no idea what he was doing. (Well, she had some idea. She wasn't a complete innocent; in fact, she had read a great deal on the subject and fully intended to explore it further once her busy schedule allowed.) When he peeled off her robe, she was, momentarily, utterly befuddled. But that didn't seem to bother Chris much. He apparently had no interest in her actively participating beyond not getting in his way. Which Gina had no intention of doing, in any case. To be honest, she wouldn't have known how. And to be really honest, she was too curious.

When Chris left an hour later, telling her it was time for her to catch the bus—for which, considering her usual fears of screwing up and missing it, Gina was as grateful as for his earlier distraction technique—she stammered, "Um, Chris?"

"Yes, luv?"

"What does . . . what did . . . what did you mean by that?"

He smiled. The same smile that caused female fans to scream and swoon when he unveiled it on the ice during a particularly sexy footwork section. He said, "What do you want it to mean?"

"I . . . It . . . Does it . . . does this mean you're my boyfriend now?"

Chris shrugged. "Sure. If you'd like." And then he told her to skate great that afternoon. Which Gina, still floating on a high she hadn't previously known existed, promptly did.

Lucian was very happy with both of them.

He was even happier when, following both Chris's and

Gina's definitive wins at the World Championship, the media picked up the story of the newly minted couple—Gina was so giddy with glee, she couldn't help telling anyone who'd inadvertently crossed her path practically before her final artistic mark was flashed on the scoreboard. And the media ran with it.

It was as if Christian Kelly and Gina Gregory had reinvented romance. (The fact that, only two years earlier, the same media had been tripping over themselves to enshrine Chris and Lauren as skating's most romantic couple ever, rarely came up.) There were talk-show and magazine interviews to give, endorsements to make, and charity galas to attend. As final proof of just how the image now superseded the skating, even *Sports Illustrated* succumbed to their off-ice appeal. For their traditional Olympic preview issue, they put Gina on the cover—which wasn't a big surprise, she was the defending Ladies' World champion, the obvious favorite for the Gold. But rather than showing her on the ice as they had all their previous skaters, *Sports Illustrated* photographed Gina with Chris. He may have been the favorite for Gold as well, but in the Men's event, which was hardly as popular as the Ladies'. And he wasn't even American, for Pete's sake! Still, there they were. America's Sweethearts. A package deal.

When Chris won his second consecutive Olympic Gold early into the Games, Gina's victory later in the week was considered a given. After all, even God himself wouldn't dare take from the media a story they were so dying to tell (and many had already written in advance). Gina skated her Long Program cautiously. It wasn't the best she'd ever performed, but it was enough to deliver the result everyone wanted, and that was all that mattered. Not a single newspaper the following day reported how many triples she'd landed or even what scores she received. Everyone was too busy speculating about how soon Gina and Chris would be trading their matching Gold medals in for a pair of equally matched gold wedding bands.

Gina never had a chance to ask. Immediately after her win, while Lucian, Chris, and even her mother (the ban on not attending Gina's competitions had been lifted once she adequately calmed down) were busy giving interviews in the mixed media zone, Gina was whisked to doping control, where she stayed for several hours waiting to be declared legal. Immediately afterwards, the dizzying whisking continued as Gina was pulled away to appear on all the morning shows. After that, it was another set of print interviews, this time for the foreign press, then the Gala Exhibition, where she skated her regular show program, followed by one encore and, when they kept clapping, a reprise of her Short Program. Gina and Chris took a bow together at the conclusion, at center ice, garnering the loudest ovation of the night and, to make the crowd go even wilder, skated a few steps together, culminating with side-by-side camel to scratch spins. They waved, and collected flowers and teddy bears, and performed an extra victory lap hand in hand. But, in that time, they also didn't manage to exchange one word that wasn't strictly business.

The exhibition was followed by a banquet so loud and so crowded that makeshift sign language was the only means of communication. Then came the bitterly cold closing ceremonies where each marched with their respective national teams, followed by Gina flying back home to the States for a parade in her hometown while Chris went to England for some kind of meet-the-Queen thing.

Gina literally didn't hear from Chris again until they met up on the first day of the Champions Tour. She was heading for the women's changing room and there he was, leaning against the opposite wall, talking to one of the Russian Pairs skaters and laughing over something Gina hadn't heard. The laughing stopped once Gina stepped into view. To be honest, everything stopped. All laughter, all conversation; heck, later, Gina would swear even the heating vents ground to a halt. The hallway was sprinkled with a handful of skaters, tour personnel, and arena workers. They all turned to look curiously at Gina, then at Chris, then back again. She wondered what they were waiting for. She wondered what she was waiting for.

Gina knew she should walk up to Chris, throw her arms around him, kiss him hello, catch up on the weeks they'd been apart. It was what any normal girlfriend would do under the circumstances. Gina was still Chris's girlfriend. Wasn't she? Why did she suddenly feel as though she was the only one who didn't know the answer to that question?

"Hello, luv." Chris seemingly took pity on Gina and her dilemma. He moved away from the Russian Pairs skater, took several steps forward, and gave Gina a kiss. On the cheek. He gave little girls and grandmothers who came up asking for autographs a kiss on the cheek, too.

"Chris?" She managed to turn his name into a question.

Which he managed to sidestep entirely with one of his own. "How was the parade, then? Wrist sore from waving at the masses?"

"I—it was fine. Chris . . ."

"Feels strange, doesn't it? Suddenly having no championship to train for? My whole life it's always been about the next competition, and now there isn't one. Takes some getting used to, wouldn't you say?"

She nodded, dumbly. Maybe that was it. Maybe Chris was right. Maybe the reason everything felt so strange now was because they were in uncharted waters. From the time she was a tiny girl, Gina had been thinking about the Olympics. Well, now they'd come and they'd gone and she'd won and now she was on her own. For the first time in her life, Gina didn't know what was supposed to happen next. Maybe that's why everything felt so disconnected. Maybe it wasn't Chris at all. Maybe it was all her.

"It does feel strange," she admitted.

"At least we've still got the tour. That's somewhat of a comfort before heading out into the cold, cruel world, no? I'll see you on the ice for rehearsal." He squeezed her shoulder, smiled, and jogged away.

Gina raised her hand to wave, but he was already gone.

There was no time to talk on the ice, of course. This being the first official day of practice, the opening number was no less than a stumbling, crashing jumble, with no one knowing where to go, when to move, or who they were even supposed to partner with for entrances and exits. Gina expected to be paired with Chris. Not only because of their relationship, but because the Men's and Ladies' Olympic Gold medalists always came out together. However, because that pairing was so obvious, nobody apparently thought it needed to be rehearsed, and so they spent the bulk of their three hours on the ice sitting around, waiting for the more complicated combinations to be ironed out before dutifully stepping through their paces and being sent to wait some more.

Gina would have thought all the downtime would be optimal for a private chat, finally. But every time she looked up, Chris was on the other end of the arena, talking with one person or another. She waited for him to look up and wave her over, but he never quite found the time.

After rehearsal, the tour manager took them all out to dinner. Chris and Gina were seated next to each other at the big banquet table. They were toasted repeatedly by their fellow skaters and asked for autographs by fans dining in the same restaurant. They were the center of attention. The center of everyone else's attention. Once, feeling bold, Gina slid her hand under the table onto Chris's thigh. He didn't pull away, but neither did he acknowledge the gesture. A few minutes later, he half stood out of his chair to reach for a steaming platter an arm's length away. Gina's hand slipped off and back to her side.

She wasn't an idiot. Gina knew when she was being dumped. In fact, her biggest concern was not that she was *being* dumped, but maybe that she had already *been* dumped. Gina wished she had someone to speak to about the issue. But, the problem was, previously, she'd taken all of her relationship cues from Chris. They'd done everything his way because Gina, to be frank, had no way. And she still didn't. She needed someone to tell her what to do. But there was no one.

There was no one to tell her how to react when the entire world seemed to know her business. Everywhere Gina went, people watched her closely, especially if Chris was in the room. They would be talking and then Gina would arrive and they would stop. It was like having a perpetual surprise party being planned for you. Where the surprise was anything but good.

There was also no one to tell Gina how to react when the entire world seemed to know her business—before she did. Gina felt pretty certain she was the last to know that Chris was now sleeping with a Swiss girl whose function on the tour was to hit the ice and bend her body into assorted pretzel shapes— most not particularly ladylike, if Gina did say so herself— while the real skaters caught their breath between acts.

And after the pretzel girl there was the television reporter who hosted the tour's network broadcast. Once they became an item, the tabloids jumped into the act, writing about Chris and Gina's tragic breakup in vivid details that never happened. You couldn't really have details where there hadn't actually been a formal breakup.

Now that it was in the tabloids, anyone and everyone felt emboldened to question her about it. Gina had thought the whispering was bad. The flat-out cross-examinations turned out to be worse.

Oh, sure, everyone tucked their queries under soft and fluffy canopies of concern. They wanted to know how Gina was doing, they wanted to know what Gina was feeling, they wondered if there was anything they could do for her.

Sure there was. They could shut up and go away. And yet they never did.

They simply multiplied, coming out of the woodwork. One magazine actually did a poll on how the public thought Gina was handling her split. Gina wondered what was more pathetic, people voting on her state of mind or her reading the results to get some idea of how she was doing.

Because, frankly, Gina wasn't certain how she was doing. She knew only that she was in constant movement. The tour was seventy-five cities in less than three months. Arena after arena, hotel after hotel, holding Chris's hand every night for the finale without looking at him and pretending not to care that he hadn't looked at her. After that tour ended, she was offered a professional contract with the Ice Capades. Gina waited to make sure that Chris had accepted his own offer with the European Holiday on Ice before agreeing to the gig. So then there was another six months of touring, this time with a company of total—although always curious—strangers. She was the headliner and got her own dressing room. Which was perfect for sitting around and brooding—and cultivating a reputation as a stuck-up bitch who thought she was too good to hang out and have a drink with nonchampions from the chorus line.

Gina would have been happy to hang out and have a drink, as long as the hanging and the drinking didn't always come with the cryptic questioning and the subtle teasing. So she compromised. She didn't hang. But she did drink.

It really was amazing how winning Olympic Gold and having her face splashed across every newspaper in the country ducked around such pesky technicalities as her not quite being twenty-one.

When Gina wasn't on tour, she was constantly being invited to movie premieres and private parties in clubs guarded by VIP lists. Designers wanted to dress her, jewelers wanted to drape her, and C-list celebrities wanted their pictures taken with her on the red carpet. Gina went along with it all. Because it sure beat figuring out what else to do.

She heard from Lucian again for the first time since the Olympics almost a year later. To his credit, Lucian was still Lucian. He didn't ask Gina how she was. He merely told her what he wanted from her. It was most refreshing. A corporate client was putting together a private VIP show of past Ladies' champions and he wanted Gina to participate. Lucian was one of the producers. There was a pile of money to be made for both of them.

Gina currently had no idea how much money she'd earned, how much she'd spent, or how much she'd managed to hold on to. But Lucian said show up, so she showed up.

And skated like crap. She'd forgotten to mention when they'd talked that Gina hadn't technically taken to the ice—even for a quick warm-up—in almost half a year.

The night of the event, Gina didn't try a sole triple jump. She fell attempting a Double Axel, then proceeded to sit on the ice for an uncomfortably long time, dazed under the spot-light. When she finally did clamber up, it was on all fours, her butt stuck up in the air like a squatting dog's. Did she mention that she'd also chosen to skate to a particularly ear-splitting version of Janis Joplin's "Take Another Little Piece of My Heart"? While wrapped in strips of black leather? That no longer quite fit, thanks to the ten extra pounds Gina had put on since having it made?

She started drinking as soon as she stepped off the ice, not waiting for the after party or even to change clothes. Heck, Gina didn't even take her skates completely off. She sat on a bench backstage, laces untied, her boots' plastic tongues flap-ping, legs splayed and stretched straight at the knees, chug-ging a zombie hastily mixed by the cowed caterer.

Lucian was walking around behind the scenes, a headset on to confer with other producers as the show progressed. He caught sight of Gina and stopped in his tracks. He took off his headset, handed it to a production assistant, walked up to Gina, grabbed her by the hand, and pulled her to her feet.

"Come with me," he said.

Lucian practically dragged Gina out of the arena and into the elevator of their hotel. He bypassed her room in favor of his own and threw her inside. She landed on her stomach, on the bed.

"Sit up properly," he ordered.

She did.

And then Lucian did a most surprising thing. He squatted by her knees so that he could look up into her face and, with seeming sincerity, asked, "What in the world have you done to yourself, little girl?"

She stared at him for a long moment. And then she admit-ted, "I don't know."

"Why?" he demanded. "Because of Christian?"

"I don't know," she repeated. And it was the truth, too. This thing, this lifestyle of hers had long ago taken on a . . . well, life of its own. She couldn't remember when she'd actually stopped thinking of Chris and just let the stream carry her along.

"You are the most naturally gifted skater I have ever taught. Ever seen, as a matter of fact. Why in the world would you throw away a blessing from God like this?"

"It doesn't matter." Gina shrugged.

"It does. It matters, because you matter."

"Right."

"No self-pity," Lucian thundered. "I won't stand for that."

She shuddered. But she also, for the first time in a long time, listened.

"I'm not exaggerating, Gina." Lucian emphasized each word with exquisite care. "I will not stand for this kind of behavior from you. You don't shred a Monet painting, you don't burn a Beethoven symphony, and you don't toss a Dickens novel in a drawer to mold. I will not let you do this to yourself. You are a work of art. You need to start behaving that way. And you deserve to be treated that way."

"Yeah," Gina snorted. "By who?"

Lucian appraised her coolly. And then he said, "Let's start with me. And then we will go from there."

She let him, of course. When had Gina ever managed to say no when given strict mandates about what she should do and how she should do it? It made no sense logically, but as soon as Lucian took over her life, she felt back in control of it again.

Gina now had a reason to get up in the morning. She knew what was expected of her, what to do to earn praise, what not to do to avoid censure, and what was coming up just around the corner for practically every minute of the day. There were no surprises, there were no unpleasant shocks, and there were no confusing decisions to be made.

Lucian rebuilt Gina's skating, her professional career, and finally, Gina herself.

She got her self-confidence back. Well, maybe not *self*-confidence; Gina wasn't convinced she'd ever really had that. But she got back her confidence that other people were confident in her. Which was just as good, really, and more comfortable, to boot.

It was all thanks to Lucian. So the least she could do to

thank him was accept his marriage proposal. Especially when, afterwards, Gina couldn't even quite recall whether he'd asked her to marry him . . . or simply told her. Not that it made a difference.

Nine

SKATINGANDSTUFF.COM
MESSAGE BOARD

FROM: SkatingYoda
Posted at 12:02 PM

You know, everyone is always getting on Lucian's case for marrying Gina but I always thought she was the opportunist there, not him. Does anyone remember how her career was in the toilet before she married him? She couldn't get arrested for traveling on her camel spin. Lucian was the one who made her a star again after the Olympics. She used him, IMO, not the other way around.

FROM: GoGoGregory1
Posted at 12:05 PM

<<Does anyone remember how her career was in the toilet before she married him?>>

You don't know what you're talking about Gina was a huge star after she won the Olympics Gina had her pick of shows and in a poll done two years after she won she was voted America's favorite woman athlete of the decade she didn't need Lucian to make her a star she was the best and everyone knew it.

FROM: SuperCooperFan
Posted at 12:09 PM

I never understood what Lucian wanted with Chris Kelly's hand-me-downs. You know how Chris is always saying Lucian was like a father to him? Well, it's pretty gross when you think of them both with Gina.

FROM: SkatingYoda
Posted at 12:11 PM

That whole Chris/Gina romance was a set-up from the beginning. It was just for publicity during the Olympics. Everyone knows Chris is gay.

FROM: Admin
Posted at 12:13 PM

WARNING: As per the written rules of the board (click **here** for refresher if you need it), skater's sexuality is off limits as topic for discussion. Thank you.

FROM: GoGoGregory1
Posted at 12:14 PM

A skater's sexuality is their own private business.

FROM: SuperCooperFan
Posted at 12:16 PM

I don't care if a skater is gay, it doesn't make me like them any less.

FROM: LuvsLian
Posted at 12:17 PM

It's offensive to speculate. Gay people should be respected as much as anyone else.

FROM: MaryQuiteContrary
Posted at 12:18 PM

So how come it's offensive to speculate if someone is gay, but not offensive to wonder if they're straight?

FROM: LuvsLian
Posted at 12:19 PM

<<So how come it's offensive to speculate if someone is gay, but not offensive to wonder if they're straight?>>

Nobody does that.

FROM: MaryQuiteContrary
Posted at 12:21 PM

Oh, yeah? Then how come the Admin didn't come in to chastise us when we were speculating about why Pryce dumped Wright for Quinn or if he was going to upgrade from Gregory to Cassidy, but she jumped right in as soon as Yoda said Kelly was gay, huh? How's that not a double standard? Don't you guys get it? Every time you go on and on about how someone's sexuality is their own business and doesn't affect how you feel about them as a skater, then turn around and have no problem discussing a straight guy's sex life, you're just reinforcing that being gay is different and needs special protection. If you responded as matter of factly to the question of "is so and so gay" as you did to "is so and so straight" that would prove how commendably open-minded you are and how you don't care one way or the other. This way, you're just PC idiots. (I know, I know, Admin, I'll just quietly ban myself. . . . Consider me a political prisoner.)

Bex asked Sabrina, "So you don't think Gina ever loved your father? Not even when she first married him?"

"Oh, who knows what goes through the mind of Gina? That whole marriage was so out of the blue. One minute it's Gina and Chris as skating's answer to Paul Newman and Joanne Woodward, and the next Gina is Celine Dion married to that ancient guy who discovered her as a kid."

"Come on, the age difference wasn't that bad."

"Hello? She's a year older than I am. Talk about ancient enough to be her father. Literally. I got the paperwork to prove it."

"You're not a fan."

"And you're really, really good at your job, aren't you?"

On another occasion, Bex might have even been offended by the swipe. But she had a lot more on her mind these days than a bitter stepdaughter with obvious, unresolved Daddy issues. Unless, of course, it led Bex to . . . "Do you think Gina killed Lucian?"

"That's kind of blunt, isn't it?"

"It's what you wanted to talk to me about."

"Not necessarily."

"You have another suspect in mind?"

"Who says I think my dad was killed?"

"Then why are we having this conversation?"

"Jeez!"

"Sabrina, I have a lot of work to do. Say what you want to say, or let me go."

"You don't have to be such a bitch about it."

"Ditto."

Bex listened to their entire exchange, wondering who the heck this person trading barbs with Sabrina Pryce was. Barbs weren't usually Bex's thing. Saucy wit, delightful self-deprecating asides, clever puns, pungent sarcasm, those were more up her alley. Bex didn't tend to go for the flat-out claws. But then again, maybe her earlier chat with Gina about the merits, or lack thereof, of marrying a widower still obviously in love with his late wife had prematurely aged Bex out of her stunted collegiate phase and into world-weary crone. She certainly felt world-weary at the moment. And it wasn't just the generic exhaustion of the job.

"Fine," Sabrina said. "It's just that everyone seems to be in such a hurry to call his death a tragic accident, I've got to wonder if maybe something else isn't going on."

"I'm going to ask again: Do you think Gina killed your father?"

"I certainly think she's wanted to over the years."

"Over the years? So why now? Had things between them recently gotten worse?"

"Felt like it. I mean, I don't see either of them that much. I live in San Francisco, you know. I have my own life, and none of it takes place on the ice. I talk to my father maybe every couple of months on the phone. To Gina, really only when I come out here, which is never more than once a year, more like every two. But this time, something was off. More than usual, I mean. The night before he died, I got the feeling they were . . . in the middle of something. Like I interrupted this thing and they were pretending nothing was going on, but it—something was still there, underneath. Nobody said anything or did anything, but they were . . . tight. Does that make any sense?"

"And then the next morning he was dead?"

"Yeah. The next morning, he was dead."

"That's awfully convenient."

"For somebody," Sabrina agreed.

That afternoon, the OTC's main rink was bustling with activity as Toni, alongside a hurriedly-drafted-into-assistant-duty Chris, attempted to choreograph an opening number for Lucian's tribute featuring a troupe of his current students that would be somber, respectful, and not deadly dull. Bex noted with amusement that, despite his never having taken a lesson from Lucian in his life, Toni had plopped Jeremy Hunt in the center of the company. Bex couldn't blame her. Jeremy was the most promising student Toni had ever coached and she was determined to get him maximum exposure—even if it meant literally spinning on Lucian's carcass to do it. It was beginning to seem as if the famed coach's death was working out rather well for a whole host of people.

Unable to help herself, Bex scanned the stands, checking

to see if Craig might be in attendance, watching his son practice. She didn't see him in the throng of eager moms with video cameras plastered to their noses. Not that Bex had honestly expected to. Craig made a point of keeping his distance from Jeremy's skating career unless directly invited to intervene. He was awfully good at giving people their space.

Too good, frankly.

She would have liked to have him around now to talk to. But it was probably for the best. Talking could only lead to more talking. Which would lead to thinking and then maybe even deciding and committing. Bex never did well with those verbs.

Instead, she settled for watching the rehearsal, trying to figure out what her next move should be. At center ice, Jeremy was attempting to land a Triple Axel on a fierce downbeat of music. It was a jump he usually mastered, but this time around, he would leap into the air, turn three and a half times, land on one foot, and just when it seemed he had it, his blade would slide out from under him, sending the boy sprawling.

After he'd failed for a third time, Toni and Chris called Jeremy over to the barrier and signaled for him to lift up his right boot. He did so obediently. First Toni, then Chris ran their fingers along the edge of his blade, conferring briefly among themselves. Then Toni reached into her pocket and pulled out what looked to Bex, from a distance, like a pumice stone. It seemed to be used for the same purpose, as well. Toni took the flat, grey rock and struck it forcefully, but with control, along the bottom of Jeremy's blade. A few more precise swipes and she indicated for him to give it a try now.

Jeremy gingerly set his foot back down on the ice and moved it cautiously a few times back and forth before taking off at full speed into a dozen backwards crossovers. He leapt into the air and completed three and a half revolutions followed by an imperfect, slanted, though upright landing. Toni and Chris nodded, satisfied, and returned to what they were doing.

Bex waited until the two coaches called a break to confer

among themselves, then promptly pushed her way through the teen throng towards Jeremy. He was sitting on a bench, dutifully wiping up the slush from his blades with a soft cloth so they wouldn't rust.

"Hey, dude," she offered, simultaneously wondering how much Jeremy knew of what was currently going on between her and his dad.

"Bex! Hey!" He looked genuinely happy to see her. Which meant he either had an idea of what was going on and was pleased about it, or he had an idea of what was going on and was happy Bex was dragging her feet. Or he had no idea at all. "Dad said you were here working on the tribute. That's awesome."

"Looks like it's going to be some show."

"I hope so. Toni gave me a solo. It feels kind of weird, since I never took from him or anything. But she said that he taught her, and she taught me, so it's to symbolize a torch being passed, you know?"

Bex contemplated what fine wisdom Lucian had passed on to Jeremy's biological parents when he'd been their coach, but decided now was not the time or place to recall that particular era.

Jeremy, however, had no such qualms. "Dad wasn't thrilled at first about me skating in a tribute to Lucian Pryce. You know, because of the . . . stuff."

"I can imagine."

"Toni talked him into it, though. She said it would be good for me to be on TV, show what I can do, especially if I want to prove that my making the World Team this past year wasn't just some fluke. Toni's real good at talking people into things they don't want to do. By the time she's done, you start thinking it was your idea in the first place."

Bex asked, "What happened to your skate blade out there?"

"Oh, that." He lifted his leg by the thigh with both arms to show her. "I think I must have caught a rut or something coming in, because I took a huge chunk right out of the front, see?"

Bex peered at the blade, noticing that there did seem to be an indentation about an inch or two below the clawed toe pick at the tip. "Looks all smoothed out now, though."

"Yeah. Good thing Toni had a stone on her."

"Do all coaches carry one?"

"Usually. It's just for quick fixes, though. I'm going to need a good sharpening when I get back home. I don't want to do it now, though. Don't want to have to break in freshly sharpened boots before the show."

"So one little knick can really make that much of a difference?"

"Oh, yeah, totally. It was throwing me completely off balance on the Axel. I could feel something was wrong, but I wasn't sure what. I thought maybe my legs just felt funny or my sock got bunched up. I was trying to skate it off. Good thing Toni and Chris figured out what was going on. I could have really hurt myself."

"I'm glad you're okay," Bex told Jeremy sincerely.

"Thanks. Hey, are Dad and I going to get to see you while we're all here? I know everybody's totally busy, but maybe the three of us could hang out?"

"I—I don't know, Jer."

"That would be cool, wouldn't it?"

Bex agreed. "Yeah. That would be cool. But there's something I need to check out first. You tell your dad I said hi, okay?"

"Sure, Bex."

She called the police station but, upon getting the runaround, decided to hail a cab and see for herself. Once there, nobody would just let Bex take a quick look at Lucian's personal effects. The cop on duty insisted that everything, including Lucian's skates, had already been packed up and were waiting to be picked up by Gina. Oddly enough, Mrs. Pryce did not seem to be in much of a hurry.

Bex thought fast. She told him they (she was deliberately vague on who exactly "they" might be) wanted to borrow the skates to construct a memorial centerpiece. For the tribute. A cornucopia of items to symbolize the stages of Lucian's life as a competitor and a coach. Since the medical examiner had already cleared the items for release, surely there was nothing improper about handing the pair over? The cornucopia was scheduled to be a surprise for Gina and Sabrina, unveiled the night of the show—that's why Bex didn't want to wait and retrieve the skates later from Mrs. Pryce. Surely, the officer could understand that? They were trying to do a good thing, here.

He looked at Bex funny for a moment.

But in the end, he did hand over Lucian's skates.

Clutching the paper bag they'd been packed in, Bex headed back to the arena.

She managed to catch Toni alone in the coaches' lounge. Making sure that no one was listening in, Bex yanked out the well-worn pair and laid them on the coffee table at Toni's feet.

"Look!" she announced.

"Lucian's skates." Toni's voice was devoid of any emotion, even curiosity. She acted as if she were confronted with her ex-partner's last skates every day of the week.

"What do you see?"

"Lucian's skates," Toni repeated. "What are you doing with these, honey?"

"Look at the blades."

Toni did. "Yes?"

"Can't you see it? They're both covered in ruts."

"Skating is a tough sport."

"Come on, Toni. I saw how you and Chris evened out Jeremy's blades today with that stone thing or whatever it's called. If he was having trouble just trying to manage one rut, how the heck was Lucian expected to stay upright in blades this beat up?"

"Jeremy was attempting to land a Triple Axel. I assure you, not only had Lucian never mastered one in his prime, but he certainly wouldn't have been trying one now."

"That's right. Lucian wasn't trying to do anything more challenging this morning than backwards crossovers. That shouldn't have been enough to knock him over. Unless some-one tampered with his blades first."

"And how do you propose 'someone' did that, Bex?"

"Easy. If a stone can take out a rut, I'm sure it can deliber-ately put one in."

"Even if that were the case—"

"Isn't it?"

"Well, I suppose so, in theory."

"So then—"

"But even if that were the case, Bex, how did this alleged killer of yours obtain access to Lucian's skates?"

"Easily. Both Gina and Sabrina were at the house with him yesterday. They could have waited for him to leave the room—"

"Lucian didn't keep his skates at home."

That took some proverbial wind out of Bex's theory. "He didn't?"

"No."

"So where did he keep them, then?"

"Here. In his office. At the rink."

"But that's even easier! Anyone could have walked in—"

"Lucian always kept his office locked. Remember, you tried to open the door this morning to call the police."

She did remember. "And Lucian was the only one with a key?"

Toni hesitated. "Actually, I have one as well. I travel here with my own students several times a year. Lucian gave me a key, oh, almost five years ago, I'd say. So I would have a pri-vate place to rest when not teaching. None of us are getting any younger, you know, Bex. Lucian thought I might need the break."

"Oh." Now it was Bex's turn to hesitate.

"Would you like to lock me up now, or after the tribute show?"

"Don't be silly. I—"

"Come now, Bex. You were happy to point the finger at Gina or Sabrina when it suited your purposes. Why not me?"

The peculiar tone of Toni's voice took Bex by surprise. She

couldn't tell if the older woman was being sincere, acting coy, or deliberately baiting Bex.

"Fine, Toni. I'll play along. *Was* it you?"

"Did I kill Lucian?"

"Sure. You seem to really want me to ask you, so I'm asking: Did you damage Lucian's skates so that he'd fall down and crack his skull? After all, you knew about his previous fractures, you knew he was vulnerable. You have means; I saw the stone. And you just told me you had the opportunity."

"What about motive? Did I have one of those as well?"

"Actually," Bex said, "that's the easiest one of all."

"Is that a fact?"

"Yeah. It is."

"And what might have been my motive to kill my oldest friend in the world?"

"He dumped you."

"He did?" For the first time, Bex got the feeling Toni wasn't playing games. She seemed genuinely surprised by Bex's assertion. "When?"

Again, her response threw Bex off-kilter, leading her to stutter. "Well, a bunch of times. I mean, most recently I guess when he left the Connecticut Training Center to come teach out here and didn't take you with him."

"I didn't want to go. My life is on the East Coast. My children are there."

"Shouldn't he have made you director of the Connecticut Center, then? You had the seniority. Instead, Igor Marchenko—"

"That wasn't Lucian's call to make. That was the board of directors. In fact, the reason Lucian took the job out here was because he was so furious at them for bringing Marchenko in to coach at his facility. Lucian didn't want Igor there, so he resigned and took another position."

"Okay, fine." Bex hadn't wanted to bring up her final point. It was impolite and hurtful, and she really didn't want to go there. But if Toni insisted on acting like this, she left Bex with no choice. "What about the fact that Lucian dumped you years ago? Right after the Olympics. He dropped you as a partner and . . . other stuff . . . so he could have a solo career. And then he married Eleanor, to boot. Lucian treated you like dirt. That sounds like a pretty good motive to me."

Ten
Toni

Mr. Sullivan, of Sullivan's Skating Stars, said, "I'm afraid . . . the problem is . . . it wouldn't be possible. . . . I can take one of you. One, not both. I'm sorry. It's one thing, just the skating. People can overlook just the skating. Maybe. But a married couple such as yourselves . . . We play a lot of small towns, you see."

They saw.

Lucian was out of his chair before Mr. Sullivan had finished speaking. The words coming out of his own mouth were ones unlikely to endear Wright and Pryce to small-town audiences—or big-town audiences, for that matter. Toni had to grab him by the arm and pull Lucian back into his seat, shooting him a warning look.

Toni smiled at Mr. Sullivan. "Thank you for explaining the situation to us, sir. Would it be all right if we got back to you tomorrow morning with our decision?"

Mr. Sullivan said that would be fine.

"It's not fine," Lucian raged as soon as they were outside. "It's not fine and it's not right, and I don't care if your precious mother and daddy would think I'm acting like a hot-headed mick. I am a hotheaded mick, and that SOB was—"

"Just telling us the facts of life. He was being honest, and your beating his brains in won't change the situation one iota. At least Mr. Sullivan had the good manners to be frank with us. The other tours didn't even bother offering that much respect."

Lucian looked at Toni sideways. "You have a most interesting way of looking at the world, young woman."

"And that's why you love me," Toni reminded.

He conceded, "Among other things . . ."

Back at the Wright home in Harlem, Lucian refused to let go of the insult they'd been dealt. (Toni had long ago noticed that Lucian seemed to take much more offense at insults to her honor than she did; she supposed it was because he'd had less practice with it.) Lucian stormed, "We don't need them. We don't need any of them, you realize. We're National champions. We're Olympians. We can have a perfectly fine professional career without any of those bastards."

Toni agreed. "I've been thinking that, too. What if we forget about the traditional tours and—"

"Exactly. To hell with them. I bet there are dozens of kids, hundreds even, who would want to take lessons from Wright and Pryce. We could set up our own school. Here in the city, or someplace else. Both our names right out front. We don't need Sullivan and his provincial audiences to make money. We can—"

"Coach?" Toni asked.

"Of course we can. I've technically already been doing it—though don't let the USFSA know; they'll be out for my hide, for sure. And you, you're a natural at any damn thing you put your mind to. I bet we could be the best in the country within just a couple of years. That will show them. They think they can keep us down—"

"Lucian—" Toni interrupted.

"What?"

"Lucian . . . I don't want to coach."

"What are you talking about?"

"Coaching. I've never really been interested in it. Well, maybe some time down the road, when I'm older and the performing opportunities . . . But Lucian, I started figure skating because I love to perform. I love being at center ice, all those eyes watching me. And then the applause afterwards. I want to be a star. That's all I ever wanted from this."

"But, Sullivan said—"

"Forget Sullivan. Let's start our own show."

"Oh, come now . . ."

"Why not? If Sullivan and his ilk can do it, why not us? You just said I was a natural at anything I put my mind to."

"Actually, I said you were a damn natural."

"Even better."

"But what do we know about running an ice show?"

"What did I know about ice skating when I started? What did you know about coaching?"

"Where would we get the money?"

"We'd raise it."

"Daddy?"

"He likes a good investment as much as the next man. Besides, there are other people out there we can talk to. You said it yourself. We're National champions. We're Olympians. Our names mean something."

"And so do the colors of our respective skins," Lucian said.

"I haven't forgotten."

"If Sullivan thinks he couldn't tour the both of us around the country, what gives you the idea we could do it ourselves?"

"We should at least try."

"And if we fail? We'll be laughingstocks. If we fail, we will never get another decent booking. And as for the skating school . . . who would want to take lessons from a pair of renowned losers?"

"This isn't like you," she said. "When did you become a coward?"

"I am not a coward, Toni. But I am a realist. Always have been, you just never noticed. It was one thing when we were on the amateur scene. I had some control there. I understood the rules and I understood how to manipulate them. I always had a Plan B. I knew that once you and I reached a certain technical and artistic level, even the damn racist USFSA would not be able to ignore us. Not without consequences, anyway. And I knew that you and I could reach that level simply by working harder and smarter than anybody else. This is different. This is asking the money-paying public to go beyond centuries of voodoo prejudice—"

"Don't lecture me about centuries of prejudice, Lucian. Your 'No Dogs or Irish Allowed' barroom signs can't compete with my arsenal, so don't even try."

"My point exactly. Aren't we on the wrong sides of this argument?"

"No. Because my side is about not giving in. How do we know that we'll fail until we try?"

Lucian sighed. "There is a very, very, very narrow window of opportunity for skaters like us to cash in following the Olympics. In one year, it will be even narrower. In four years, no one will remember our names."

"Unless we give them something to remember."

"Like a coast-to-coast failure?"

"I never expected this from you," Toni said.

"And I never expected you to be so blind. And so stubborn."

"Stubborn—and a good degree of closing my eyes—got me this far. Why give it up now?"

"Because," Lucian said softly. "How about because I'm asking you to?"

She hesitated then. After close to an hour of arguing all the while knowing in her heart that she was absolutely right and nothing Lucian might counter could sway her, Toni hesitated. She'd had all her answers prepared for when Lucian tried to tell her what to do. She had nothing to offset his asking her.

"You're asking me to—"

"Yes. I am. For both our sakes. We had a plan, Toni. You and I were going to be married and we were going to have a professional career in skating. Together. Well, as it turns out we can't have one performing. But coaching—coaching, I'm certain, is still within our reach. But only if we act now. So I'm asking you, Toni. Come with me. Let's do what we always planned on doing."

"We planned on performing."

"We planned on being together."

"We still could be."

"No. Not your way. I won't risk looking like a fool."

"So it's your way or—"

"I didn't say that," he warned.

"You are asking me to give up my dream."

"I'm asking you to accept that it won't happen."

"You know, that's the first time you've ever said that to me?"

"This is a problem, Toni, that even I can't fix."

"I understand," she agreed. "But maybe I can."

He had nothing to say in response to that. And Toni, for her part, had nothing to say—to his dismay. She wanted to reach out and touch him, to reassure somehow that everything was still all right. But it was as if one of them were standing in place, and the other swiftly being swept away. Toni figured it was a testament to how many years they'd spent working on moving as one entity, that, even now, she couldn't tell which of them it was that was standing and which one was disappearing. All she knew was that the distance between them was suddenly insurmountable.

As if he were already gone, Toni heard Lucian positing, "I guess you had better contact Sullivan and tell him you're taking the headlining spot on your own. He should be happy to hear it, I'm sure. A woman is always a better draw on these things than a man."

"No. I told you, Lucian. I've made up my mind. I am going to be a star on my own terms. I am not going to take crumbs from some second-rate tour and be grateful somebody's willing to have me. I'm starting my own show. In fact," she said, "I think you're the one who should call Sullivan. Take the solo spot. Even if it's just for a year or so. Nothing better than touring the country for getting your name out there. It will help the coaching career. I'm sure it will."

"We're both rather certain of ourselves, aren't we, Toni? We both think we know exactly what's right and what's wrong and what everyone should do."

"That's why you love me, isn't it?"

"Among other things . . ."

Toni didn't speak to Lucian for six months after he left on Sullivan's tour. Her life was simply too busy. And hearing his voice, even on the phone, would have simply hurt too much.

She did as she'd promised. She attempted to start up her own skating tour. She didn't expect it to be easy, and on that count, the experience didn't disappoint.

While Lucian could make cracks about Toni turning to Daddy for funding, the fact was, even if Toni had made that her first approach, her father didn't have the means or the interest. He thought Toni's idea was as ridiculous as Lucian had and, when she revealed she'd turned down Lucian's offer to coach alongside him, agreed with her ex-partner that it was a strategic mistake on Toni's part. (On the matter of their broken engagement, he stayed mum. After all, if he'd pretended not to be aware of it being on, he could hardly comment one way or the other about it being off.)

Toni went looking for capital from alternate sources. Banks turned her down flat. Even Negro institutions like Carver Federal, Unity Bank, and Citizens Trust told her that they saw little profit to be made from subsidizing an ice show, especially one whose unique selling proposition was a black girl as the star.

She tried pitching the tour as a nonprofit and turning to companies that offered artistic grants to dance companies and the like.

"Figure skating isn't art," she was told.

Toni even attempted appeals in churches, suggesting that such a national ice show could be seen as a community event, an inspiration to young people, proof that they could be anything they wanted to be if they just put their minds to it.

"No, they can't," she was told. "And there's no point in your filling their heads with nonsense."

It was while getting her hair straightened at the same Harlem beauty parlor she'd been going to since her mother took her in the second grade, that Toni thought to turn to the women who both ran and patronized such institutions.

She pointed out to the owners that women were the primary audience for figure skating shows. So what better venue to spread the word about their salons? It took her months of literally going door-to-door to beauty parlors—black and white—in all five New York City boroughs before Toni collected enough sponsors to put on her first exhibition. "One Night Only!" the signs trumpeted; Toni neglected to mention that one was all she could afford. It was held in a barely upright 2,500-seat Harlem theater outfitted with artificial ice; Toni was the main attraction and five other girls of indeterminate color—two were Puerto Rican, one was Chinese, and another was something called a Sephardic Jew—served as a makeshift chorus line. She rehearsed them for four weeks; she designed and, with a little help from the other girls, sewed their costumes. She cut the music, hired and trained a lighting director, and wrote advertising copy. She made multiple appearances at every school, Scout troup, Jack and Jill club, Ladies Auxiliary, and church that would have her, talking up the show, all but begging—all right, begging—people to attend.

Ultimately, they did. After expenses, Toni earned a whopping $3,786 profit. Less than twenty-four hours later, she'd poured it into another show in another town. She invested in her own sheet of artificial ice and proceeded to take it on the road. She toured the South and the Midwest and, even though people told her she was crazy, played three sold-out shows in Hollywood. There, everyone said the public turned out to see the novelty of her. Toni didn't care. They came, they paid, they watched, and they applauded at the end. She was a star. And on her own terms, at that.

She said as much to Lucian when they finally hooked up, by phone. She was in San Francisco, high off another successful engagement at Playland, a small outdoor amusement park in the Ocean Beach area. Her music had needed to compete with the pounding of the waves and the harking of overweight seals, but again, there were applauding audiences and bouquets of flowers and her picture in the newspaper. Lucian was back in New York, on a break from his tour and already coaching a couple of promising skaters part-time. He told Toni about one girl in particular. Eleanor Quinn, her name was. He said she had, in his opinion, incredible potential.

"And that's why you love her?" Toni guessed. She hadn't spent every day with the man for the past decade not to recognize the signs when she heard them.

"Among other things," he conceded. And then, "Toni . . ."

"What?"

"If you'd consider—"

"No."

"Just come back and visit. See what we could have here."

"No, Lucian. I can't. I've got momentum now. People have heard of me. I've actually had to turn down two bookings because I could honestly tell them I was too busy. You're the one who taught me how important momentum is in this business. I can't let people forget who I am. So what if I'm just the flavor of the month? What difference does it make? I've got to stretch it out as long as I can."

He sighed. "Eleanor is a beautiful girl."

"I'm sure she is. And I'm sure you'll make her an incredible skater."

"Keep in touch, Toni," he asked. "Promise?"

"I promise."

And Toni did. She even fully intended to make it to Lucian and Eleanor's wedding when they invited her, if only a chance to skate at a 7,500-seat venue in Atlanta alongside several former World champions hadn't come up at the last minute. (She'd be filling in for someone more important, but as always, Toni didn't care what number she was on the guest list as long as she could be a part of it.) She sent her regrets and told everyone who asked that she was genuinely happy for the bride and groom.

She never did understand why no one seemed to believe her.

A few years later, Lucian didn't manage to make it to Toni's wedding, either. Eleanor was eight months pregnant with Sabrina and couldn't travel as far as New York from where they were then living in Seattle. They both sent their best wishes, though, and Toni, for one, had no reason to believe they weren't sincere.

Her husband-to-be, an accountant named Keith whom she'd initially hired to help keep her tour's books and make sure all her taxes were properly paid—and deducted—observed, "It's a shame. After everything you told me about him, I was really looking forward to meeting the great Lucian Pryce."

"You'll get your chance," Toni promised.

And he did.

After Toni's older son, Keith Jr., was born and she realized that, good intentions aside, there was no way she was going to manage hitting the road with a newborn who needed more accessories and support staff than her entire chorus line put together, Toni called Lucian, by then working at the Olympic Training Center in Connecticut, and told him, "I'm ready to coach now."

"It's about time!" he exclaimed.

For the next month, as Toni and Keith prepared to relocate (or, technically, since they'd never lived anywhere for more than a few weeks at a time, actually *locate*), everyone in skating whom Toni told about her new position would hesitate, lower their voices, and with a concerned hand resting on either Toni's shoulder or her knee, nervously ask, "And how do you feel about that?" (It was the 1970s; people's feelings were the main topic of conversation under any circumstances.)

"Fine . . ." Toni answered the first several times, unaware of the subtext that was making everyone look so concerned.

Then, when she got a clue, she asked, "You mean because Lucian and—"

"Yes, exactly," they gulped in relief, happy not to have to spell it out for her.

"Oh, Lucian and I are fine. We always were."

"Right," they said. "Of course. Be brave, Toni. We're all behind you."

Which was a nice thing to hear, she supposed. Even if she had no idea what they were talking about.

Eleven

**SKATINGANDSTUFF.COM
MESSAGE BOARD**

FROM: Sk8luv4ever
Posted at 3:18 PM

My friend who skates at the OTC told me Jeremy Hunt is going to be in the Tribute show. I can't wait to see him. I totally fell in love with Jeremy at Nats last year. He's got what it takes to be World Champion.

FROM: SkatingYoda
Posted at 3:22 PM

<<He's got what it takes to be World Champion.>>

I beg to differ. Jeremy Hunt is barely 14 years old. The puberty monster hasn't gotten him yet. He could be a total flash in the pan as soon as he grows a little and loses all those precocious jumps of his.

FROM: SuperCooperFan
Posted at 3:23 PM

Jeremy Hunt might have quads, but he skates like he's 10 years old. It's called MEN'S Singles, not BOYS.

FROM: LuvsLian
Posted at 3:34 PM

And I'm sure your opinion about Jeremy has nothing to do with him almost beating your precious Super-Cooper at Nationals this year.

FROM: SuperCooperFan
Posted at 3:35 PM

In your dreams. Jeremy didn't take a single judge away from Coop. That second place was a gift from the judges. And speaking of being biased, you only don't like Coop because he cheated on YOUR precious Lian.

FROM: Sk8luv4ever
Posted at 3:37 PM

Does Jeremy Hunt even take from Lucian?

FROM: SkatingYoda
Posted at 3:39 PM

No. He takes from Toni Wright. But I heard he was going to switch to Lucian this summer. Lucian coached Jeremy's bio dad, Robby Sharpton, so they thought he could work his magic on Jeremy, too, since they skate so much alike. Toni was furious about it. Her best students always end up leaving her for Lucian.

Toni said, "Do people still think that? Goodness, how many years has it been? Forty years after the fact, are you telling me people still think I'm carrying some sort of torch for Lucian after the man done me wrong?"

"Well, Toni, it's just that, the way everything happened—"

"Nobody knows what happened. Nobody but Lucian and I. Everything else has just been speculation and innuendo, and totally unfounded rumors. In fact, the truth of the matter is . . ."

Toni trailed off. Just when things were getting interesting.

"What? What's the truth of the matter?"

"Nothing. Nothing that's any of your business, in any case."

"I was just—"

"I know what you were doing, Bex. You're not my first television researcher, you understand. I know perfectly well what your job is. But I'm afraid I'm not going to be able to help you. Not this time. If you were hoping for a confession about how I broke into Lucian's office with the spare key he gave me and sabotaged his skates so that he would fall down, crack his head on the ice, and die all to avenge some long-ago romantic slight, I am sorry. What is it you call it in the television business? A story line? That story line will not be available for you to wrap up in a pretty ribbon and summarize in four minutes during your broadcast."

"I'm sorry," Bex said. Unlike Toni, she wasn't nearly as clear as to what exactly she was apologizing for. But clearly an apology was needed, nonetheless.

"You're certain that Lucian was murdered, Bex?"

"Certain? No," she admitted. "But, it feels that way."

"Well then, I wish you luck in getting to the bottom of this. You know, Lucian wasn't exactly everyone's favorite person. But he did have his good side. Please keep that in mind as you so untiringly dig for the bad."

For the next few hours, Bex hung out at the rink, finishing that part of her job that didn't include looking for murder suspects. She watched Gina, Chris, and Gabrielle run through the programs they were going to perform at the tribute. She took notes on their music choices and on each technical element so that the 24/7 commentators, Francis and Diana Howarth, would have all the key information in front of them once they arrived to host the on-air show.

Chris and Gabrielle, as a one-night-only ice dance team, were skating to "I'm Still Standing" by Elton John.

"I thought it was a pretty appropriate tune for a skater." Gabrielle sang softly, *"I'm still standing after all this time/Picking up the pieces of my life without you on my mind."*

"Referring only to skating, of course," Bex said.

"Yes, of course," she said, brightly. "What else could it possibly be referring to?"

Chris had picked a classical piece, or rather several of them, all vaguely familiar selections by Puccini.

When Bex inquired about the symbolism, he explained, "This was my first Olympic Long Program. The night I won my Gold medal, it was the happiest I had ever seen Lucian be. It was the happiest I'd ever been in my life, as well. I thought it was perfect for a tribute. Wouldn't you agree?"

As for Gina, her program was, according to Bex's earlier notes, supposed to be "In My Life" by the Beatles. But when Gina took her spot at center ice to rehearse, what came through the sound system was that Green Day song that was all the rage a couple of years earlier:

> *It's something unpredictable, but in the end it's right.*
> *I hope you had the time of your life.*

At least, Bex was pretty certain it was Green Day. Ever the good researcher, she pulled out her laptop while Gina was still skating and double-checked before putting it down as fact in her report for Francis and Diana. A few clicks revealed that Bex had been correct on one count. The song was by Green Day. But her initial assumption about its title was wrong. It wasn't called "Time of Your Life" (despite that particular phrase being repeated at least four times); it's actual title was "Good Riddance."

• • •

𝓑ℰ𝓍 was about to ask Gina about the meaning of—and reasons for changing—her tribute number when she was distracted by Sabrina walking through the swinging doors and into the rink. Lucian's daughter paused at the elevated barrier, taking in the activity going on below in her father's name. She crossed her arms, resting her elbows on the rail, and continued watching without expression. The only time she so much as acknowledged the skaters was when Toni waved from the ice and Sabrina offered a perfunctory nod in return. When Chris also raised his arm in greeting, Sabrina pretended she hadn't noticed.

It was a bit harder for her to ignore Bex, seeing as how the intrepid girl-researcher chose to pop up right next to one of Sabrina's propped elbows and then get about as much in her face as she could to a person who was looking in the other direction.

Bex said, "This must feel so strange to you."

"Hmm," was all Sabrina deigned to reply.

Okay, well, then, let's try the opposite track. Bex said, "On the other hand, I guess being at a rink is like coming home."

Sabrina snorted. "Hardly."

"Really? I'd have assumed you grew up around the ice. All the other coaches' kids that I know—"

"My mother used to bring me. When I was very young. She helped Lucian teach sometimes. Did some choreography, especially for his girls. She'd set up a playpen in the corner and she'd have one of the skating parents, or even some of the girls, keep an eye on me while she taught. Soon as I could walk, though, I got as far away from the ice as possible."

"You didn't like spending the day with your mother and father?"

"When my father was at the rink, all his attention was on his students. And when my mother was at the rink, all her attention was on my father."

"Your mother must have loved him very much."

"She adored him. I never got why, but adore him she definitely did."

"Not like Gina, I suppose?"

Another snort. But Bex had obviously said something pleasing. Sabrina actually snuck a look in her direction.

Bex pressed on. "Sabrina, you mentioned before how you thought something was off between your father and Gina the night before he died."

"Yeah. They were both acting weirder than usual."

"Do you think maybe you could talk a little more to me about it? Maybe, if you described exactly what happened, you and I could—"

"I don't know exactly what happened. I wasn't there all night to watch them play *Who's Afraid of Virginia Woolf?* I flew in that morning from the city, spent a couple of hours in forced bondage—sorry, bonding—with dear ol' Daddy and the stepmonster—here at the rink, of course; God forbid anyone should have been at the house to welcome me when I arrived—and then, soon as I could, I got out of there. I had a date for dinner. Thank God. Don't know how much Lucian and Company I otherwise could have taken."

Something wasn't adding up for Bex. "I thought you said you hardly ever visit your father."

"Yeah. So?"

"So you're only in town a couple of times every couple of years, and you had a date your first night here?"

Sabrina stared at Bex queerly. "Not that it's any of your business, but I happened to run into a former boyfriend that afternoon. We decided to go out and catch up on old times. What does that have to do with anything?"

"Nothing," Bex admitted. "It's just that, in my business, it's important to make sure all the facts fit together. Or else it's impossible to see the big picture."

"Well, excuse me for living," she snapped. "What, were you hoping to catch me in a lie so you could pin Lucian's death on me?"

Actually, Bex had been doing exactly what she said, making sure the facts she already had corroborated each other enough to form a whole picture. But if Sabrina wanted to discuss possible culpability in her father's murder, who was Bex to stop her?

"Like I explained, it's important to know where everyone was at a given time so you can reconstruct—"

"Yeah, yeah, yeah, I've seen *CSI*. I know the drill." Sabrina turned away from Bex, towards the door. "Look, you don't believe my story? Check it out at the source. My boyfriend, he just walked in." She finished completely turning her back on Bex so she could greet the man then entering the rink. She pointed to her boyfriend.

Craig Hunt.

He'd just walked in, a few inches behind Jeremy, who was carrying his skate bag over one shoulder. Craig carried the garment bag with Jeremy's costume for the show.

Sabrina all but jumped for joy and gave a little squeak when she saw them and, blowing by Jeremy completely, sprung up on her tiptoes to give Craig a kiss. On the lips.

He seemed surprised by the gesture.

But not as surprised as, over Sabrina's shoulder, he was to see Bex.

Craig raised his free arm to gently set Sabrina back down on the ground, detaching his lips in the process. Discombobulated by the rejection, Sabrina looked around to where Craig was staring. She realized that it was Bex and proceeded to peer suspiciously from one to the other. Well, that made two of them.

The only one looking more confused than Bex, Sabrina, and Craig was Jeremy. But, unlike the rest of them, he decided not to pursue the issue.

"I'm going to get ready for my run-through, okay, Dad?" Jeremy asked.

Craig nodded.

Jeremy gave the assembled adults one last look, shrugged, and moved on.

Bex wished she could do the same thing. But the odds of that happening weren't seeming so good.

Someone had to speak first. Bex hoped it wouldn't prove

to be her. Nothing that she could think of to say at the moment struck her as particularly productive.

Craig said, "Hey, Bex."

Not exactly productive. But noninflammatory. She could go with that. For now. "Hey, Craig."

"You know each other?" Sabrina managed to make her four-word statement sound like a question. No, better, a four-page accusation.

"Yes," Craig said.

"And you and Sabrina know each other." Bex hoped her own, longer phrase didn't sound nearly as accusatory. Unless it should have.

"Yes," Craig said. "From a very long time ago. High school."

"It wasn't that long," Sabrina trilled.

For the first time since she and Craig started dating, Bex felt vaguely smug about her relative youth. For her, high school actually wasn't that long ago. Which she hoped, under the circumstances, was a point *in* her favor and not against.

She said to Craig, "But I thought you grew up in Connecticut."

"I did."

"So how . . ."

"Lucian didn't move to Colorado until I was in college," Sabrina explained. "I went to high school in Connecticut, too. You can imagine what a shock it was for me, running into Craig here of all places. I had no idea his little boy skated."

"Yeah," Bex said. "Jeremy is really good. He can do two quads, you know."

Discussing Craig's son's mastery of the Quadruple Toe Loop and Salchow seemed to be the safest avenue to pursue.

"Well, that's just great," Sabrina said, dismissing Bex even as she was pretending to address her. She told Craig, "You said you and Jeremy would be here this afternoon for the rehearsal, so I thought I'd stop by and say hello."

"That's nice," Craig agreed.

"I was thinking, maybe afterwards, you and I—"

Bex didn't need to hear the rest of the invitation. She stomped off.

Ғоr the next half hour or so, Bex pouted. Not visibly, of course. Bex was much too professional and mature to allow her feelings to surface while at work. But even as she conferred with the camera crew about where would be the best spots for them to set up based on the notes she'd taken diagramming the various skaters' performances, Bex kept one eye on Craig chatting with Sabrina. And she pouted. On the inside.

When Toni called a break, Bex did, too.

She picked up her laptop and headed inside to the snack-bar area, meaning to look busy typing away. She'd barely opened the lid and rebooted when Craig sat down across the table from her and said, "You're pouting."

"Am not."

"Bex . . ."

"Am not."

"This is silly. I ran into an old friend. She suggested dinner. Jeremy was going out with the other skaters that night, so I said sure. We had a nice time reminiscing about the not-so-good good old days, and then I took her home."

"You went on a date."

"Let's try this again. I ran into an old friend. She suggested—"

"A date."

"Bex . . ."

"You know, I didn't say no. When you proposed. I may not have said yes, but I didn't say no. We're not over." Bex swallowed hard. "Are we?"

"You're acting silly. And jealous."

"So?"

"So. It's cute."

"Are you sure you don't mean juvenile?"

"You know, Bex, the one who keeps having a problem with our age difference isn't me. It's you."

"What does Jeremy think?"

"About what? Sabrina? He's never even met her."

"About me."

"He likes you; you know that. He's always liked you."

"He liked me when I was some skating researcher who came down to his rink to ask him questions for a TV show. He liked me when I was hanging out with his dad—at least, I think he did. How much do you think he'll like me if he knew you asked me to marry you? Does he know?"

"No. Jeremy's had enough happen to him this past year. I have no intention of upsetting his life any further until I know exactly where we're headed."

"So I'm right. You think this will upset him."

"Upset in the sense of change his life? Absolutely. I intend for it to. I intend for it to upset all our lives. But upset in the sense of being unhappy about it . . ."

"That high school you and Sabrina attended must have been for the gifted and talented. You're awfully good with words."

"Actually, words are more your area, Bex. You're the one skilled at using them to hide behind."

"So did you have a good time? With Sabrina?"

"It was a pleasant evening."

"Just like old times?"

"Not exactly."

"Meaning what?"

"Meaning, it was good to see that Sabrina has calmed down since I first knew her. She was very . . ." Craig struggled to select just the right word. "*Intense* in high school. Tightly wound. She seems to be doing better now. I gather she's very successful professionally. Has a nice life in San Francisco. I'm happy for her."

"What was she so wound up about in high school?"

"Oh, some usual things. Some not so usual. Grades, popularity, college. It's all the same wherever you go. Then again, her mother had died a few years earlier. I know that was hard on her. And, of course, she and her father didn't get along very well. She really had some strong feelings about him then."

"Seems like she's still got some pretty strong feelings about him now."

"Oh, no. No, this is nothing. In high school, there were times I honestly thought Sabrina wanted to kill him."

"Really? How do you know that?"

"Because she asked me to help."

Twelve
Sabrina

Sabrina started plotting her father's demise even before he returned from the World Championships following Eleanor's death. Her first plan involved calling Interpol—or whoever was in charge of security in Europe—and telling them that Lucian Pryce was a registered Fascist, or maybe a Communist, bent on overthrowing their government. She ultimately decided against that particular scenario when she guessed that the word of an American teen might not carry that much weight in international circles, and that even an arrest wouldn't necessarily lead to Lucian's guaranteed death. He'd probably just get off with a warning or something.

Her next fantasy involved his plane crashing. Sabrina particularly liked that one because it would leave her a very media-friendly tragic orphan, deserving of sympathy as the daughter of two skating legends. She might even get to go on *Oprah* and meet Duran Duran. At the very least she might get to shoot one of those "I'm going to Disneyland" commercials.

Unfortunately, plane crashes were out of Sabrina's hands, no matter how many hints she offered up to God in the three days before Lucian's homecoming. Her father ended up landing safe and sound on American soil. Sabrina didn't go to meet him at the airport, despite knowing that there would probably be reporters there, shoving cameras and microphones in his face and asking questions about his marriage to America's late sweetheart. Even if Oprah herself came, Sabrina still didn't want to be anywhere near her father under the circumstances.

She could barely stand looking at him once he finally arrived at the house.

"Are you all right, Sabrina?" he asked, standing awkwardly in the hallway, suitcase on the floor between his legs, garment bag slung over his shoulder. For a moment, Sabrina actually let herself believe that Lucian was truly interested, that he really cared how she was holding up after being in the room with her dying mother, watching her trying so hard to breathe, then, all of a sudden, not breathing at all.

She might have answered him; she might even have cried and told him the truth. But a moment later, the door behind Lucian opened. And Chris Kelly walked in.

Who cared if he technically lived there? Who cared if he, even more than Lucian, looked concerned about Sabrina's well-being? He shouldn't, he couldn't, he didn't belong there. Not today. Not after Eleanor. Not after what Lucian had said on TV.

"Why don't you ask your only reason for living these days?" Sabrina snapped to her father and stormed out of the room.

She slammed her bedroom door and sat up all night, waiting for one or the other to come up and apologize to her.

Nobody did.

The next morning, she got dressed, went downstairs, and upon Lucian's orders, climbed dutifully into the car for the ride to the cemetery for Eleanor's funeral. She didn't say a word to her father the entire way there. She didn't say a word to him at the church or at the graveside or on the way home. She didn't say anything to Chris, either, even when he sat up front with them in the family pew, or stood on the condolence line afterwards.

She wanted to scream, "She wasn't your mother!" but Sabrina knew it would do no good. Lucian was more Chris's father than he was hers, and that, ultimately, was all that mattered.

Afterwards, life at home fell into a routine. Sabrina and Lucian did their best to stay out of each other's way. He hired a housekeeper whom Sabrina neither liked nor disliked. A housekeeper meant that their place stayed sparkling clean, the bills were paid on time, and their meals were cooked—though Sabrina made a point of eating separately from Lucian. He continued to give Sabrina an allowance—via the house-keeper—meaning her personal needs were taken care of. He continued to travel frequently—especially during the fall and winter months—which meant keeping out of his way didn't prove to be much of a problem.

Inside, Sabrina felt like she was about to explode. At first, she thought her feelings were grief. Grief over her mother, grief over her life, grief over the mess her relationship with Lucian had devolved into. But after a while, she realized that it didn't feel exactly like grief. Sabrina wasn't sad or weepy or melancholy. . . . Sabrina was something else. She just didn't know what exactly.

Externally, however, Sabrina Pryce was perfectly fine. No, even better. Externally, she was perfect. After all, she wasn't Eleanor Quinn's daughter for nothing. Even as she woke up every morning suffocating from a horrible, all-encompassing sense she couldn't quite name, on the surface, Sabrina was the poster child for adjustment. Her grades didn't dip after Eleanor died like her teachers had logically expected. In fact, they went up. She continued cheerleading as before, then joined Junior Achievement for good measure. She dressed beautifully as always, eschewing the latest trends (it was the 1980s; passing up neon leg warmers, shoulder pads, and ear-rings larger than her head wasn't too big of a sacrifice) for classic looks her mother had taught her would never go out of style. She wore her ebony hair long, though never feathered, moussed, or, God forbid, teased out. And she continued dat-ing the same types of boys she always had. Nice, clean-cut, wholesome, all-American types, maybe leaning a tiny bit towards the science nerds, but never so much that they didn't also play soccer or tennis or run track on the side. It wasn't difficult for her to get dates. Boys had always liked Sabrina. She'd listened to Eleanor and made a point of seeming a little mysterious, a little unapproachable, and always, always expecting to be treated like a lady. Eleanor hadn't seen anything insincere or manipulative in such behavior. It was simply the way one behaved. Was it insincere or manipulative to have good table manners or to use proper grammar? There was a right way to behave and a wrong way. Eleanor Quinn Pryce expected her only child to behave in the right way. And to reap the benefits of such behavior accordingly.

Which meant that boys—especially certain types—had always liked Sabrina. And she thought she liked them, too.

Until Eleanor died, and Sabrina doggedly continued on as if nothing were wrong, only to discover that those certain types of boys, for some reason, suddenly didn't appeal to her at all.

She blamed herself, at first. She figured she must still be in mourning, that's why their small talk about school and college plans and music and some television miniseries about giant lizards disguised as human beings was driving her up a wall. But as time passed, Sabrina began to blame them for being so friggin' boring. Didn't they ever think about anything larger than their stupid little lives lived in a stupid little town surrounded by stupid little people? They were getting as annoying as the idiots at Lucian's rink, who could only discuss jumps and spins and who might be at Regionals this year. Didn't they know there was a whole world out there? Didn't they realize that there could be more to life than . . . than . . . than . . . well, whatever the hell they were talking about at the moment? Didn't they know what it was like to trudge through your day, acting cheerful and upbeat while inside your head, something was pounding. Something dark and shapeless and nameless and desperate to get out, only you couldn't risk that, not until you understood what it was, for fear that, once out, it would simply swallow you whole?

Sabrina thought that there was only one boy in the entire Senior class who might know what that shapeless thing was.

His name was Craig Hiroshi. He was in Sabrina's math class. He sat in the back, minding his own business, never speaking up unless called on, always arriving just before the bell rang and then escaping the moment it rang again. He had dark hair and dark eyes and wore jeans with simple white T-shirts and a gold stud in one ear; he didn't belong to any clubs or participate in any extracurricular activities and was the exact opposite of everything Sabrina had been told she liked in a boy. And yet, she couldn't keep away from him.

Because once, in the hall, they'd passed each other going in opposite directions. Somehow, by accident, maybe because it was crowded and there was nowhere else to look, their eyes had met. And in that instant, Sabrina thought she saw behind his lashes the same pounding, nameless thing that regularly tried to claw its way up her chest and into her mind. Only, unlike her, Craig seemed to have the monster under control.

And, unlike her, he didn't seem to take any notice of his demon's mirror image passing him in the hall.

Or maybe it was just Sabrina he took no notice of.

She did everything she could think of to get his attention. She sat next to him in class. She asked him questions about their math homework, which he answered dutifully (and, she was a bit surprised to note, correctly). She wore her nicest outfits and took extra care with her makeup.

But none of Eleanor's tactics were working with this boy.

Finally, Sabrina said to hell with ladylike propriety and, as they were both heading out the door one Friday afternoon, cornered Craig before he pulled his usual disappearing act. She asked, "Why don't you want to talk to me?"

She wondered if he would deny it. She wondered if he would pretend not to know who she was or what she was referring to. But instead, Craig simply looked Sabrina right in the eye and said, "Talk."

Boy, did she ever.

At lunch, which they had outside, alone and away from the din of the cafeteria (not to mention the curious glances

Sabrina was sure to attract for straying so far off her usual social circle), Sabrina did nothing but talk. She told Craig everything. About Lucian and his treatment of her mother. About Eleanor choosing to die rather than upset him. About Chris and about every other skater who mattered more than she did and, finally, about this feeling that Sabrina couldn't shake. Or name.

Craig listened. He proved to be an excellent listener, though Sabrina figured she should have expected that, what with him never talking. He listened without interrupting, and when Sabrina was finished, he said, "You're not crazy."

Sabrina had never asked him if she was crazy. She'd never even wondered if she were going crazy. The possibility never entered, crossed, or settled in her mind.

And yet, the moment Craig deemed that she wasn't, a feeling of relief so profound washed over her that Sabrina could barely speak.

She wasn't crazy.

Oh, thank God, thank God. She wasn't crazy.

"What you are," Craig said, "is angry."

That possibility hadn't made an appearance, either.

Oh, sure, Sabrina knew she was mad at Lucian. But she'd been mad at Lucian for most of her life, on and off, with peaks for crucial Olympic seasons. Mad was a gnawing, hip-hopping, skipping little nibble of a feeling. It wasn't something that tore through you with the power of a buzz saw. Mad was something easily controlled, easily dismissed, easily ignored. What she was feeling couldn't possibly be anger. Sabrina wasn't capable of getting that angry. Why, if she ever did, who knew what would happen?

"Angry," Sabrina repeated.

Craig shrugged and didn't say more.

"What about you?" The question escaped before she could stop herself. Because if what Sabrina was feeling was, indeed, anger, then anger had to be what she'd glimpsed in him as well.

"All the time."

"You're angry . . . all the time?"

"Yeah."

"And that doesn't freak you out?"

"You get used to it."

"How?"

"It's like breathing. How do you get used to that?"

"What are you so angry about?"

"Stuff."

"And it never kind of gets, you know, away from you?"

"Like what?"

"Like, you start thinking these things. Things you know you really shouldn't be thinking."

"Like what?" Craig proved just the right amount of genuinely curious and laid-back blasé for Sabrina to take a risk and tell him.

"I think about killing my dad."

"So?"

"I mean, I think about it all the time. I see a car on the street, and I think, I could run Lucian over with a car. I see a building going up, and I think, I could bury him under a pile of bricks. I've even thought stuff like, my dad has these badly healed skull fractures from when he was a skater, so if he falls a particular way, it could kill him. I've thought, when we're alone together in the house, I could trip him. Make it look like an accident. And that would be that. Nobody would ever know. The perfect crime."

"Okay," Craig said.

"You don't think it's wrong to walk around constantly coming up with ways to kill your father?"

"Depends on the father, I guess."

"Lucian doesn't beat me. He doesn't molest me or torture me. He just kind of ignores me. He's not that bad, objectively speaking."

"So why do you want to kill him?"

"I just do. I mean, I don't even know if I do. I only know that I think about it."

"Are you going to finish your fries?" Craig asked.

"No. Help yourself."

So he did.

And afterwards, Sabrina guessed they became a couple. Everyone who thought they knew her was shocked. Craig wasn't her type, they said. Well, maybe he wasn't. But he didn't judge her. And he didn't bore her. And at the time, that was plenty.

However, that he also didn't seem to like Sabrina as much as she liked him was a problem she resolved to fix.

It wasn't that Craig mistreated her exactly; it was simply that, while she thought about him constantly, even when he wasn't around (in a way, thoughts about Craig had replaced her fantasies about orchestrating Lucian's demise, which Sabrina saw as another positive outcome of their relationship), Sabrina got the feeling that out of sight was out of mind when it came to her place in Craig's world. He always acted happy to see her when she popped up or called, but he never initiated any of the calls himself. She planned their dates, and he went along. She chased, and he allowed himself to be caught. She pulled, and he didn't resist. It wasn't very romantic.

Sabrina attempted to solve the inequality by becoming a better girlfriend. She tried to not talk only about herself, to show an interest in what was important to Craig.

She asked him, "Why is your last name Hiroshi? You don't look Japanese."

"I'm adopted," he said. "My dad's Japanese. My real name is Craig Hunt."

"Oh, I didn't know you were adopted. Were you a baby when it happened?"

"Seven."

"Did you live with your real mom and dad before that?"

"Jenny and Michael Hiroshi *are* my real mom and dad," he snapped. "It was foster homes before that."

Okay. So obviously the way to this man's heart wasn't through a rousing game of *This Is Your Life*.

Sabrina tried a few more avenues, eventually learning that Craig wasn't interested in talking about his past, his present (including school, pop culture, or sports), or his future (including college and/or professional postgraduate plans).

So if Craig wasn't willing to talk about *his* life, what was left for Sabrina to cling to, to keep the conversation going, but hers? Noting that the only subject he'd ever really expressed an interest in was her initial confession about wanting to kill off Lucian, Sabrina found herself turning back to that more and more often, if only to have something to say.

Finally, Craig demanded, "Are you just going to keep talking about this, or are you actually going to do something?"

She didn't want to bore him. Because then Craig might take off. And what would Sabrina have in her life then?

So she said, "Well, yeah, of course I'm going to do something."

After that, her plans became less conceptual and more concrete. No more divine-intervention plane crashes or magic bricks collapsing of their own volition. If Lucian Pryce was going to die for what he did to Eleanor—and what he did to Sabrina, too; but mostly Eleanor; Sabrina needed to believe that she wasn't being petty here—then it would have to be at the hands of his daughter. After some serious consideration, Sabrina decided that an ill-timed fall was the best way to go. Skaters fell all the time. No one would suspect. The only questions that remained were how to set it up, where, and when.

"I'm thinking that maybe the house isn't the best place to do it," Sabrina mused to Craig, jabbering faster and faster in an attempt to keep his attention focused on her. "It would seem too weird. He whips around the rink at lightning speed and then people are supposed to believe he came home and tripped over linoleum?"

"Humph," Craig said.

"So I think the rink would be better. When he's on skates, either on the ice or off. One little shove or trip . . . I even thought, what if all the lights suddenly go out, just for a minute or two. It happens all the time, at the rink. The place uses so much electricity, they're always tripping the circuit breaker. And anything could happen in the dark, don't you think?"

"I guess . . ."

"Will you come to the rink with me, Craig? Help me scope out the landscape, you know? See if you get any ideas?"

"I guess . . ."

It wasn't, in retrospect, the best idea Sabrina ever had. And not merely because, years later, she and her therapist would come to the conclusion that dreaming up new and vicious ways to kill your father was probably not the soundest basis for a relationship. Even, granted, in a setting as melodramatic as high school. They also agreed that Sabrina switching obsessions from getting Lucian's indifferent attention to trying to break through Craig's equivalent apathy did not testify to stalwart mental health, either.

But taking Craig to the rink proved to be a rotten idea because the day Craig did accompany her for the first time was also the first time he laid eyes on Lucian's prize Pairs skater, Rachel Rose. And that, as they say, was that.

Not that Craig broke up with Sabrina on the spot. On the spot, nothing much happened beyond a perfunctory conversation on where might be a good spot for Lucian to die. But afterwards, things definitely changed.

Where before Craig had been willing to go along with Sabrina's suggestions about what they should do, when, and where, now he was visibly resistant. He started breaking dates. Politely, honorably, and never at the last minute, but breaking them all the same. And when he began showing up at the rink when Sabrina wasn't there, that's when she knew for sure.

Sabrina didn't so much accuse him as state the obvious when she told him, "You're in love with Rachel, aren't you?"

"Yes," Craig said.

"Why? I mean, what does she . . . I don't understand. Tell me. What's so great about Rachel?"

"When I'm around her," Craig began, and, in his romantic state, managed to utter the longest sentence Sabrina had ever pried out of him. "When I'm around her, I don't feel angry anymore."

And that, again, was that.

Thirteen

SKATINGANDSTUFF.COM
MESSAGE BOARD

FROM: GoGoGregory1
Posted at 4:11 PM

So now Jeremy Hunt is skating in the tribute also with him and
Gabrielle Cassidy its like let's make a list of the no-names is
Gina just going to get on the ice and wave now looks like there
won't be time for anybody else like the real champions to do a
number!!!

FROM: IceIsNice
Posted at 4:15 PM

I'm sure all the big names will get their numbers. Chris Kelly is
skating a solo and a dance with Gabrielle Cassidy.

FROM: DanceDiva
Posted at 4:16 PM

OMG!!! Chris Kelly is ice dancing now!!! I always thought he should have been a dancer. He's got those long limbs and he moves so smoothly on the ice. This is like a dream come true for me!!! Do you think they'll compete as a team???

FROM: SkatingYoda
Posted at 4:21 PM

<<Do you think they'll compete as a team???>>

That's the plan. It's why Chris moved to Gabrielle's training center last year. They're getting their OD and FD ready now for next season.

FROM: DanceDiva
Posted at 4:22 PM

Any word on what country they'll be representing?

FROM: SkatingYoda
Posted at 4:30 PM

Great Britain. England hasn't had a world quality dance team in years. They're so excited about Chris and Gabrielle they've basically guaranteed them the win at Nationals and a trip to Worlds if they'll represent Great Britain. Gabrielle is in the process of getting her citizenship rushed through now, so they'll be Olympic eligible by the next one.

$\mathcal{B}$ex had two questions, and she went with the most pressing one first.

She asked Craig, "You used to wear an earring?"

He shrugged, equally amused. "I did a lot of . . . interesting . . . things at eighteen."

"Speaking of interesting, you didn't think it was interesting enough to mention to me earlier that Sabrina Pryce is obsessed with killing her father?"

"Was obsessed. Past tense."

"Are you sure?"

"Bex, I don't know about you, but I most certainly am not the person today that I was at eighteen—the earring stud being only Exhibit A. Why would you presume Sabrina hasn't changed since high school?"

"Well, for one thing, because her father is dead."

"She's hardly the only one with a motive."

"Did she say anything about it during your date?"

"It wasn't a date."

"Your friendly dinner, then. And by the way, Craig, Sabrina thinks it was a date."

"No."

"Not even in a nostalgic sort of way? You know, like: Remember when we used to plan to kill my father? Wasn't that totally *Badlands* of us?"

"I don't think she was serious about it, not even then. She was an angry, messed-up kid whose mother had just died and whose dad didn't give a damn about her. It was just a way to blow off some steam and impress the school's resident bad boy."

"You were the resident bad boy, Craig?"

"You don't believe me?"

"It's a little tough to picture. I mean now, you're so . . . so . . ."

"Old?"

"No!"

"Stodgy?"

"Would you cut it out?"

"Would you like me better if I dug up the earring again?"

"I like you fine now."

"Good."

Bex knew he was deliberately teasing her, and she hated herself for going along so gullibly. But she really wished he wouldn't keep reminding her of how much older he was than she. Or how, when he was playing bad boy in high school, she was still playing with her paper dolls.

"Good," he repeated. She expected him to go on. To maybe bring up his proposal or their relationship or anything personal, really. But all Craig did was stand up, stretch, and tell her, "I'm going to check on Jeremy. Good luck with your sleuthing."

She watched him walk away. She wasn't the only one. When Bex looked up, she noticed that Sabrina was standing across the rink, staring daggers at both of them through the glass partition that separated ice from snack bar.

Never one to back down from a challenge, Bex stared back.

After a moment, Sabrina looked away.

Bex felt very pleased about that.

Boy, she *was* young, wasn't she?

Attempting to regain her dignity and act like the professional on assignment she supposedly was, Bex mentally apologized to Sabrina for her lapse, stood, picked up her laptop, and moved out of the snack bar, rounding the corner towards the coaches' lounge.

She was moving relatively quietly, which is probably why the two figures standing intertwined at the very back of the lounge, by the window, didn't hear her come in. With the light streaming through right behind their backs, it took a moment for Bex to identify the shadows as Chris Kelly and Gabrielle Cassidy.

It took her less time, however, to identify what they were doing.

Bex wasn't *that* young, after all.

Chris had his arms around Gabrielle, fingers linked at the base of her spine, palms lightly massaging her back. Her own hands were braced on his chest, and she was looking up at him, their lips barely touching. Yet it was obvious they had been. And very recently.

Well, Bex thought, *this is certainly interesting.* Even if she wasn't sure exactly why. After all, no one had told her for a fact that Chris and Gabrielle weren't romantically involved. She had no reason to be so surprised. Even if Gabrielle was technically Chris's boss, this was the twenty-first century, stuff happened. Still, nothing about their body language or the way they'd interacted earlier, either at Lucian's house or at the rink, suggested an intimate relationship. Plus, there was the whole separate-hotel-rooms thing. If they were a couple, why the separate rooms? Who were they trying to fool and for what purposes?

Of course, to be fair, Bex and Craig were technically romantically involved as well (nebulous current relationship status be damned). And, while here, neither had given any indication of it, either through body language or verbal interaction. And they were staying in separate rooms, too. So who was Bex to judge?

Except that Bex was here for work and Craig was here with his son and the whole thing had come up suddenly. That wasn't the case with Chris and Gabrielle.

Bex had a million questions to ask. And no idea how to frame a single one. So, in a show of newfound maturity that both startled and impressed even her, rather than simply babbling unrehearsed nonsense off the top of her head, she quietly withdrew, still unseen, deciding to table her queries for another time.

Bex was heading away from the coaches' lounge, towards the snack bar, passing Lucian's office, when the lights went out.

At first, her brain didn't register what was happening and her feet automatically kept walking. She didn't freeze in place until she was overwhelmed by the cacophony of screams coming from the ice surface as speeding skaters crashed into each other and the walls in what Bex could only presume was a tangle of freshly bruised, possibly bleeding arms and legs. The audible panic reminded her of the possible dangers inherent to overwhelming blackness combined with sharp objects strapped to people's feet.

Because the blackness was total. The rink itself, unlike the offices in the back, was entirely without windows, so not even a sliver of light peeked in to break the dark. It was worse than being outside at night, where at least streetlamps softened the gloom. This was infinite nothingness. Bex could feel her limbs and she could move them, yet she couldn't see them. It was rather nerve-racking. But her situation, she presumed, wasn't nearly as chilling—no pun intended—as that of those trapped on the ice when the lights went out.

The bulk of the shrieks were coming from their direction, and it took a few moments before Toni's voice was able to rise above the general din to command, "Calm down, now. Calm down, everyone. Just stay where you are. Freeze."

The scrape of a dozen skates indicated her order had been obeyed. Toni's orders were always obeyed.

"Good. Now. Who knows where the circuit breaker is here?"

A silence. And then a woman's voice—Bex tried to place it; Gina?—piped up. "I do."

"Excellent. Would you be so kind as to turn it on for us? Everybody else, freeze where you are and don't move. The last thing we need is a panic or a stampede."

Bex agreed wholeheartedly. Which was why, as per Toni, she remained precisely where she was, despite the curious, darkness-induced sensation of free-falling into some vast, bottomless pit.

The person directly behind Bex, however, must not have gotten the message. He/she barreled straight ahead, presumably towards the exit, knocking Bex down in the process.

She fell forward, another unpleasant sensation. With the lights off, Bex couldn't see the floor, and so thrust her arms out in a random panic, having no idea of actual distance. She locked her elbows and felt both creak in protest as her palms scraped the wet, padded floor sooner than expected. Bex's left wrist buckled from her weight and her hand slipped out from under her. Her chin and her chest hit the ground as, at the same instant, she felt a sharp, flaring pain in her side. It was like falling on something sharp. Or being kicked—deliberately—with a skate blade.

She groaned and instinctively rolled away from the blow, smacking into the opposite wall and laying there, curled up in a fetal position, trying to catch her breath and ward off any other whack that might be in the offering.

No other blow came. But neither did the person who'd knocked Bex down follow the trajectory she'd anticipated.

Bex assumed her assailant, panicked by the darkness, was making a mad dash for the exit despite Toni's warning to stay still. Bex craned her neck towards where she recalled the door being. She figured she'd at least get to see who it was that had so rudely blindsided her as soon as the figure made it to the light of the outside. But instead of heading forward, Bex's attacker seemed to have withdrawn back in the direction of Lucian's office. Either out of guilt for the hit-and-run, or some other reason.

Bex whimpered and awkwardly attempted to roll over onto all fours, hoping there wouldn't be a rerun encounter with the sharp object that had grazed her side. She was feeling her sweater, noting that the kick had actually been hard enough to rip through the knitted material, when the lights came back on.

Everyone cheered just as Bex was able to confirm that the wetness coating her fingers wasn't merely leftover melted sludge, but actual blood drawn from the encounter.

And she noted something else, too.

From her vantage point on the floor, Bex was able to lift her head and notice that the doorknob to Lucian's office now sported a key . . . a key that had most definitely not been there before.

"Bex!"

She was still down on all fours, shaking her head slowly from side to side to make sure the key wasn't a weird hallucination caused by her full body check, when Craig came running up at full speed, slipping both hands under her arms and helping her to rise.

"My God, what happened?"

"I—I got knocked down. . . ." She spoke slowly, as if trying to chew paste.

"Are you all right?"

"I think so. . . ." The paste was now in her throat. She coughed to clear it.

"You're bleeding!"

"Oh." She looked down at her side. "Yeah . . . I'm not sure . . . I hit something maybe when I fell?"

Craig looked around. "What? I don't see anything."

"I don't know. . . ."

"Come with me." Supporting her weight, Craig helped Bex take the few steps necessary to enter Lucian's office.

As he turned the knob, she shrieked, "No!"

"What?" He turned to her, panicked. "What's wrong? Did I hurt you?"

"The knob. The key. Fingerprints."

"What?"

She sighed. Craig's palm was gripping it securely. Any evidence that may have been left had already been wiped away. "Nothing. Sorry. I'm okay."

Craig nudged the door open the rest of his way with his foot, settling Bex into the nearest chair and proceeding to search for a first-aid kit, easily locating it behind Lucian's desk. "Let's get that disinfected. When was the last time you had a tetanus shot?"

"What?"

"Tetanus shot. Who knows what you cut yourself on. It could be dangerous."

"No, really, it's—the skin is barely broken."

"Can't be too cautious."

"Craig?"

"Yeah?" He was kneeling by her side, pouring some hydrogen peroxide onto a sterile piece of gauze. Outside, people were milling about, a few peeking curiously into the office window to see what was happening, then moving on. One of the curiosity seekers, Bex noted, was Sabrina. She paused, taking in the sight of Craig by Bex's side, then pursed her lips and moved on.

"Craig, didn't you tell me that one of Sabrina's plots for knocking off her dad was to turn off the rink lights and trip him?"

"Yeah, so what, she . . ." Craig trailed off and looked up. "You're not serious?"

"Well . . . the lights went off. And somebody tripped me."

"For one thing, this is an ice rink. It uses a ton of juice. The circuit breaker trips all the time; even I know that. For another, Lucian is already dead. Why would Sabrina want to hurt you?"

"Your date the other night . . ."

"I told you it wasn't a date."

"She thought it was."

"Don't be silly."

"Okay, fine. This has nothing to do with you and her. Maybe Sabrina is trying to keep me from figuring out that she was involved in Lucian's death. She could have easily messed with his skates."

"You have no evidence of that. Besides, even if Sabrina did do it, you're no threat to her."

"*Somebody* tripped me, Craig."

"It was dark. Accidents happen in the dark."

"I didn't just fall down." If she hadn't been certain of it before, she was now. "I was kicked, too. By a sharp object. Like a skate."

"Well then, it couldn't have been Sabrina," Craig pointed out reasonably. "Sabrina doesn't skate."

He had her there.

Trying to regain ground she'd lost, Bex indicated the office door. "Key," she said.

"I see it."

"It wasn't here before."

"What?"

"Lucian's office was locked. The morning that he died, I definitely know it was locked, because I tried to get in to call 911. And it was locked this morning, too, because I looked, out of habit, when I came in. There was no key in the door before the blackout, and afterwards, there was."

"Okay. So?"

"I don't know. But it's got to mean something."

"Couldn't the key have been inserted between this morning and the blackout, and you just didn't notice?"

"Maybe. But who would leave a key in the door?"

"Someone who wanted to come back and open it later?"

"Would you stop being so reasonable?"

"Bex," Craig said as he ripped a strip of tape to affix the gauze into place, "you're in shock. You're not thinking straight. Let me take you back to your hotel. You can rest—"

"I can't rest. Lucian's killer is here, right now. I'm certain of it."

"You're getting a little hysterical about this. What did Freud say? Sometimes a cigar is just a cigar? What if, in this particular case, an accident is just an accident?"

"Et tu, Hunt?"

"I just feel like you're grasping at straws. This has been a very stressful week for you. Your first time field producing and all . . . If I had known this was coming, I wouldn't have put the extra pressure on—"

"How did this become all about you?"

"Me?"

"Yes, you. You think that just because you proposed to me I've lost the ability to think straight and now I'm hallucinating imaginary murders just to keep my mind off what my answer is going to be? Boy, you've got some ego!"

"Bex." Craig stood up. He closed the first-aid kit and returned it to its place. He said, "I am now going to slowly back up out of the room. I am going to go to the snack bar and I am going to sit there until it's time to pick up Jeremy and take him home. I will make no sudden moves, noises, or accusations. I will let you get on with your work and I will silently cheer you on—from the other side of the rink. Yay, Bex, go Bex, et cetera."

He was being patronizing and condescending, and by every right she should have been furious. But Bex couldn't help it. He was also being damn cute. She laughed.

"How the heck do you put up with me?"

"I'm a peach of a guy." For a moment, he looked like he was going to bend down and kiss her. She wished that he would, no matter who might see.

Professional, shoshmessional. Sometimes, a girl just needed to be kissed.

But Craig thought better of it. He winked instead,

mouthed, "I love you," and took off as promised, moving slowly out of the room, no sudden moves.

Bex didn't deserve him. That much would have been obvious to a blind man. The question remained: Would she take him in spite of that? And, if she didn't, then what?

$\mathcal{B}ex$ waited until the throbbing in her side had subsided to a guitar pluck rather than the drone of a massive base before venturing out of Lucian's office. She ended up back in the coaches' lounge, where this time, Gabrielle was sitting alone. Massaging her calves and pulling off her skates.

Skates. When Bex saw Gabrielle and Chris together earlier, had they both been on skates? The coaches' lounge was only a few steps away from the office. Either one of them could easily have run from one to the other to slip the key in the knob, knocking over Bex and kicking her in the process.

Of course, in that case, the question was, how would either Gabrielle Cassidy or Christian Kelly have gotten their hands on a spare key to Lucian's office? Why would they have been so desperate to return it? And most important, how could either have snuck into his office the night before Lucian's death to sabotage his skates when both hadn't arrived in town until the following day?

Gabrielle looked up, saw Bex, and, indicating her skates now sprawled on the ground, sighed. "You forget how painful it is. I rarely get out on the ice anymore." She noticed the tear in Bex's sweater and gasped, "What happened to you?"

"During the blackout, I was standing outside Lucian's office. Somebody bumped in to me, knocked me down, and kicked me."

Bex watched Gabrielle closely for a reaction. There didn't seem to be one beyond, "Ouch, are you okay?"

"I'll live." And then she said, "It must have freaked you and Chris out, being in here all alone when the lights went out."

This time, there was a reaction.

Gabrielle blushed. And developed a sudden interest in

loosening a knot in her boot that, as anyone could see, had already come loose a few minutes ago. "Chris and me—how did you know we were—I didn't realize anyone had—"

"I walked in a few minutes before the blackout. Saw you."

"We didn't hear . . ."

"I didn't want to interrupt."

"We . . ."

"It's no big deal."

"But, it is. I mean, it isn't. Chris and I—we're not—"

"I'm not going to tell anybody if you don't want me to."

"There's nothing to tell."

"That's fine."

"I mean, not anymore. We're not . . . anymore. A couple of months ago, it was already over. We just didn't want Lucian to know. . . ."

"Why would Lucian have cared?"

"About us? No, he probably wouldn't have cared about us. I mean, he wouldn't have thought I was good enough for Chris—nobody was good enough for Chris as far as Lucian was concerned, not Gina, not Lauren. But that wasn't our worry. Well, it wasn't mine. If Lucian knew we'd ever been involved, though, he might have figured out that . . . Never mind. He's dead. It doesn't matter now."

Bex took a gamble. She said, "Why was it so important for Chris to return the key to Lucian's office while the lights were out?"

Gabrielle gasped. She tried to hide it, but it was too late. And they both knew it.

"How did you . . ."

"You guys were the closest ones to the office. The lights weren't out that long. Means, opportunity, motive . . ."

"It wasn't my idea," Gabrielle swore. "I didn't know Chris was going to do it. I'd never ask anyone to break the law to help me. He only told me afterwards. You've got to believe me, Bex."

Fourteen
Gabrielle

Initially, Gabrielle assumed that the hardest part of opening her Alternative Ice Skating Training Center would be raising the money, building the facility, and attracting customers, preferably paying ones. And none of those things was easy, by any means. But what really surprised her was that the most, most difficult part of the entire endeavor proved to be hiring coaches, and especially a head coach.

Initially, when she put out feelers, Gabrielle was inundated with responses. Ice rinks were expensive propositions; it wasn't as if new ones, especially elite ones, were established every day, and everyone was interested in at least hearing more about a brand-new facility. They came enthusiastically to meet Gabrielle and get a tour of the grounds. And then they heard what she was trying to do: Create champions without the stress and trauma mandatory in other centers.

And then they laughed.

Vaguely evil laughs.

"It's impossible," everyone said. "It can't work."

"You need pressure to make a diamond."

"No pain, no gain."

"If you can't stand the cold, stay out of the ice rink."

If there was a cliché Gabrielle missed during the process, it wasn't due to lack of trying. In the end, she assembled a smaller staff than she wanted, but at least all of them were publicly committed to coaching with her ideals in mind (Gabrielle didn't want to know what they said about them in private). But she knew she still needed a head coach, one with international name recognition preferably, if she really wanted her program to blink on the skating world's radar.

Chris Kelly was not who she had in mind. But Chris Kelly was who she got.

He just showed up in her office one day, no appointment, no introduction. He obviously expected her to know who he was.

Gabrielle wondered if she was also supposed to genuflect.

"You're looking for a head coach," he said.

"The sky is blue," Gabrielle replied. When he looked at her blankly, she explained, "I assumed we were exchanging declarative statements. Your turn."

Obviously, grammar humor wasn't Chris's cup of tea.

"I am willing to do it," he said.

"And 'it' would be . . . ?"

"Willing to take the head coach job. I know nobody else wants it."

"Do you have any experience in the field, Mr. Kelly?"

"Like what, now?"

"Oh, let's start simple: Have you ever coached before?"

"Certainly."

"Really? I don't think I've ever heard of you—"

"Well, in a matter of speaking. I choreograph all my own routines."

"So you're used to working with difficult students."

"And for the past few years, on tour, I have done the group numbers as well."

"That's not exactly coaching."

"Close enough, I'd say."

"Shouldn't you be on tour right now? It's the middle of the season."

"I had a bit of an injury. Knees aren't what they used to be. I'm to be out for the next few months, they tell me. So I thought . . ."

"This is a full-time position."

"I told you I was out for a few months. Won't be going anywhere."

"And after that?"

"Who thinks that far ahead?"

"People who run training centers and enroll students based on the promise of a coach being there when he says he will."

"Look, life is mercurial, is it not? Nobody knows where they'll end up one day to the next. I said I'm available for the next few months. What say we leave it at that and see where it goes?"

"Why do you want this job so badly, Mr. Kelly?"

"Didn't say I wanted it. Said I was willing to do it. Now are we on or not?"

Gabrielle wanted very much to throw Chris out of her office. She couldn't imagine dealing with his arrogance for even the vaguely promised few months.

On the other hand, she *could* imagine printing up the new season's brochures without a big-name coach to advertise. And what her response would be.

She asked Chris, "When can you start?"

As Gabrielle was giving him a tour of the dual-rink ice surface, the ballet studio, the weight-training room, the dorms, and the cafeteria, she clarified the center's philosophy. "You are familiar with our policies, correct? We are a no-pressure, no-abuse, no—"

"Yes, yes, yes." He nodded absently. "I heard. We'll see about that, won't we?"

To Gabrielle's surprise, from his first day there, Chris followed her policies to the letter. He didn't yell at the kids; he didn't call them names. He didn't tell the girls to lose weight or the boys to do more reps at the gym. He didn't pressure, he didn't belittle, and he didn't threaten. Because, as Gabrielle figured out soon enough, he didn't care.

He would tell a student to execute a move. The student would do it and, more often than not, fail. Chris would simply tell them to do it again. Sometimes, he might suggest a change or an improvement. But if the student failed to execute it as told, Chris would simply shrug and move on to something else. No one was getting browbeaten. But no one was learning much, either.

Whenever Gabrielle tried to speak to him about it, Chris would challenge her. "Rather I yelled at them?"

"Well, no . . ."

"So everything's dandy then, isn't it?"

It was at moments like this that Gabrielle spied the obvious and rather frightening anger Chris seemed to be constantly holding in check. But she couldn't quite discern whom it was directed at or, frankly, what to do about it.

She felt it was her responsibility to get to the bottom of things. Not only because she had a duty to protect her students but also because, well, frankly, she was curious.

Gabrielle hadn't known Chris well when they were training together at Lucian's. He was so much older and already a champion when she got there. She knew about what had happened with Lauren obviously, but he'd recovered from that, moved on with Gina, and then with half the global female population. Whenever she'd caught glimpses of him on television since, he'd seemed perfectly fine and in control. So why all the fury now? And more important, what did it mean for Gabrielle and her facility?

She attempted to broach the subject in a roundabout way, telling Chris, "You know, I'm a little concerned. . . ."

"Have there been complains from the parents?"

"What?" Gabrielle was taken aback. "No, no, nothing like that."

"So everything's fine then."

"I don't think so," she said. "You, Chris. You don't seem . . . fine."

"You said there were no complaints."

And another conversation would unceremoniously come to an end.

Good thing Gabrielle had a doctorate in psychology. Or else she might really be making a mess of things now.

The aforementioned things went on along in the same vein for another three months. And then, one afternoon, Chris was back in Gabrielle's office, again with no warning, appointment, or preamble to announce, "Remember that commitment you wanted? Well, you've got me. Indefinitely, long haul, ad infinitum, that would be all she wrote, good-bye, farewell, and amen."

"Excuse me?"

"It didn't help."

"What didn't?"

"The doctors couldn't think of anything more to do. They already tried operating. Several times. Cleaned the cartridge out of my knee so often, orthopedist said last time in, there was nothing more to remove. I attempted the holistic route myself. Acupuncture, acupressure, hot, cold, poultice on the outside, roots and sprouts on the inside, vitamins, binding. None of it worked. Last-ditch attempt was to give it some rest. Stop jumping for a spell, they said. Maybe that would help. It didn't help. I can barely land a Single Axel now. Can you imagine? I once fancied trying a quad. Didn't need it when I was competing, of course, but it was something I believed within my grasp. May even have done one or two in practice. Not anymore. Not even a single. Leg buckles right under me. It's all over. So I guess I'll be staying here, then."

And then he walked away, leaving Gabrielle speechless.

And inexplicably heartbroken.

"I'm sorry" was all she could think of to say later that evening when she knocked on the door to the apartment Chris received as part of his salary package, on the top floor of the skaters' dormitory.

Yup, certainly was a good thing Gabrielle had that doctorate in psychology. Otherwise, she might have been reduced to a blathering idiot.

Chris opened the door, accepted her condolences in silence, shrugged, and, leaving it open so she could come in, walked away from the door and towards a table. He sat down and continued with what he'd been doing before she arrived. Studying a stack of what appeared to be X-rays and medical reports and photocopied magazine articles, all without a trace of enthusiasm. Or hope.

Gabrielle stood across from him, desperately searching for something to say but coming up frustratingly empty. For a moment, neither of them moved. And then, in the silence, Gabrielle was struck by an epiphany. All of her years of talk therapy—as both a patient and a practitioner—were useless in the face of a person mourning his damaged physicality, a physicality that had long ago become his most expressive means of communicating. All of Chris's achievements had come about without words. They were physical and tangible and visible. And they deserved to be commemorated in the same manner.

So Gabrielle gave up trying to think of something to say. She simply sat down on the chair next to Chris and took his hand in her own, squeezing it lightly.

He didn't respond at first. Just kept sifting through the paperwork with his free palm, looking for something, anything that might fix his dilemma. Gabrielle didn't try to stop him. She didn't try to do anything. She simply continued sitting there, holding on to Chris's hand, until finally, he shoved all the paperwork angrily away. Pages fluttered and slid to the floor. Chris reclined in his chair, head back, eyes closed, and took several deep breaths. He didn't let go of Gabrielle's hand until he, at long last, opened his eyes. He met her gaze and smiled.

"Okay," Chris said calmly. "Plan B."

Neither one of them initially expected that Chris's Plan B—was Gabrielle imagining it, or had she heard an echo of

Lucian in Chris's pronouncement? Lucian, after all, always had a Plan B—should necessarily include Gabrielle in anything but a professional capacity. And yet, it did.

In a way, Gabrielle supposed that she should have predicted it. The training center was located on an isolated stretch of land in Southern California. When it came to social company, her and Chris's choices were limited to the kids, the parents who periodically drove up to make sure everything was going all right, and the coaches. The latter were all nice people, but as far as romance was concerned, Gabrielle was definitely not the male staff's type. Chris had a rather easier time of it with the women coaches. Gabrielle felt positive more than one was interested in him—and not shy about expressing it.

But Chris seemed exclusively focused on her. Which Gabrielle found flattering . . . and disconcerting.

But what she found even more disconcerting was that, as the months went on and she and Chris grew closer and closer, Gabrielle couldn't shake the nagging sensation that their relationship had more than the requisite duo in it. There was her. There was Chris. And then there was . . . Lauren.

It wasn't obvious. It wasn't even omnipresent. It was just . . . cumulative.

Chris wore his wedding ring along with Lauren's on a chain around his neck. Up in his apartment he had a photo of the two of them after his win at the Olympics. He reminisced about places they'd visited and restaurants they'd eaten at and people they'd both known. He remembered her favorite movies, her favorite books, her favorite music, her favorite TV shows. When he looked at his first Olympic Gold medal, framed in a velvet-lined box on the wall, Gabrielle practically could see him remembering Lauren. When he saw a young couple holding hands on the street, he thought of Lauren. When he told stories from a decade ago, even when Lauren wasn't mentioned by name, she was still somehow in them.

Which was all normal, Gabrielle supposed. She shouldn't be disturbed by it. And yet, she *was* disturbed by it.

But not as much as she was by the fact that she and Lauren kind of looked alike.

Well, not exactly alike. This wasn't a cheesy horror movie or even *Vertigo*. Their resemblance was surface, not precise. They were both petite, blonde, with shoulder-length hair they pinned up in a French twist, blue eyes, small features, and a nose that turned up just a bit at the end. It was a description applicable to a lot of young women. (How did that joke go? "I'm one in a million. That means there are three hundred people in the United States alone who are just like me.")

Gabrielle just wasn't too thrilled about it applying to her and the late Lauren.

She tried broaching it with Chris. But when he refused to grasp—or refused to admit to grasping—what she was getting at, Gabrielle finally gave up and flat out told him, "I don't think you've gotten over her yet."

"Of course I haven't," Chris said.

Oh. Well. Gabrielle should be happy to be right, shouldn't she? Why didn't she feel happy?

"I am never going to get over her. She was my wife, I loved her, and she died for absolutely no reason. Why should I get over it? On the other hand, what does that have to do with you and me?"

"I'm not sure I'm thrilled with the idea of being second choice."

"What second choice are you talking about? Lauren is not here. I am not making a choice between her and you. I am with you. There was no choice to be made."

He made it all sound so reasonable.

"How can I be certain that you're in love with me and not just with some woman who happens to look like your late wife?"

"Which you happen to do."

"Yes."

"You are not making this easy for me, Gabrielle. What do you want me to say? Do you want me to say that you do not remind me of Lauren? That would be a lie. I do see some similarities. But so what?"

"I'm sorry. I can't explain it any better."

"Gabrielle. Luv. How do you expect me to deny an accusation that you can not even coherently make?"

"It's a stumper, all right," she agreed.

"I love you," he said, calmly. "I love you for being you. Not Lauren. I love you for the way you start sentences that you don't know how to finish. I love you for the way you are always energetic in the morning while the rest of us are still trying to stumble toward the coffee machine. I love you for how you'll cling to an argument even when you can't recall which side you are on. And I love you for the way you've bucked every traditional assumption and historically tested method to open this training center, against the odds."

"You think my bucking every traditional assumption and historically tested method is stupid."

"Indeed I do. But I admire your gumption in futilely attempting it." He smiled and touched her cheek gently with one hand. "I love you, Gabrielle. I love you for being you. And I think I know a way I can prove that."

Unfortunately, Chris's idea of proof involved larceny.

Gabrielle was rather not expecting that.

A few days after their conversation, with Gabrielle feeling no more reassured about her place in Chris's life vis-à-vis Lauren than she had before embarking on their disastrous chat, Chris asked for a long weekend off. She granted him the minivacation, despite his tight-lipped refusal to reveal where he was going.

When he returned, he handed Gabrielle an unlabeled floppy disc and said, "There. If that doesn't prove that I love you, I don't know what will."

"What is it?"

"A disc."

"Yes, thank you, I can see that. Anything on it?"

"Funny you should ask. . . ."

"It seemed appropriate."

"It just so happens that, on this disc, are records of every lawsuit ever filed against Lucian Pryce and the Olympic Training Center."

"Wow," Gabrielle said. "Average men just send flowers. At most, jewelry. What prompted you, Chris, to go with information I have no use for?"

"I beg to differ."

"I beg you to clarify."

"Don't you see? All these lawsuits, they were filed by parents of students that Lucian injured in some way through his training methods. We are not just speaking of a broken bone here and there. There are records of life-altering back injuries, head injuries, knees—not to mention the psychological issues."

"I don't need a disc to tell me that." Gabrielle held up both her arms, the faint scars on her wrists still visible above each sleeve.

"But the rest of the world does. Think about it, Gabrielle. We release all this information to the press. Someone is bound to do a story on it, especially as we head into the Olympic season. The right reporter can make Lucian and his training methods sound positively Draconian."

"So?"

"Which is where you come in. With Lucian being vilified right and left, that puts you in the perfect position to promote your center as the alternative."

"Oh . . ."

"Now do you see?"

"Where did you get this, Chris?"

"From Lucian's computer."

"What?"

"That's where I was this weekend. Colorado. Stopped by to say hello to Lucian, Gina, and along the way . . ."

"He just gave you this information?"

"Not exactly."

"You stole it?"

"Technically, the information is just where he last left it. I merely made myself a copy."

"How?"

"I pressed 'Save As,' Gabrielle. It's not that difficult."

"How did you get on Lucian's computer?"

"The 'On' button is traditionally a fine place to start."

"He doesn't have a password?"

"No."

"And he just keeps his computer out in the open, where anyone can jump on and read his personal documents?"

"Well, not exactly. The man's not a fool. It is located in his office, at the rink. For goodness' sake, Gabrielle, why are you being so petty? I wanted to demonstrate how much I care for you, how much I believe in you, how much I support what you are trying to do here."

"By breaking, entering, and stealing."

"By George, I think you've got it!"

"This isn't funny."

"Actually, I was shooting for romantic, so I'm glad."

"I can't do this, Chris. It would be wrong."

"Fine. Do with it what you like. It isn't my business. I just wanted you to see how far I was willing to go for you. Maybe then you'd believe that Lauren has nothing to do with you and me being together. She is my past and she will always be my past. She will always be there. But she has nothing to do with my present."

"Chris . . ."

"What, luv?"

"How could you do it?"

"I told you, office, computer, 'On,' 'Save As.' . . ."

"No. How could you do this to Lucian? I mean, I don't think I'm going to release this information, it's too . . . too exploitive; I'm not ready to go that far, yet. But you . . . you were willing to throw him to the wolves."

"For you. I am willing to do this for you."

"Only for me?"

Chris shrugged. He looked away.

"Chris . . . I thought . . . I thought that Lucian was like a father to you. You're crazy about him. At least, you always act like . . ."

"I know what I act like."

"You mean, it isn't true?"

Another shrug. "It doesn't matter."

"It does to me."

"Well, it shouldn't."

"Why were you so eager to betray him?"

"Honestly? It's none of your business."

"It is when you were planning to use me to do it."

"For God's sake, Gabrielle. Here I am, trying to do something nice for you, and you, as usual, are looking for an ulterior motive!"

"Chris, I'm just trying to understand—"

"Enough with the understanding! Enough, do you hear me? Why can't a person just live around you? Why does everything have to be analyzed and scrutinized until even the pleasant things have been twisted into something devious and, frankly, mad?"

"Because I'm a shrink, okay? It's how I was trained to think."

"Well, it's insane, to borrow a spot of the terminology. How is a person supposed to function when every action is allegedly fraught with hidden motives?"

"The idea, actually, is that you're supposed to function better once you know what the hidden motives are."

"Bullocks."

"Okay."

"Take the disc, Gabrielle. Use it, don't use it, I can't quite summon up the energy to care anymore. But just let me and my motivation be. I am happy the way I am, living a life as unexamined as Socrates preached against. What a shame you'll never be able to claim feeling similarly."

"What? Unexamined?"

"Happy."

Fifteen

FROM: GoGoGregory1
Posted at 6:46 AM

Getting the laptop and camera phone ready for our big trip
West any requests I'll try to get all the pictures and autographs
I can let me know who you want!!!

FROM: DanceDiva
Posted at 7:10 AM

Will you please, please, pretty please, get a picture of Chris
and Gabrielle skating together? I want to start a website for
them and would love some pix to get it going. Action shots and
off-ice too if you can. Maybe they'll even let me do their official
site.

FROM: SkatingFreak
Posted at 7:14 AM

Good luck getting Kelly to pose off the ice. He's a real jerk. A friend of mine asked him for an autograph after a show a couple of years ago and he walked right by her and onto the bus without even looking in her direction.

FROM: SkateGr8
Posted at 7:16 AM

Chris Kelly is super-nice. I've gotten his autograph three times at three different shows and he's always nothing but polite and respectful to his fans.

FROM: MaryQuiteContrary
Posted at 7:19 AM

<<he's always nothing but polite and respectful to his fans.>>

Fans, maybe, but definitely not his students. He's teaching at Gabrielle Cassidy's fruity-crunchy academy, though "teaching" is a nice way to put what he's doing. I hear he yells at the kids, hogs the best ice time from the other coaches, and then cancels lessons at the drop of a hat if he's got something better to do. And by better, I mean more glory in it for Chris. No wonder that place stinks. I'd never send my kid there.

FROM: GoGoGregory1
Posted at 7:23 AM

I met Chris a bunch of times right before the Olympics when he and Gina were dating and he was a very gracious young man then I think after he and Gina broke up it just maybe made him more cynical and that's why some people had bad experiences with him afterwards.

FROM: LuvsLian
Posted at 8:10 AM

Does anyone know why Chris and Gina broke up? They seemed so in love.

FROM: SkatingYoda
Posted at 8:14 AM

Chris Kelly was a typical man who couldn't stand his girlfriend getting more attention and being more successful than him. It was fine when he was the reigning Oly champion and she was just an up-and-comer. But when Gina won the Gold and got more famous than him because she was American and a lady and Ladies' skating is much more popular, Chris threw a fit and broke up with her. It happens all the time. Look at all the movie stars who get divorced or break up right after they win Oscars. Halle Berry, Hilary Swank, Reese Witherspoon. Chris Kelly is just another insecure chauvinist.

FROM: SuperCooperFan
Posted at 8:19 AM

<<But when Gina won the Gold and got more famous than him because she was American and a lady and Ladies' skating is much more popular>>

I like Men's skating much more than Ladies'.

FROM: TwirlyGirl
Posted at 8:22 AM

I think most real skating fans prefer the men, but the majority of casual viewers like the Ladies' event, it always gets the big ratings and its who the networks hype. Plus, Chris was English, which means he'd never be as popular here as Gina. That's tough for a lot of guys to take, and he seems like the type who always has to be the center of attention and make it all about him, jmho, of course.

"It wasn't my idea, Bex," Gabrielle repeated. "I didn't know Chris was going to do it. He only told me after he'd already broken into Lucian's office and stolen the file. I never would have let him go ahead if I'd known in advance."

"How did he get the spare key?"

"I don't know. He never told me that, either."

"But you did know he was going to turn off the lights and secretly return it today?"

"Yes."

"In fact, you must have helped him. Chris couldn't have been in two places at once. The fuse box is way on the other side of the rink from the coaches' lounge."

"Yes," Gabrielle admitted. "I turned off the lights. He returned the key."

"Why? I mean, why did he bother? With Lucian dead, nobody would care about that copied file now."

"Frankly, Bex, it was you."

"Me?"

"With all your accusations about Lucian's death not being an accident, Chris didn't want to get caught with anything suspicious."

"So Chris doesn't think Lucian's death was an accident, either?"

"He thinks you think it wasn't, Bex. And we all know how tenacious you can be with these things. Honestly, your reputation really does precede you."

That was a nice thing to hear. If Bex couldn't be loved, respected, and revered, what the heck, feared was always good.

"What do you think?" she asked.

"About Lucian possibly being murdered?"

"Yeah."

"Well, he wasn't one of my favorite people."

"And you did stand to gain from his death."

"How do you figure?"

"He was the competition. With Lucian Pryce gone—"

"You think his students would have turned to me?" Gabrielle laughed. "Oh, no. No, I don't think so. Sure, this training center might have lost a kid or two. Kids who specifically came out here to study with Lucian and would accept no substitutions. But honestly, nothing much would have changed. All of his Colorado students would have found a new coach. A new coach who was, in the end, an awful lot like their old one. Believe me, if you subscribe to the Lucian Pryce school of skating, you would not have ended up at my rink."

"But don't most people subscribe to Lucian's methods? Or at least believe they're necessary to make champions?"

"That would unfortunately be correct."

"So how do you expect to make a go of your place?"

"I don't know. Honestly, Bex, I don't. Now, I didn't tell my investors that. For them, I had a nifty proposal with all sorts of charts and graphs and convincing arguments. But off the record, the bulk of my game plan is to just keep hoping that someday enough people will wake up and realize that crippling a child—physically, emotionally, or both—simply isn't worth the hunk of gold it gets you."

"Gabrielle?"

"Yes?"

To Gabrielle, Bex's next question would probably sound as though it came out of left field. But the fact was, Bex had been trying to think of a way to slip it in ever since Gabrielle first brought up the suggestion up. "Did you . . . did you really break up with Chris because you thought he was still hung up on his dead wife?"

Gabrielle hesitated for a moment, wondering when they'd switched topics. Then, deciding that this one was still preferable to the original, she answered honestly, "Well . . . it didn't start out that way. And *I* technically wasn't the one who broke up with *him*. But ultimately, yes, I guess that's what happened."

"Though when I walked in here before the blackout," Bex pointed out, "you and Chris didn't exactly look . . . broken up."

"Oh. That. Old habits die hard. People slip. The problem with the human brain is that it's programmed to forget the bad stuff much quicker than the good stuff. You blank on the reasons why you broke up a lot sooner than you do on the ones that brought you together in the first place."

"You know, Gina talked about feeling as if Lucian was constantly comparing her to Eleanor, too."

"That would be a neat trick. Gina is nothing like Eleanor. Sounds like Lucian had quite a challenge ahead of him."

"Gina thinks their marriage never really had a chance because of it."

"Lot of that going around, I guess."

"Tell me about it." Bex sighed.

Sabrina was in Lucian's office, listlessly going through a stack of papers on his desk, when Bex finally got up the courage to go in and apologize. She wasn't sure how precisely one went about apologizing for suspecting a person of doing something she didn't do—specifically, knocking Bex over in the dark, then kicking her for good measure—when the person in question didn't know she'd ever been under suspicion. But Bex's conscience was driving her to at least to say something vaguely conciliatory before moving on.

"Hi," Bex said.

"Oh. Hello." Sabrina's greeting could have been hostile. Or it could have been indifferent. Hard to tell with her.

"Going through your dad's stuff?"

"Someone has to, I guess. It's not very interesting. Bills and competition notices and flyers from boots and blade manufacturers."

"What about his computer?"

"What about it?"

"Might be confidential stuff there. Things he didn't want other people to see."

"You mean like figure skating trade secrets? It's not exactly Homeland Security around here. Besides, what difference does it make? He's dead. Even if something's going to embarrass him, he's still dead. Which reminds me." Sabrina looked up, no longer indifferent. "Any idea who did it yet?"

Reluctant to admit that Sabrina was still at the top of the list, Bex waved her arm vaguely and, as a stalling tactic, mused, "Well, without a concrete motive, I have to start by looking at means and opportunity. If we assume the means is someone sabotaging Lucian's skates the night before our shoot—or maybe very early in the morning, that's a possibility, too—then opportunity is narrowed down to the people who were already in town prior to Lucian's death. That leaves people like Chris and Gabrielle off the hook, since they didn't get in until after Lucian already—"

"No," Sabrina said. "No, that's not right."

"What do you mean?"

"I don't know when Gabrielle got here, but Chris was in town the night before. I know this. I saw him."

Bex felt like a cartoon character screeching to a halt. Cautiously, she said, "Gabrielle told me she and Chris took the same plane up yesterday morning. They were sitting right there in your living room when Toni and I came in."

Sabrina shrugged. "Yeah, they arrived together from the hotel that morning. But Chris was already in town the night before. Don't know when Gabrielle got there."

"He was at your house two nights ago?"

"Yes, Bex, geez, pay attention. He had dinner with Dad and Gina. I didn't stay. As soon as they started in on old times, that was enough for me. Besides," Sabrina added, "I had a date."

Yeah. Right. That. As if Bex could have forgotten. But, believe it or not, at that moment, she honestly cared more about what Sabrina was revealing than about what she and Craig might be hiding. Which Bex figured probably wasn't a good indicator for her relationship. But that could wait.

"So you have no idea what they talked about."

"I can guess. . . . Let's see, first Chris gushed to Lucian how wonderful he was, then Lucian agreed. Then Lucian told Chris how wonderful he was. Chris agreed. Then they discussed how terrific all three of them were to have won two Olympic Gold medals in the same year. Rinse. Repeat. Stick your finger down your throat."

"You said earlier you thought there was a weird vibe going on between your dad and Gina the morning he died. Did that start the night before? With Chris?"

Sabrina gave it some thought, then shook her head.

"Maybe. Who knows. Like I said, when those three get together, all I want to do is get the heck out of there."

Logically, the next person Bex should have spoken to was Chris. But when she left Lucian's office, he was back on the ice, trying to coax a cohesive performance out of the Junior corps de ballet with Toni at his side.

Gina, on the other hand, was waiting rinkside. She'd changed out of her skates and was now sitting on a bench, wrapped in a heavy coat over her workout clothes, blue hands clutching a cup of steaming, dirt-colored hot chocolate. She was periodically blowing on it, sipping, wincing, blowing again, then wincing again.

Bex skipped the preliminaries. She plopped down right next to the Olympic champion and, confident that blaring music combined with the scrape of two dozen blades would keep eavesdroppers at bay, flatly stated, "You lied to me."

The instant swell of panic in Gina's eyes told Bex her blunt approach had been the best one.

"What—what do you mean?" Gina stammered, the hot chocolate sloshing in her cup. A drop spilled out and left a red mark on her hand. Gina didn't appear to notice.

"You told me Chris arrived with Gabrielle after Lucian was already dead."

"No, I didn't." Gina wasn't so much contradictory as she was confused. "You never asked me when—"

"Okay, let's put it this way. You didn't tell me Chris was in town the night before Lucian's . . . accident."

"You never asked me."

"You didn't think it was relevant?"

"To what?"

"To who had means and opportunity to kill Lucian!"

"You think Chris killed Lucian?"

"I think I'd like to know why everyone was keeping it a secret that he could have."

Gina didn't say anything. She didn't say anything for so long that Bex felt the need to prompt her.

"Isn't this the part where you're supposed to tell me that

Chris couldn't have killed Lucian? That he was crazy about him? Loved him like a father and all that?"

Gina slowly shook her head from side to side. "Well, not exactly . . ."

Sixteen
Gina

Of all the many edicts that Lucian issued to her during their marriage, the one Gina found most difficult to follow was his insistence that she and Chris remain friends. Not friendly. Friendly, Gina could have dealt with. Friendly was waving to Chris when they crossed paths at various international or professional competitions. Friendly was saying nice things about him when reporters wanted to talk incessantly about their double win at the Olympics. Friendly was making small talk when Chris called before swiftly handing the phone over to Lucian.

But friends . . . friends was a skate of a totally different color. Friends meant that Lucian expected her to stay and chat with them when Chris came to visit. Friends meant that she was supposed to have no objections to Chris spending the night at their house whenever he was in town. Friends meant that Gina was to act as if what had happened between them meant absolutely nothing and she was completely over it and everything was just hunky-dory. Well, it didn't and she wasn't. But Lucian said that it was. And, as always, it proved easier to just go along with him.

Chris, for his part, was certainly happy to jump on the friends bandwagon. He behaved as if the fiction Lucian insisted on for all three of them was absolute fact, treating Gina like a combination of little sister and old buddy. He always acted genuinely happy to see her, sweeping her into a hug, kissing her on the cheek, and launching into a banality of surface conversation. At least for the first couple of years. Eventually, Chris seemed to fall under the delusion that their sham of a friendship was genuine, and started segueing into more and more personal topics. It was on such occasions when Gina first began to long for the days of banality.

Now, instead of telling her about where he'd last traveled, Chris was telling her about the problems with his knee, the surgeries and treatments he'd undertaken, and his fears that he'd never be able to skate again.

Since, to be honest, the only response Gina could summon up upon hearing his concerns was "Good," she mostly kept her mouth shut and nodded a lot as he went on and on.

After the Saga of the Knee, they moved on to Tales from the Coaching World, with Chris lamenting about having to switch sides of the barrier and now being reduced to training spoiled brats who didn't realize how lucky they were to still possess bodies that worked and could fly through the air—crappily, sloppily, lazily; but Chris could fix that if they'd only listen to him. And if only Gabrielle Cassidy would let him coach the right way, instead of through a muzzle of touchy-feely love and self-esteem.

Gradually, however, Gina began to notice something very odd. Slowly, almost imperceptibly, Chris's stories about the training center and Gabrielle—especially the ones about Gabrielle—began to switch from what hell it was to work under such conditions to wasn't it awesome though for Gabrielle to be trying so damn hard to create something new and unconventional? He stopped calling her a kook and a fool and started using words like "pioneer" and "trailblazer."

That was when Gina realized that Chris had fallen hard for the good doctor.

And that, because of Lucian's orders, she was doomed to hear all about it.

At first, she went along her usual path, smiling, nodding, and in her mind, playing random selections of her favorite music like an in-cranial iPod. But then Chris would ruin the mood by asking her a direct question, forcing Gina to actually listen and, even worse, summon up a coherent response or reasonable facsimile thereof.

It was easy when the questions were limited to, "Do you really think I can do this? Not just coach, but coach the way Gabrielle wants me to?"

"Sure, Chris, why not?"

"She is so depending on me. I would hate to let her down."

"You won't."

"But what if I simply cannot do it? What if I can only teach in the same way that I was taught?"

"You'll be fine, Chris."

"Gabrielle has poured every cent she has into the training center. She's staked her professional reputation on it, not to mention her personal well-being. I want to help her in any way I can. That's why I'm turning to you, Gina."

"What?" She'd gone on automatic pilot after the second or ninth, "Yahoo, you can do it, go, Chris, go," and so had missed what exactly he was asking of her. "What do you need me to do?"

"I need you to make me a copy of Lucian's key to his office."

"What? Why? You can go into his office any time you want. Just ask Lucian."

"I'm afraid I can't do that. Not this time."

"Why not? What do you need from there?"

"It's not important."

"So I'm just supposed to hand over this key to you, and you're not even going to tell me why?"

"It's better if you don't know, Gina."

"Oh, I seriously doubt that. Spill it, Christian."

He looked around, once over each shoulder, as if expecting Lucian to materialize in his living room where Chris and Gina were sitting on the couch. "I want to copy one of Lucian's computer files. The one detailing all the lawsuits with skaters and their parents that he's settled over the years."

"Why?"

"To help Gabrielle. So she has some ammunition to fight with when people want to know why her training method is superior to Lucian's and his ilk."

"Those lawsuits are confidential. Lucian settled them specifically so that the cases wouldn't go public."

"I know."

"You're ready to ruin him? For some . . . girl?" Gina wasn't quite up to uttering Gabrielle's name out loud yet. She hoped her pronunciation of the word "girl," however, made it perfectly clear how she felt about Dr. Cassidy in particular, and Chris's plan in general.

"Not for any girl, but yes."

She should have been horrified. But horror had to wait until the jealousy was completely washed out of Gina's system. She suspected it would be a long wait.

"You're willing to trash Lucian in public? Lucian, your mentor, your idol, your best friend in the world. All so that your girlfriend can feel better about herself?"

"Again, Gina, you are oversimplifying, but . . . yes. Will you help me?"

"Why should I?"

"Because," Chris said, "I am very humbly asking you to."

"God!" Gina leapt up off the couch. "You're some piece of work, aren't you? You treat me like crap, dump me without so much as a 'Dear Gina' letter, then force me to listen to your going on and on about the pioneering genius of Gabrielle Cassidy, and now I'm supposed to help you help her by bringing down my husband?"

"I thought we were friends."

"Actually, we're not. I don't know what we are, but friends isn't it. And, I repeat, Lucian is my husband. Why should I side with you over him?"

"Because." He sighed. "You know that you want to."

She hated him.

If Gina thought she had hated him before, that was nothing compared to the odium flowing through her now. She hated him for being so smug. She hated him for making assumptions about what she would or would not do. She hated him for knowing her so well and for always being able to play her. Most of all, she hated him for being right.

"This isn't about you," Gina told Chris when she handed over the copied key to him a few days later. "I have my reasons for doing this, and it isn't about you."

"I understand completely."

"Well, I don't understand. Fine, Gabrielle is the greatest thing since sliced bread and you want to make her little science project a success. But how could you even think about destroying Lucian in order to achieve that?"

"I have my own reasons, too," Chris said.

And that was the end of that particular discussion.

For days, then for weeks afterwards, Gina waited for something momentous to happen. She waited for Gabrielle to expose Lucian; she waited for Chris to go public with his beloved coach's failings. But a month passed, and nothing did.

Chris came to visit them again and everything seemed the same as before. He and Lucian traded war stories and hearty slaps on the back and all the usual, nauseating, good cheer they always exchanged.

One thing was different, though.

This time, when Chris walked through the door and offered Gina his usual hello hug and kiss, his hands landed not on her waist, but on her butt. His lips not on her cheek but on her mouth. It all happened so fast, Gina couldn't even be sure it hadn't been an accident. Until it happened again.

And again.

He sat closer to her than was necessary on the couch and at the dinner table. He followed her with his eyes wherever she went. Most important, for the first time since . . . well . . . ever, Chris let Gina get a word in edgewise. He listened to her now. He asked her questions about her life, and then he actually listened to her answers. He showered her with compliments and attention, and he listened to her.

She didn't know what to think.

No, that wasn't true; she did.

Gina channeled her best inner Dustin Hoffman to ask, "Mr. Kelly, are you trying to seduce me?"

He grinned.

"Why?"

"Because you're worth it."

"Uh-huh." His wickedly tossed-off words made her heart and its surrounding organs do a Triple Toe Loop from a standing position, but she fought to keep it from showing. "And what happened to the sainted Gabrielle?"

"It's over."

"Really?" She hoped she sounded more disbelieving than hopeful.

"Yes."

"Why?"

"Stupid reasons; you know how it is in relationships."

"Stupid reasons like what?"

Chris sighed and looked away before answering. "Gabrielle . . . thought . . . she thought I still had some unresolved issues. From my past."

"Like what?" Gina pressed. She had to admit, being on the side of making Chris uncomfortable rather than having him do the same to her was most pleasant. She hoped to keep it going for as long as possible.

"Gabrielle thinks that we shouldn't be together as long as, in her opinion, I am still fixated on another woman."

Gina's breath caught in her throat. Was Chris saying what she thought he was saying?

"Another woman? From your past?"

"Yes." Chris still wouldn't look at her. But then again, he didn't have to. It was obvious what he was trying to tell her. "Gabrielle is under the impression that everything I do is a result of these unresolved feelings of mine. Well, I do guess that is what happens when one chooses to become involved with a psychologist."

Gina took back every nasty thing she'd ever secretly thought about Gabrielle Cassidy. Obviously, the woman was a psychological genius. It made perfect sense when you looked at it her way. Chris's out-of-character desire to publicly humiliate Lucian could come from only one source: his jealousy over Lucian's having married Gina—a woman he was still in love with! No wonder Gabrielle refused to accept Chris's pilfered offering as a sign of his love for her. And no wonder she wanted nothing more to do with him. Gabrielle realized that Chris was still in love with Gina!

It was almost too much to take in at once. Gina, who prided herself on never getting dizzy, no matter how many revolutions in a jump or how blurred the spin, now felt as if she could barely stay upright. Finally, after all these years, after everything he'd put her through, Chris was telling Gina he loved her.

- Well, not exactly.

He wouldn't be Chris if he could express such a sentiment easily. But what else could his tale about Gabrielle's suspicions possibly mean? Chris Kelly loved her!

Now, the question remained: What were they going to do about it?

Initially, the answer was easy.

That they would sleep together was a no-brainer—Chris had already confirmed he was trying to seduce her; to acquiesce under the circumstances was only polite. That the one-night (okay, afternoon) stand would turn into an affair was even more predictable.

However, after five months of sneaking behind Lucian's back (a thrill almost equal, for Gina, of hearing Chris say he loved her; it was, as far as she could recall, the only time she'd ever felt like she knew something her husband didn't), Gina felt it was time to move up to the next level.

"We have to tell Lucian about us, Chris."

"All right, then."

That was disturbingly easy. She had expected Chris to put up more of a protest. Something along the lines of why rush, why ruin a good thing, why rock the boat. His prompt agreement threw Gina off somewhat. She'd had a much longer discussion planned.

"Oh . . . okay. Good. Great. So it's settled then."

"Absolutely."

"The question is, when should we do it?"

"No time like the present, I say."

"The present? Chris, Lucian's tribute is next week."

"Exactly. This way, neither of us shall have to feel hypocritical, getting up there and saying all sorts of flowery things about him. The fact is, he was an excellent coach. We can say so with all impunity. But, as a man . . . well, he left much to be desired, didn't he? Why should you have to lie about it? I say we get everything out into the open, then head into the tribute with a free heart."

"You want to tell him *before* the tribute?"

"What say tonight? We are all having dinner together, are we not?"

"Well, yes, but Sabrina . . ."

"Sabrina already said she won't be attending. Met some bloke she used to know, they're going out. It will only be the three of us. Just like old times."

"Old times . . ." Gina repeated.

She could hardly wait.

She could hardly breathe.

She felt certain Lucian knew something was up the minute he walked through the door. How could he not? Gina was shaking like a leaf, babbling even more than usual. Chris, for his part, appeared absolutely calm. He acted as if nothing at all were out of the ordinary as he greeted Lucian and walked with him to the dining room table, chatting all the while about some gymnastics move he'd seen on television that he thought might be adaptable, with a few modifications, for the ice, and did Lucian think it would keep within the new rules?

They must have gone back and forth on the subject for hours, though the clock in the kitchen stubbornly insisted only twelve minutes had passed before Gina couldn't take it anymore and blurted out, "Lucian, Chris and I want to tell you something."

"Not now, Gina. Can't you see we're in the middle of—"

"Yes, now. We need to talk to you right now. Listen to us."

Lucian sighed. It was the same sigh he heaved Sabrina's way when she was being particularly obstinate about something. It made Gina feel like a ten-year-old.

"Fine," Lucian said. "What is it?"

"I—" She turned her head, looking for reinforcements. "Chris?"

She knew he'd find a way to break it to Lucian gently. Maybe he'd bring up the history he and Gina shared, the reality that neither had ever truly gotten over the other, no matter how much time had passed. Maybe he'd invoke how much they had in common, being closer in age and having gone through the intense Olympic experience together (not that Lucian hadn't been a part of it as well, but it wasn't the same, standing by the barrier versus being out on the ice all by yourself, knowing that, in the end, no one could help you, that it was under your control and your control only, and that there would be plenty of people to thank if you won, but only yourself to blame if you lost).

Chris wiped his lips with a cloth napkin, returned it to his lap, leaned back in his chair, and politely informed Lucian, "Gina would like you to know that I've been screwing your wife for the past five months."

Gina gasped.

Lucian, however, merely continued with the forkful of lasagna he'd been raising to his lips before Chris even started speaking. "You don't say."

If Chris's blasé attitude had earlier thrown Gina for a loop, then Lucian's equally nonplussed reaction appeared to have the same effect on Chris.

"Er . . . yes," he began. Then didn't quite know what to say next.

Lucian looked from Chris to Gina and inquired, "And what would you like me to do about this, then?"

"Do?" Gina asked.

"Yes. Do. I assume you had a reason for sharing this revelation with me. What might it have been?"

"We—" Gina said.

"I—" Chris said.

"Go on then. Out with it."

"I'm leaving you," Gina blurted. "For Chris."

"Yes." Chris hopped gratefully on her lead, seizing Gina's hand across the table. He was squeezing too hard, but Gina figured now wasn't the time to wince. "She's leaving you, Lucian. We're running off together. What do you think of that?"

"Running far, are you?"

"Why are you acting like this?" Gina demanded, leaping up from the table, nearly knocking over Chris, who was still clutching her fingers for dear life.

"How would you prefer me to act?"

"Don't you care? Aren't you upset? Even just a little? Chris is stealing me away from you!"

"So he says. . . ."

"What do you mean?"

"Christian, my dear boy." Lucian turned to face him. "Do you honestly expect me to believe this is what you want? This hysterical child following you around for the rest of your life?"

"Chris loves me!"

"Does he now?" Lucian shrugged. "Then I wish you both the very best."

"Now, see here." Chris loosened his grip off Gina's hand and focused his attention exclusively on Lucian. "Are you saying you're giving us, what, your blessing?"

"Who am I to stand in the path of true love? You want her, Christian, you take her."

"Bloody hell, I don't want her!"

The words were out of Chris's mouth before his brain registered the confession. He attempted to backtrack; Gina could see his lips desperately moving in an attempt at correction, but no adequate sentiments proved forthcoming.

"What I meant was—"

"I know what you meant," she said quietly.

"No, Gina, listen to me. What I meant was, I didn't want to hurt Lucian, so—"

"Actually, I think that's exactly what you wanted to do. You tried it first by giving Gabrielle that disc."

"Disc?" Now they had Lucian's attention. "What disc?"

"But she wouldn't do your dirty work for you. She saw right through you. You are always telling me how smart she is, aren't you?"

"What are you talking about?" Chris snapped. "Why does everyone always think they know my own mind better than I do?"

"What disc?" Lucian repeated, the amusement and gaiety that sprinkled his earlier conversation completely gone. He was all business now. Because now the topic at hand was actually important.

"Gabrielle had you figured out. First, you wanted to use her to hurt Lucian. When that didn't work, you turned to me. Only I'm not as smart as she is. I fell for it. I really thought you loved me. I really thought you wanted me for me."

"Christian," Lucian demanded, "what is she talking about?"

"Nothing. She has no idea. She's just angry."

"What is this disc she keeps talking about?"

Chris looked Lucian right in the eye. He said, "I haven't the slightest idea."

"Were you really trying to hurt me, son, with this little pantomime?"

"No." Chris shook his head. "It just . . . happened. You know how it is."

Gina could have sworn she'd heard those words before. Except that now they sounded hollow and banal and so false she could hardly believe when Lucian offered Chris an avuncular chuckle and a hearty, "Oh, yes, certainly. I know exactly how it is, my boy."

Gina wanted to stomp her foot. She wanted to shake her arms and scream and yell, "Hey, what about me?"

But that would have been pointless. Because she knew now that this had never, ever been about her.

Seventeen

FROM: SkatingFreak
Posted at 9:02 AM

So how come Chris gets all the blame on here for the Chris/Gina breakup? Anybody ever consider the possibility that she was a real bitch? I always figured she was boning Lucian on the side the whole time she and Chris were supposedly "in love." Isn't that what happened with Lucian and Eleanor? He was her coach, he married her and made her a star? Gina probably figured it was the only way to win, following in ol' Ellie's footsteps.

FROM: SkateGr8
Posted at 9:15 AM

I heard Lucian and Toni Wright were engaged and she was on tour and one day she opens the paper and reads that Lucian up and married Eleanor without even telling her.

FROM: IceIsNice
Posted at 9:15 AM

So it wasn't bad enough that Gina went from Chris to Lucian,
she was doing them both AT THE SAME TIME??? AT THE
OLYMPICS!!! GROSS X 2!!!

"So that was it?" Bex clarified. "You told Lucian you were
leaving him for Chris, Lucian said go ahead, and then Chris
said, nah, thanks anyway?"

She hated being so blunt, but Bex had to be sure she understood this dysfunctional dynamic correctly.

"Pretty much," Gina agreed. "And then, to top it all off,
they went on as if the whole confrontation never even happened. It was like hitting a reset button."

"That's . . . that's . . ." Bex searched for the right word.
"Sick."

"Isn't it? I'm glad you agree. Because, frankly, I've been
wondering if I was the crazy one. I mean, I know I had an
irregular upbringing, delayed adolescence and all that. I'm
certainly not as experienced in the whole relationship field as
some women my age, but all in all, I have to say, yes, this
whole thing struck me as rather sick."

"Chris didn't end up spending the night at your house, did
he? He was supposed to, but he left?"

"Yes. Under the circumstances, maybe even Chris thought
that would be pushing things."

"So he flew back to California, then took the next plane
back up with Gabrielle? Didn't you find that a little weird?"

"Compared to everything else that happened that night?
No."

"Do you think he was setting up an alibi?"

"For what?"

"For killing Lucian. It wouldn't have held up under any
sort of investigation, but on a surface level, well, when
Gabrielle told me they'd flown up together that morning, it
never crossed my mind that Chris could have been at the rink

earlier to sabotage Lucian's skates. It left him covered in case anyone asked questions."

"I have a question," Gina said.

"What?"

"Why would Chris kill Lucian? It certainly wasn't out of any love for me. It's not like Lucian put up a fight, challenged him to a duel, and Chris had to defend my honor."

"You make a good point."

"Yeah. I thought I did."

"I'll get back to you."

She cornered Gabrielle by the vending machine. Bex asked, "You didn't find it odd that Chris flew to Colorado in the afternoon, flew back home in the evening, then flew out with you once again the following day?"

Gabrielle dropped her quarters in the vending machine's slot but was too surprised to punch the button with her order. "He did what?"

"You didn't know?"

The machine beeped insistently. Gabrielle stared at it for a moment, then, suddenly unable to remember what she'd wanted, hit the key to return her coins. "All I know is that Chris and I always intended to fly out together in the morning. We made our reservations maybe a month in advance."

"So you had no idea that Chris actually flew out earlier?"

"No. I mean, Chris said he had some stuff to do that day, so I gave him the time off, but I figured he had last-minute errands to run before the trip. Why would Chris fly back and forth like that?"

Bex said, "I'll get back to you."

She told Craig, "So what I have is means and opportunity. Motive, on the other hand . . ."

They'd left the claustrophobia of the ice rink (yes, such things were technically allowed, Bex had learned her second year on the job) for the privacy—and warm weather—of a bench underneath a tree in the park across the street from Lucian's rink. Jeremy had asked if he could stay and have lunch with the other kids from the show, leaving Bex and Craig on their own for at least an hour.

Previously, the thought of an uninterrupted moment where all sorts of uncomfortable personal topics were likely to pop up when least expected might have led Bex to a glut of creative excuses and/or simply running screaming in the other direction. But with her mind on Chris and his rather unique frequent-flyer plan, she was more interested in having Craig as a sounding board.

"You're certain Chris is your killer?"

"He was in town, he had a key to Lucian's office, plus the special stone to mess up his blades."

"Which are only relevant facts if Lucian was indeed killed by someone deliberately ruining his skates."

"I saw them, Craig. No way would a pro like Lucian leave his equipment in that kind of condition. If they'd been damaged accidentally, he certainly wouldn't have gone out on them. Not in front of a television crew!"

"What about your other suspects? Don't any of them have the lucky trifecta?"

"The only other person who had means and opportunity was Toni. But she has no motive that I can see. Gina has motive and means, but I don't know about opportunity— wouldn't Lucian have noticed if she snuck out of the house early that morning or late that night? As for Sabrina, she had motive, she had opportunity, but I wonder about means. I don't see her walking around with a handy stone in her pocket."

"Which brings us back to Chris."

Bex summarized her earlier conversation with Gina. To her surprise, the more she talked, the more concerned Craig seemed to grow. By the time she got to the end of her story, with Chris and Lucian both basically informing Gina that neither one particularly wanted her, then sharing a manly laugh about how wacky life could be, Craig appeared downright alarmed.

"Bex . . ." he began cautiously.

"What?"

"I—um . . . Have you noticed something peculiar about the motives you've been collecting for all the potential suspects?"

"You mean that this is one creepy, pathetic bunch?"

"Not exactly."

"Then what?"

"Well, it seems like . . . to me, anyway . . . it's looking like there's a . . . theme . . . to all of these stories."

"A theme?"

"A theme."

"Like in a book?" Bex had a General Knowledge degree from Sarah Lawrence. If there was one thing she knew about, it was literary themes and their sundry devices.

"You could say that. Everyone you told me about, their big issues with Lucian or, well, with the world in general, seem to be that of a past relationship affecting a present-day one."

She considered his words. "Okay. So?"

"So . . ."

"That's short for 'so what?' "

"Remember when Gil accused you of being so accustomed to ferreting out murders at skating events that you've started seeing murders where none exist?"

"Yeah. You told me he was wrong. You agreed with me. You said you thought there was something fishy going on here, too."

"I did. I did agree with you. About that."

"But you don't agree with me about—"

"Bex." He was doing his best to lead her independently to the obvious conclusion. "Think about it. The theme of a past relationship affecting a present one . . ."

"I admit, it's a little too coincidental, but . . ."

"Bex, come on. Lucian, Eleanor, and Gina. Chris, Lauren, and Gabrielle. Heck, even Toni, Lucian, and Eleanor to some degree. It all doesn't remind you of anything?"

"This isn't about Rachel."

Craig exhaled, happy at least to stop talking in metaphors and circles.

"I didn't say that it was. I'm just suggesting that, when your mind is on something, there becomes a tendency to start seeing references to your situation everywhere, even when they aren't necessarily there."

"So? What? Because of you, me, and Rachel, I made up Lucian, Eleanor, and Gina? Or Chris, Lauren, and Gabrielle?"

"Made up? No. Given them more weight in the narrative of Lucian's possible killer than they probably deserve? Possibly."

"That's it!" Bex said. She jumped off the bench.

Craig blinked. "What's it?"

"You're a genius!" The lower half of Bex's body was already on her way back to the rink. The upper, however, stopped, grabbed Craig's face in her hands, and kissed him more fully than she had in days. "You're going to be the first one I thank in my Emmy acceptance speech."

Dumbfounded but pleased, Craig asked, "You've solved your case?"

"No. But I know now who can."

It wasn't easy to get Toni, Gina, Gabrielle, and Sabrina alone in a room where they wouldn't be overheard or interrupted. Even harder was just getting all four women to show up at the same time. Bex felt as though she was corralling drops of mercury. Every time she got three in one spot long enough to go in search of the fourth, one of the original three would wander off. Finally, however, as the afternoon's rehearsals wound to a close, she managed to sequester them all in the ladies' locker room. To make sure no one would come in while they were talking, Bex put a sign on the door advising that there was a leak in the bathroom and everyone should keep out.

"Are we about to chant the opening to *Macbeth*?" Sabrina asked dryly.

"Too many witches," Toni warned.

Bex said, "I need your help. All of yours."

"To do what?" This was from Gina.

"To prove that Chris killed Lucian."

"You're nuts." Gabrielle stood up and was already heading for the door.

Only Bex's caveat of, "Or to prove that he didn't," stopped her.

"So you don't know for sure," Gabrielle clarified.

"No. I don't. And I just realized—well, a friend helped me realize—I'm not the one who is in a position to find out."

"Meaning what?" Gina asked.

"Here is the thing," Bex explained. "I came into this whole situation like a TV producer. Do you know how we prepare a skating special for air? We all sit around a big table, and we ask ourselves, 'What's the story line we're telling?' We create a narrative thread in advance, and then we show only those bits of footage that fit with our story line. Everything else we ignore and throw away."

"No kidding," Toni, Gina, Gabrielle, and Sabrina said in a frayed version of unison.

That did take Bex back a bit. She had no idea TV's tactics were so transparent. And here they all thought they were terribly clever. Or at least subtle.

"How many profiles of me do you think 24/7 has done, focusing on the Eleanor Quinn replacement angle?" Gina mused.

"Or my—what do you all call it? Historical significance to the sport?" Toni added.

"The only time I ever get called for a quote on skating is in relation to suicide," Gabrielle piped in. "Creativity isn't exactly television's forte."

"I don't think you guys have ever met a cliché you didn't like," was Sabrina's final comment.

Okay, okay, Bex got it. She was a hack. They didn't have to harp on it.

Bex said, "That's why I'm turning to the four of you. I've been looking at Chris through a prism. I got a story in my head, and I couldn't let go of it. I was so close to the issue that

I couldn't even see what I was doing. A friend had to point it out to me. He was wrong about my motivation, of course. But he was right in that I couldn't see the big picture. I couldn't figure out Chris's motivation for killing Lucian because, as an outsider, I'll never be able to see the whole person that Lucian was. All I'll ever get is snippets of him here, snippets of him there, three-minute up-close-and-personal profiles that barely scratch the surface of the man."

Speaking of sounding familiar . . . Wasn't that what Craig told her days ago, perched precariously on the unfolded sofa bed in her apartment? That it wasn't so simple to peg people based on a few, stray facts? That nobody ever fully understood another person's motivations?

"Is this about Lucian or about Chris?" Gabrielle asked.

"It's both. Because to figure out why Chris may have done what he did, I need to fully understand both men. And I realize now that I never will."

"But," Toni pointed out, "you could say the same about any of us. We all only know a small piece of both men, as well."

"Yes," Bex agreed. "But together . . ."

"What do you want us to do?" Sabrina asked.

"I'm thinking," Bex said, "of an intervention of sorts."

"Meaning?"

"A couple of months ago, at the Nationals, I had a confession from a killer—"

"Oh, yes," Gina bubbled. "I saw that. He killed that poor girl, then strung her up to make it look like an accident. You got that monster to confess live on TV!"

"Well, not exactly. What I actually had was a confession he made only to me, one that I couldn't prove. I then set him up to confess to someone else. What he didn't know was I had a camera running the whole time. That was the confession we broadcast."

"You want us to do something similar here?" Toni didn't look at all pleased by the prospect.

"Well, optimally, if I could set it up . . ."

"No," Toni said. "Absolutely not."

"Toni," Gabrielle offered diplomatically, "if we do what Bex asks, we can prove that Chris wasn't responsible for Lucian's death. We can get this settled once and for all."

"I am not against speaking to Chris, per se," Toni clarified. "I just don't want to have it videotaped. The fact is, we have no idea what sort of information might come out of this—what did you call it, Bex? This intervention? I am not about to offer it up to 24/7 for their infinite free use."

"She has a point," Gina agreed.

"So you'll do it?" Bex asked. "If I promise no cameras, just the four of you in a room with Chris—and, well, me, too. You have to let me be there. I've been living and breathing this case for days. I have to see how it ends. You'll do it?"

They all exchanged nervous glances. The wordless communication in the room could have made an abstract ballet.

Toni finally spoke for the entire group. "We'll do it."

Eighteen

"What exactly is going on?" Chris asked.

He'd walked into the coaches' lounge at Bex's request,

only to come face-to-face with an all-female swarm. And Bex locking the door behind them.

Chris looked from Gabrielle to Toni to Gina to Sabrina to Bex. He said, "Can't help feeling there's a *Macbeth* joke just dying to come out."

"Did it already," Sabrina responded dryly.

"Apparently," Gina added, stealing a peek in Toni's direction, "we're several witches over the limit."

"Ah, well. So what's this about, then?"

Suddenly, none of the assembled had anything to say. The room became a roller derby of eyes meeting, then quickly recoiling away, of awkwardly shifting feet, of hands that couldn't find a spot to settle, and of heads diving into hunched shoulders, turtle style.

Chris gave them a minute to come up with a single, coherent thought. When that wasn't forthcoming, he said, "Well, we're a few months off my birthday, so this can't be a surprise party. My immigration status has been settled—special talent visa, thank you very much—since I was fourteen, so you all aren't planning to turn me over to the INS. And I don't suppose Bex needed the lot of you on hand to conduct my pre-interview in advance of the tribute. So I'm going to step out on the proverbial limb and presume that we've all gathered here today, this one man and five women, to cross-examine me about our mutual, dearly beloved, dearly departed friend, Lucian Pryce."

"Wow," Bex said. "And I thought *I* could pretzel any simple phrase into an overcomplicated mess."

"I come by it honestly. I *am* English."

"This is about Lucian," Gina agreed.

"Bex thinks . . ." Sabrina began.

"We wanted to hear your side of the story," Gabrielle interjected.

"Because God knows, you're good at keeping secrets." That was from Gina.

"Bex did make a convincing argument. . . ." Toni said.

"Did you kill Lucian?" Bex, tired of the runaround—and

afraid he might start doing linguistic gymnastics again; that was her job—cut to the chase.

Chris looked at Bex. He looked at Toni, Gina, Sabrina, and finally, for the longest time, at Gabrielle.

He was still looking at her when he said, "Yes."

Bex was the one who'd initially entertained the possibility of Chris being Lucian's killer. She was the one who'd concocted the entire scenario of how and when. Yet, in the end, she was also the one who appeared most shocked by his (surprisingly effortless) confession. Everyone else barely blinked. After fighting Bex over so much as questioning Chris only an hour earlier, each woman now looked as if she'd known the truth all along.

"Why?" Sabrina demanded.

"That would be my business, darling."

"Oh, no." Was Gina actually enjoying this now? She sure sounded like she was enjoying it. "I'd say it was all our business. We all might have had moments of wanting to do Lucian in. But you're the only one who actually went ahead and did it. I'd say we deserve an explanation."

"Or a vicarious thrill," Sabrina piped up. No question there, Lucian's daughter was definitely getting a kick out of the proceedings.

"Hush, Sabrina," Toni said. And then, in an equally firm tone, "Christian, we're waiting."

"For what? For me to draw you a color diagram? What would be the point? I'm certain Miss Levy here has already drawn all the necessary arrows."

Bex said, "You flew up from California the night before he died. You had dinner with him and Gina—" A quick, pleading look from the newly widowed Mrs. Pryce told Bex that while Gina was eager to hear the details of Chris's sins, she wasn't nearly as enthused about the prospect of airing her own. And so Bex declined to elaborate on his evening with the Pryces. "Then, afterwards, you used a copy of the key to his office to break in and mess up Lucian's skates with your handy-dandy blade-sharpening stone. Then you hopped back on a plane, returned to California, and arrived back with Gabrielle the next morning."

"That's a pretty lame alibi," Sabrina offered.

"It wasn't supposed to be one," Chris said.

Bex asked, "You mean you didn't plan this in advance? Killing Lucian? It was some kind of spur-of-the-moment thing?"

Chris shrugged, but he didn't deny.

"Then why the two flights back and forth?"

Chris looked first at Gina, then furtively at Gabrielle. "I—I had something I needed to discuss with Lucian. Privately."

In other words, Chris hadn't wanted Gabrielle to know that the evening before they were scheduled to fly to Colorado together, he planned on flaunting the fact that he'd been sleeping with Lucian's wife in the great man's face.

Sabrina asked, "But weren't you scared Gina or I would tell the police you were in town earlier?"

"The police?" Chris swept one arm around the room. "Do you see the police here anywhere? An old man falls down while skating. What's there in such a tale to be of interest to the police?"

"Bex figured it out," Gina said.

"Bex works for *television*."

"I still don't understand why," Toni said softly. "You loved him, Christian."

"Not as much as we all apparently thought," Gina chimed in.

"I did love him," Chris admitted. "And he claimed he loved me. He claimed he wanted what was best for me."

"He did," Toni insisted. "Lucian was a good coach. He cared about his students."

"He loved you like a son," Sabrina concurred. "No. He loved you more than that."

"He made you a two-time Olympic Gold medalist," Gina said. As if there was no better evidence of Lucian's devotion.

"Yes. And the first time, I couldn't have been more grateful."

"The first time . . ." Gabrielle repeated. She hadn't spoken a word up to that point. While the other women gleefully descended on Chris for detail and clarification, Gabrielle had hung back, never taking her eyes off of him.

"Yes." He, too, even while answering the questions being snipered at him from all sides, had focused exclusively on Gabrielle.

"Lauren," she said.

"Lauren," he said.

"Lauren?" Gina asked in surprise.

"I wanted to quit." Chris's upper lip snickered tentatively upward, as if it were the only part of him still amused by how naïve he'd been. "After that first Olympic win. I wanted to quit. I wanted to live a normal life. Have a wife and a family and all that boring crap. With Lauren. We had plans. But Lucian convinced me to stay. Just until the Worlds, he said. Just through the tour, he said. Just one more season. He said he didn't have anyone else as good as I ready to get on the world stage. I didn't want to leave him without a champion, did I? I wouldn't do that to him. Not after everything he'd sacrificed for me."

Bex thought she saw Sabrina gag a bit at that.

Chris went on. "I did love Lucian. And I was grateful to him. So I did what he asked. I stayed in. Even when I didn't want to. And I kept training. And Lauren moved to be with me while I did it. And one night, a driver ran her off the road. And she was dead. Because she was driving in a town neither of us wanted to be in. But we were. Because of Lucian."

"You blamed Lucian for your wife's death," Sabrina whispered practically to herself. And smiled. Was that an expression of peace Bex glimpsed settling into every nook of her being? "Fair enough."

But no one was paying attention to Sabrina. Gina said, "So you hated him? All these years you just pretended?"

Chris shrugged. "Yes. No. Everything in between. Life's never that jolly simple, is it? Not all black and white."

Or so everyone seemed to be telling Bex these days.

"So this was about Lauren," Gina said. "Lauren was the relationship Gabrielle accused you of not being over?"

"Of course. Who else could she have been talking about?" Gina shrugged. "Doesn't matter."

"Why now, Christian?" Toni asked.

"Because of the tribute. Because I couldn't stomach the thought of an evening of paying homage to him and his skaters. Knowing that I would be held up as his shining example. The two-time Olympic Gold medalist. I thought, a few months earlier, I thought I'd found a way of paying him back. But it didn't work out." Bex wondered if she was the only one who could see how furiously Gina was blushing. "So, before I went back to California, I had this idea . . ."

"Did you mean to kill him?" Gabrielle asked.

"I don't know," Chris confessed. "Maybe I just wanted to embarrass him, put him out of action for his own tribute. Or maybe I did want to kill him. I don't know. I just did it. And when I heard he had died . . . I was crushed. I didn't think I would be. I was crushed."

Bex remembered his tearful reaction to the news. And she believed him.

After that, there really wasn't much left for anyone to say. The silence now wasn't so much awkward, like it had been in the beginning, but subdued. Everyone was swirling in their own thoughts, reluctant to put forth another question only to receive back an answer they didn't actually want to hear.

Bex broke the silence. Again. She said, "You know, we're going to have to tell the police."

No one spoke. Chris turned to look at Bex. The others followed.

Finally, Gabrielle said, "I didn't realize that taking two flights on two consecutive days to the same location constituted a crime, Bex."

Bex blinked. "Say what?"

"Unless I've misunderstood, your only evidence against Chris is the flight he took to Colorado and back prior to the one he arrived on with me."

"Well, that's not the only . . . "

"All coaches carry a stone, Bex," Toni chimed in. "It isn't a pistol. A permit isn't necessary."

"And about the copy of the key I gave Chris," Gina said. "Lots of people have a copy of that key. Lucian's office is practically a public space."

"Are you all out of your minds?" Bex asked.

She scanned the room frantically. *Sabrina. Sabrina still has possession of her senses. Sabrina will . . .*

"Chris did come up to see my father and Gina the night before Lucian died. It was so they could work out the details of the tribute's opening routine. Chris never intended to stay beyond dinner. He always intended to fly back for Gabrielle. He didn't even bring a suitcase that first time."

Okay. To the question of "Are you all out of your minds?" the answer was obviously "Yes." Cumulatively, they all were.

"Why?" Bex demanded. "He admitted to killing Lucian. You all loved him. Each in your own weird way, but you all did. Chris killed him. Don't you care?"

"Of course we care," Toni said. "We cared about Lucian. And we care about Christian. We have to look out for him now."

"He's one of ours," Gina said. "You wouldn't understand, Bex."

"He's family." Sabrina shrugged.

"This doesn't make any sense."

"Maybe not to you," Gina agreed. "But then you don't really know us. You never will. No matter how many TV pieces you produce."

Bex told Craig, "You were right, I was wrong."

"Always nice to hear. Any clue about what and when? Why would be good, too."

"Chris Kelly killed Lucian. Toni, Gina, Sabrina, and Gabrielle all know it, and they're all covering for him. Also, judging by the way she was looking at him, I'd say Gabrielle was ready to do a lot more than cover for him."

"Wow," Craig said.

"My sentiments exactly."

She'd asked Craig to take her as far away from the rink as

possible. Short of running all the way home to New York, they'd settled for a touristy mountain spot. From its peak, even looking in all four directions, there were only trees, lakes, and an assortment of clichéd, perfect nature. No ice to be glimpsed for miles.

"I don't get it," Bex trilled. "Why would they do that? Everything they've said or done up to this point . . . I was sure that if we got Chris to confess, they'd be tripping over each other to turn him in. But then, Gina—Gina, of all people; hardly the voice of reason or, most of the time, even sense— Gina told me that I was presumptuous—"

"Presumptuous? Gina Gregory actually used the word 'presumptuous'?"

"I'm summarizing."

"By using bigger words instead of smaller ones?"

"It's how I summarize."

"Go on."

"Gina suggested it was presumptuous of me to think that I could predict how any of them would react or why. She said I didn't know any of them, really. A couple of interviews didn't make me an expert."

"And that would be the part where my being right came in?"

"Yes."

"I can't say I'm completely surprised. Not about my being right. Well, about that, too . . ."

"Yes, yes, yes, you're brilliant. That was already established. What do you mean you're not surprised?"

"Remember, Bex, I've seen the skating world close ranks before. Everyone at the rink knew that Robby was abusing Felicia while they were skating together, and even after they were married. Nobody said a word. The reason Rachel never bothered charging Robby with rape was because she knew it would come down to he said/she said, and the entire skating world would be on his side. You protect the skating first, then the skater. All outsiders come in a distant third."

"But Lucian was a skater, too."

"He's a dead skater now. Chris is alive. Chris is who they

owe their allegiance to. Besides, a scandal of this sort wouldn't be good for anyone. To start with, it would ruin a perfectly good, tear-jerking tribute. And no one wants that."

"Not Gil, that's for sure."

"Well, there you go. You have a motive for keeping this under wraps. So why can't you understand that those other women might, too?"

"You're making this sound so simple. Weren't you the one who told me that people and their motives are a lot more complicated than what can be conveyed in a single, pithy sound bite?"

"I'm summarizing. Only using small words. Perhaps that's why you didn't realize it."

"I don't know if I can do this anymore, Craig. I became a researcher because I liked understanding things. I liked finding facts and filing them away into neat little columns until I saw the big picture. Until I thought I saw the big picture."

"I wasn't trying to give you an existential crisis."

"In one week, you've asked me to marry you and then completely upset my entire world view. What did you think was going to happen?"

"Well, I was hoping you'd say yes."

"So this has all been a clever plan on your part? Lucian's death, the illogical behavior of those who supposedly loved him the most. That was all you?"

"Yes," Craig deadpanned.

"You're incorrigible."

"There goes another big word."

"Yes," Bex said.

"You mean yes, that was a big word?"

"Yes, I'll marry you."

That shut him up. Bex kind of liked that.

She expected him to sweep her into his arms and kiss her deeply while the camera swirled around them, taking in both the breathtaking passion and scenery. At least that's the way it happened in the movies.

But instead of the sweeping and the smooching, Craig actually took a small step back. He asked, "What prompted that?"

"Well, you did propose. And I did promise you a reply."

"Under these circumstances?"

"Pretty romantic spot."

"You know what I mean."

"I thought we could never fully understand what another person really means?"

"Yes, yes, yes, you're brilliant. That was already established."

She smiled. "Thank you."

"Oh, Bex, what am I going to do with you?"

"In the immortal words of that Calgon commercial: 'Take me away.' I don't care if I never see, hear, or speak to another skater as long as I live."

"No," Craig said. "You want to quit working in skating, that's your business. But you don't get to use me as an excuse for yourself, or for anybody else. Besides, there's Jeremy, remember? He's in the ice chips up to his spangly shoulder pads. If you're with us, you're going to be in skating anyway, whether you like it or not."

"I'm sorry, but aren't you doing exactly what I did earlier? Assuming you know my motives for agreeing to marry you, and reacting accordingly?"

"It's surprisingly seductive."

"So I'm hesitant to marry you because I think you're trying to replace your dead wife, and you're hesitant to marry me because you think I'm using you to quit working in skating. That's not a ringing endorsement for till-death-do-us-part, is it, Craig?"

"No." The banter was gone. From both of them.

"So. What do we do now?"

He shrugged.

And she had nothing to counter it with.

Epilogue

The night of the actual tribute show, Bex was so busy running around, mostly trying to keep out of Gil's field of vision, that she ended up with very little time to ponder the fact that there was a killer on the ice, paying homage to the man he'd killed. She'd spent the week before Gil, Francis, and Diana arrived for the telecast conducting interviews with the major players then picking out the best sound bites for use during the show. Her subjects, initially, seemed a bit reluctant to sit down with her. But every single one of them recognized they couldn't very well flat out refuse without providing 24/7 with a good reason. And since no one was willing to provide said good reason, the interviews went on as scheduled.

From Toni, Bex got: "Lucian Pryce never let anything stand between him and his goals. He never encountered a problem he couldn't solve. One way or another. If his first solution went up in flames, Lucian always had a Plan B."

Sabrina said, "My father loved my mother. He really did. She loved him, too. I'm lucky, I think. A lot of people never get to see that. They have no idea something like that can even exist. They both left me a lot to live up to."

Gina summoned, "If it weren't for Lucian, I wouldn't be living the life I have today. He made me who I am."

Even Gabrielle managed to admit, "I didn't know how strong I could be until I was tested. I guess I have Lucian to thank for that." And then she plugged her training center for the next ten minutes. Bex let her ramble on. That's why there was such a thing as an editing room.

Chris proved the most difficult to talk to. Even if, at the start, he was the least averse to doing it. In fact, Lucian's killer actually seemed somewhat cocky about the whole thing. He sauntered into the hotel room Bex had booked for these sessions as if he were almost challenging her to try and trip him up. Bex had no intention of doing that. To be honest, she was trying to forget that she knew anything about this man at all, beyond what his public was allowed to know.

Chris took the seat across from Bex, one leg crossed over the other, arms raised and draped over the back of the chair, looking her right in the eye. *Go ahead,* he seemed to be saying, *hit me with your best shot. I'm ready.*

Bex didn't think she was doing any such thing. Yet, when she started off with a softball question about Chris's childhood under Lucian's tutelage, rather than with a combative one focusing on his death, Chris appeared discombobulated. He actually stumbled through a query Bex expected to be a no-brainer. One about his and Lucian's first meeting.

"I—It was when I first came to the States. I'd never met him before. My coach back home, she'd sent him a video of me skating. He'd never seen me in person. I was so nervous. I had this fantasy he'd see me step off the airplane and it would be: This isn't the package I ordered; send it back postage due. Problem was, I had no place to go back to. My mum and dad split up and neither one was dying to have me. I was living with my older brother, but I knew his girlfriend wasn't too keen on me being there, either. Lucian Pryce was my only shot. If he hadn't taken me in . . . If, the minute he saw me, he hadn't marched straight across the room and told me I was welcome . . . He called me 'son.' That first night, he called me 'son' . . . I don't know what I would have done. Probably burst into tears right at the gate. That would have been a jolly sight, wouldn't it?"

For a minute, the now-adult Chris looked as though he was
going to burst into tears right then and there, too. Bex supposed he might be playing her, of course. But she didn't think
so. He sounded so sincere. Heck, all the women she'd interviewed earlier had also sounded sincere. And as far as Bex
knew, they'd even told her the truth. Granted, she didn't know
what facts and opinions they'd left out of the broadcast, but
everything they'd put in was, in fact, technically true. Viewers
of 24/7's special on the life and death of Lucian Pryce would
be left with an impression of a man loved by his colleagues,
students, and family. Gil would get the "tear-jerking tribute
show with world-famous skaters sobbing about their sainted,
dead coach and how much he meant to their lives and careers"
he'd demanded. It would be heartfelt and unambiguous and,
let's not lose focus of the ultimate goal here, highly rated.

The rest of the preproduction week, Bex spent noticing
things she'd never noticed before. Like the fact that life apparently went on outside 24/7's camera lens. Previously, if
someone had asked Bex, in an abstract sort of way, "Say,
Bex, do you think every important thing that happens at a
sporting event happens in front of a camera?" Bex would
have said, "No, no, of course not. What are you, crazy?"
Yet, she'd come to realize that it seemed she believed exactly that. The week before Lucian's tribute, Bex found
herself noticing that all sorts of conversations were taking
place in corners and at rinkside, and presumably even outside the rink. Chris and Gabrielle, Chris and Gina, Toni
and Sabrina, Gina and Sabrina, Gabrielle and Gina, Chris
and Sabrina. All of them were having pow-wows outside
Bex's hearing. They were arguing and crying and laughing
and reconciling. She'd seen it all before. She'd just never
cared. But now, Bex viewed every conversation as further
evidence that she was planted very far outside of a loop
she'd once thought she understood completely.

The night of the main event, Bex stood rinkside for the beginning of the ninety-minute performance portion. Television
cameras perched in wait at every corner of the gleaming oval.
The stands were packed with fans, though due to the somber-

ness of the occasion, it wasn't quite the carnival mood of a usual exhibition; some had even worn a respectful black. Toni and Sabrina sat on a special platform of honor erected at the end furthest from the entrance. Backstage was a blur of sequins, hair spray, and muffled skate blades clanking over carpeted floors.

Chris skated out first, holding Gina by one hand and Gabrielle by the other. Earlier, as they waited a few feet away from Bex to take the ice, Chris had turned to kiss Gabrielle gently on the lips, followed by Gina on the forehead. All three smiled at each other, then made their entrance under a gold-tinted spotlight, to thunderous applause. Chris, Gabrielle, and Gina glided to a smooth stop in front of Sabrina and Toni, kicking up a small shower of ice spray. They bowed. The two women atop the podium rose in response, kicking off a standing ovation. Sabrina and Toni beamed. Chris, Gabrielle, and Gina beamed back.

Bex had to turn away.

She walked as quickly as was possible without drawing unnecessary attention, all the way to the back of the rink, ending up practically next to the room housing the cooling equipment. It was no use; she could still hear the applause and the music that signified the kickoff of the first tribute number.

"Bex! Wait!" Craig's voice crowbarred through the darkness a split second before the rest of him caught up. The two of them huddled under a single bulb, the only sane couple in the place. Give or take a person.

She said, "I couldn't do it. Couldn't stand there and watch all that fawning when I know that—"

"What?"

"You know what. Chris killed Lucian. And now he's out there, getting ready to skate to 'Wing Beneath My Wings,' or whatever claptrap Gil insisted on for the closing."

"I believe it actually is 'Wind Beneath My Wings.' I saw Jeremy rehearsing it earlier. Only the Gary Morris version, not Bette Midler."

"That makes it much better then, thanks."

"Try not to take it so seriously, Bex. This isn't about you. It's about them. This is their problem. Let them deal with it."

"It's my problem, too. I used to think I understood people. How am I supposed to do my job if I don't have a clue what people are really like or what they're capable of?"

"Who cares?" Craig asked lightly.

"Couldn't you at least fake an interest in my future?"

"I don't mean, who cares about your future. I mean, who cares about what people are really like? You're not a psychologist, Bex, or an FBI profiler. You're in television. You're in the business of creating fantasies. The characters you put on the air are no more real than . . . than . . . the *Friends* friends. Or all the people who love Raymond. Or whoever it was that slayed vampires. They're a collective illusion created by you, the camera, the skater, and the viewer."

Another rousing burst of applause almost drowned out the last of Craig's lecture. Bex couldn't resist; she had to poke her head around the corner for a peek at what was driving them all so wild.

On the ice, underneath a screen flaunting a huge projected portrait of Lucian in all his Master of the Universe glory, Toni had put on her skates, too. Dignified as ever, if somewhat slower than in her prime, she led a line of former students, not just Chris, Gina, and Gabrielle, but another dozen, lesser champions, ranging in age from thirtysomething to no more than twelve. The tune playing during their procession was ABBA's "Thank You for the Music:"

> *So I say thank you for the music*
> *For giving it to me. . . .*

Bex watched the skaters laughingly hold hands and twirl in a giddy circle beneath the portrait. She watched the audience wipe away tears and cheer until they were hoarse.

Bex asked Craig, "Is this as big of a sentimental, manipulative piece of claptrap as I think it is, or is it, you know, kind of . . . moving?"

"Why does it have to be one or the other? Why can't it be both?"

"Are you being deep again?"

"I'm being pragmatic."

"Isn't that usually my job?"

"Look at that audience, Bex. Really look at them. They're having a great time. That's what they came here for. To be moved and uplifted and swept up in the fantasy. So who cares if the skaters on the ice are sincere, or what their reasons are for being in this show?"

"I care."

"Why?"

"Because the truth matters."

"Sure it matters. But to what end? Why does it matter why people do what they do? Isn't *what* they do finally more important?"

Bex tore herself away from the ABBA-vaganza to focus completely on what Craig was saying. She sensed it was very important, and she wanted to make sure that she understood it in exactly the same way as he meant it. "Translation?"

"Ok. Example: Gabrielle Cassidy is here to plug her training center. But her being on the ice again is making people happy. They're remembering how much they enjoyed watching her compete once. Or maybe they're remembering how young they once were, while they were enjoying watching her compete. It doesn't matter what their motivation for the enjoyment is, just like it doesn't matter what her reason for being here to bring them that enjoyment is. She's happy, they're happy. What else matters?"

"We're not just talking about skating anymore, are we, Craig?"

"I want to marry you. You want to marry me. Maybe we should just focus on that instead of constantly drilling the other person about why. Most of us don't know why we do the things we do, much less why other people do what they do. So to hell with why. Let's stick to what. What do you say, Bex? Will you marry me?"

"Yes." It was that easy. She didn't have to think, she didn't have to rationalize or dissect or second-guess. She simply said, "Yes," without hesitation.

Craig grinned. When he grabbed Bex to kiss her, there were no swirling cameras, no fabulous mountaintop views, no lush, swelling soundtrack (well, unless you counted ABBA still blaring from the ice). But it felt as if there were. All that and more, actually.

The first thing Bex said when they pulled apart was, "We have to tell Jeremy."

"Agreed. But he's a little busy right now."

They both turned their heads just in time to watch Craig's son land a perfect Triple Axel, exactly on the spot he'd been practicing to hit all week.

"Yahoo!" Craig pumped his fist, as proud as any dad whose son had scored a winning touchdown or knocked in a home run.

Bex jumped up and down and clapped her hands. "Go, Jeremy!"

Craig noted her genuine excitement and, amused, asked, "So. Still thinking of giving up the skating gig?"

"Well . . ." She gazed thoughtfully over the ice. Jeremy's Axel was being followed by each skater performing their signature move under a spotlight that changed colors according to their costumes. Toni, in forest green, did a still more than presentable lay-back spin; Gina, in hot pink, her change-foot Biellman; Gabrielle, in yellow, a Choctaw so deep her hair was practically brushing the ice when she leaned back; and Chris, in dark blue, a delayed Axel that seemed to hang frozen in the air like a basketball player mid-dunk.

Bex said, "It is terribly pretty. . . ."

"It is," Craig agreed. "It really is. . . ."

SKATINGANDSTUFF.COM
MESSAGE BOARD

FROM: GoGoGregory1
Posted at 6:46 AM

OMG guys the Lucian Tribute was the best skating show I've ever seen in my life so beautiful and so moving and everyone was great even the people I never heard of and oh you should have seen Chris and Gina together there was definitely something going on there take my word for it in a few months they're going to announce that they're back together maybe we'll even get our wedding this time remember you heard it here first!!!!

FROM: MaryQuiteContrary
Posted at 6:49 AM

Yeah, well, I don't believe a word of it. Not until I see it on TV.